PRAISE FOR M

Tom Clancy fans open to a strong female lead will clamor for more.

— *Drone*, Publishers Weekly

Superb!

— *Drone*, Booklist starred review

The best military thriller I've read in a very long time. Love the female characters.

— *Drone,* Sheldon McArthur, founder of The Mystery Bookstore, LA

A fabulous soaring thriller.

— *Take Over at Midnight,* Midwest Book Review

Meticulously researched, hard-hitting, and suspenseful.

— *Pure Heat,* Publishers Weekly, starred review

Expert technical details abound, as do realistic military missions with superb imagery that will have readers feeling as if they are right there in the midst and on the edges of their seats.

— *Light Up the Night,* RT Reviews, 4 1/2 stars

Buchman has catapulted his way to the top tier of my favorite authors.

— Fresh Fiction

Nonstop action that will keep readers on the edge of their seats.

— *Take Over at Midnight,* Library Journal

M L. Buchman's ability to keep the reader right in the middle of the action is amazing.

— Long and Short Reviews

The only thing you'll ask yourself is, "When does the next one come out?"

— *Wait Until Midnight,* RT Reviews, 4 stars

The first...of (a) stellar, long-running (military) romantic suspense series.

— *The Night is Mine,* Booklist, "The 20 Best Romantic Suspense Novels: Modern Masterpieces"

I knew the books would be good, but I didn't realize how good.

— Night Stalkers series, Kirkus Reviews

Buchman mixes adrenalin-spiking battles and brusque military jargon with a sensitive approach.

— Publishers Weekly

13 times "Top Pick of the Month"

— Night Owl Reviews

CONDOR

A MIRANDA CHASE THRILLER

M. L. BUCHMAN

Buchman Bookworks

Published by Buchman Bookworks, Inc.

Receive a free book and discover more by this author at: www.mlbuchman.com

Cover images:

Antonov An-124-100 with 2 Sukhoi Su-27s at the 2010 Moscow Victory Day Parade © Sergey Kostov | Wikimedia

Dark story sky and colorful rainbow - church on rock © Evgeniy_Bobkov | Depositphotos

Other works by M. L. Buchman: *(* - also in audio)*

Thrillers

Dead Chef
Swap Out!
One Chef!
Two Chef!

Miranda Chase
*Drone**
*Thunderbolt**
*Condor**

Romantic Suspense

Delta Force
*Target Engaged**
*Heart Strike**
*Wild Justice**
*Midnight Trust**

Firehawks
MAIN FLIGHT
Pure Heat
Full Blaze
*Hot Point**
*Flash of Fire**
Wild Fire
SMOKEJUMPERS
*Wildfire at Dawn**
*Wildfire at Larch Creek**
*Wildfire on the Skagit**

The Night Stalkers
MAIN FLIGHT
The Night Is Mine
I Own the Dawn
Wait Until Dark
Take Over at Midnight
Light Up the Night
Bring On the Dusk
By Break of Day
AND THE NAVY
Christmas at Steel Beach
Christmas at Peleliu Cove
WHITE HOUSE HOLIDAY
*Daniel's Christmas**
*Frank's Independence Day**
*Peter's Christmas**
*Zachary's Christmas**
*Roy's Independence Day**
*Damien's Christmas**
5E
Target of the Heart
Target Lock on Love
Target of Mine
Target of One's Own

Shadow Force: Psi
*At the Slightest Sound**
*At the Quietest Word**

White House Protection Force
*Off the Leash**
*On Your Mark**
*In the Weeds**

Contemporary Romance

Eagle Cove
Return to Eagle Cove
Recipe for Eagle Cove
Longing for Eagle Cove
Keepsake for Eagle Cove

Henderson's Ranch
*Nathan's Big Sky**
*Big Sky, Loyal Heart**
*Big Sky Dog Whisperer**

Love Abroad
Heart of the Cotswolds: England
Path of Love: Cinque Terre, Italy

Other works by M. L. Buchman:

Contemporary Romance (cont)

Where Dreams

Where Dreams are Born
Where Dreams Reside
Where Dreams Are of Christmas
Where Dreams Unfold
Where Dreams Are Written

Science Fiction / Fantasy

Deities Anonymous

Cookbook from Hell: Reheated
Saviors 101

Single Titles

The Nara Reaction
Monk's Maze
the Me and Elsie Chronicles

Non-Fiction

Strategies for Success

Managing Your Inner Artist/Writer
*Estate Planning for Authors**
Character Voice
*Narrate and Record Your Own Audiobook**

Short Story Series by M. L. Buchman:

Romantic Suspense

Delta Force

Delta Force

Firehawks

The Firehawks Lookouts
The Firehawks Hotshots
The Firebirds

The Night Stalkers

The Night Stalkers
The Night Stalkers 5E
The Night Stalkers CSAR
The Night Stalkers Wedding Stories

US Coast Guard

US Coast Guard

White House Protection Force

White House Protection Force

Contemporary Romance

Eagle Cove

Eagle Cove

Henderson's Ranch

*Henderson's Ranch**

Where Dreams

Where Dreams

Thrillers

Dead Chef

Dead Chef

Science Fiction / Fantasy

Deities Anonymous

Deities Anonymous

Other

The Future Night Stalkers
Single Titles

ABOUT THIS BOOK

The Antonov AN-124 Ruslan "Condor"—the heavyweight champ among production cargo jets. Russian tanks, American firefighting helicopters, rescue submersibles, satellites, city-sized power transformers...the Condor hauls them all over the world.

But when one lifts a top-secret payload rated as too dangerous, the US government decides it must take action. Untraceable *action. Call Delta Force? SEAL Team Six?*

No. They call Miranda Chase, lead crash investigator for the National Transportation Safety Board to fake a crash. Miranda refuses, but the stakes grow higher and higher. Soon she may be too late to stop the new Cold War from becoming the final war.

PROLOGUE

Spieden Island, Washington
1 hour ago
(9 p.m. Pacific Standard Time)

"FAVORITE AIRPLANE?"

"Oh, c'mon, Jeremy, ask a real one. We all know Miranda's favorite plane," Holly chided him.

"My F-86 Sabrejet," Miranda answered with an easy certainty that she at least knew this one answer. For twenty years she'd flown the old jet and knew it as well as the back of her hand. She liked its familiarity. Just as she liked the familiarity of this house. She'd grown up here.

She knew all its ways. The way the old wood creaked when the Pacific Ocean storms roared over Vancouver Island and slammed into the San Juans. The way the air didn't smell of the sea, but rather so fresh it seemed as if no one had ever breathed it before.

The high-vaulted living room with its beach cobble hearth, dark beams, and Douglas fir walls could seat twenty comfortably, four as it did now, or be cozy for just one as it usually was.

It was *slightly* uncomfortable having visitors to her island, thereby decreasing her favoritism for her house over her jet if one were to expand the parameters to "favorite place at this moment in time."

No, not uncomfortable. Merely...unfamiliar. Yes, that was a better way to think of it. Even though it was only Friday night and the rest of the chill March weekend loomed uncertainly ahead. Despite the new descriptor, she remained uncertain of her preparations to entertain them.

"Ehhhh!" Holly made a rude sound like a plane's stall-warning buzzer. "So not on, Miranda. It's not your Sabrejet." Holly's Australian accent was even thicker than usual as she sipped her second beer of the evening.

Before Miranda could respond that she knew her own mind—which she wasn't always sure of, though she was this time—Jeremy raised his hand.

"Wait! I know. I know!"

"Don't have to raise your hand, buddy." Mike winked at Miranda from his armchair near the fire. He sat as neatly as ever—a slim, elegant man with short dark hair, a dress shirt, and custom-tailored slacks.

Miranda sat on the sofa with Holly. Actually, *she* sat on the sofa whereas Holly slouched so low she was almost horizontal—her feet on the coffee table, sticking her toes out toward the fire. Her socks didn't match.

"It's any plane that hasn't crashed," Jeremy proudly announced his answer.

While the others laughed and nodded, Miranda considered. The four of them *were* the lead crash investigation team for the National Transportation Safety Board. Yes, any plane that was fully functional *was* a very good thing.

But still, she liked her old Sabrejet very much.

"Jeremy's favorite site investigation tool?" Mike called out.

Holly giggled.

Miranda had no idea why.

Holly whispered to her, "Can you figure him picking out a *single* favorite tool?"

"Oh," Miranda understood the joke now but had learned that laughs that came too late were better not laughed at all.

Jeremy always had a bigger field pack than the other three of them combined.

"That handheld military-grade thermite torch he used to slice evidence out of the old DC-3's wreckage," was Miranda's estimation. He had been particularly enamored of its ability to melt quickly through steel though it was no bigger than a two-D-cell flashlight.

"His hammer," Holly suggested. "The one he actually offered to that colonel who wanted to bust up his phone for constantly giving him bad news of more planes that had carked it."

Jeremy Trahn blushed brightly enough that it could be seen by the firelight.

"No, his program for reading Cockpit Voice and Data Recorders, even if he isn't supposed to have one. He secretly wishes he was James Bond," Mike ribbed him.

"No," Holly shook her head hard enough to flutter her

rough-cut blonde hair over her shoulders. "He wishes he was Q, Bond's equipment geek."

"No," Jeremy spoke up a little hotly, "but *he* wishes you both had fallen into the ocean and been eaten by orcas on the way here."

"You'd have been fish food right along with us." Mike accurately pointed out. He had flown the three of them out to her island in Washington State's northern Puget Sound for the weekend.

Holly was the one who'd suggested the spring solstice was a good excuse for a party. Though this March was chilly enough that "spring" didn't come easily off the tongue yet.

"Whale food," Jeremy corrected, then mumbled, "Would've been worth it."

There was a brief silence in which the only sound was logs shifting in the fireplace. Miranda watched the curious turbulence patterns as the sparks rose up the chimney.

"What *is* your favorite tool, Jeremy?" Because now she was curious.

He looked down, and she was afraid that she'd somehow embarrassed him even further than Mike and Holly had.

Then he reached for his shirt pocket and pulled out a pen.

"A pen, mate? Fair dinkum?" Holly turned to Mike. "Have you ever seen him even use a pen? Everything in the world is on his tablet."

Mike just shook his head.

Miranda could remember three instances. They'd been together as a team for almost six months, yet three was all she could recall.

"You gave it to me on the first day I joined your team. It's everything I ever dreamed of."

"Miranda's *pen?*" Mike scoffed.

"Being on Miranda's team," Jeremy said softly.

Holly, who never looked touched, looked touched. She turned to Miranda.

"He's so damn sweet," she whispered, but loudly enough for everyone to hear. "Can we keep him?"

Miranda didn't know why she wouldn't. He was an exceptional airplane systems specialist despite his youth.

"Holly's favorite soccer team?" Mike asked in a sudden, bright tone, completely changing the mood.

"The Australian Matildas," they all called out in unison. Their four Matildas baseball hats were all lined up on the mantel.

This time Miranda was fairly sure that her timing was right when she joined in on the laughter.

Helsinki Airport, Finland
11 hours earlier
(10 p.m. Eastern European Standard Time)

CAPTAIN DMITRI VOSKOV HUNCHED AGAINST THE MARCH chill and wished he was anywhere else. No matter where he shifted, the hard-blown ice pellets, which only looked like a light snow flurry, kept stinging his frozen cheeks as if he was being shot by a porcupine-quill gun.

Instead, all he could do was try to stay out of the wind

and watch as his plane was loaded—*the* heavyweight champ for cargo hauling.

Known as "Condor" in the west, his Ukrainian Antonov AN-124-200 Ruslan could carry up to a hundred and sixty-five tons in a single load. Its lone big brother, the AN-225 Mriya "Cossack" didn't really count as there had only ever been one in existence.

For dinner, he'd gone to the restaurant along the Helsinki Airport cargo road for a change of pace from their own onboard cooking. The smell—like week-old cooked cabbage—should have warned him, but he'd been hungry and cold enough to go in anyway. The meat soup could have been century-old reindeer hide—it had certainly tasted like it—and the waitress had been a dour battleax. Not even any fun flirting to break up the monotony.

At least there was no deadhead this time. As a specialized cargo-hauler-for-hire, too often they flew empty from a delivery to the next pickup.

Here in Finland, they'd dropped off a geothermal power generator built by the Brits and were picking up a load of Russian helicopters—helicopters that defecting Russian pilots had delivered into Finnish hands. No surprise that the Finns were handing them over to the Americans, so greedy for examples of Russian technology. He hoped that they'd gotten the better of the Yankees in whatever trade deal they'd worked out.

His real mistake was delaying at the restaurant too long over scorched coffee and the last slice of Brita-kakku pie, which was even worse than it sounded. The fluffy layers supposedly soaked in light cream were like sludge soaked in white grease.

The loadmasters had started the loading while he'd been at dinner. Now, it was near midnight, his gut was roiling with the heavy meal, and he couldn't get to the cockpit.

Much of the Condor's design had been taken from the American's C-5 Galaxy, but made bigger. Dmitri rubbed his hands together to no effect, then jammed them back into his pockets. he just wished the designers had provided flight deck access during loading.

The four-engine cargo jet was a massive open tube. At the rear, a ramp folded down from behind towering clamshell doors. In front, the nose swung up like a king-sized garage door to expose the front ramp. The Condor could even kneel—lowering its front landing gear to facilitate drive-on loading.

However, during loading, the stair up to his cockpit home was cut off. That left him to stand in the biting cold and watch his loadmasters do all the work.

All he could do was look longingly up at the nice warm living area four stories above him. He should be kicked back on his bunk, sleeping or watching a Scarlett Johansson movie (he had every one of them, at least all the ones she was blonde in, and most of Jennifer Lawrence's, even *The Hunger Games* when she wasn't blonde).

"How much longer, Portnov?"

"You whine too much, Captain."

"Fine. When we're done, I'll just leave you here to freeze your ass off."

"Then who would unload your helicopters in America?" Portnov slapped him on the back and returned to loading the next helo into the Condor. A painfully slow process even with two of the best loadmasters in the business running the loading team.

Of course, the least gouge in his hull could ground them for a week. And if everything wasn't perfectly balanced fore and aft, he'd crash on takeoff.

Dmitri paced back and forth because it was that or die cold in Helsinki, which sounded like a bad movie that he wanted no role in. He was always amazed at the volume Portnov managed to move in and out of their plane. Somehow it looked so effortless when Portnov was the senior loadmaster.

Damn but this took longer than a Ukrainian spring.

With its nose raised, his plane looked like a whale's maw gobbling up anything they fed it.

He glared across the field at the now darkened restaurant along the cargo road. She was long gone, but right now even that dour battleax looked like a better option than this.

Helsinki Airport
23 minutes later

Elayne Kasprak, her most commonly used name, had watched the whole operation since the Antonov AN-124 had landed before she'd decided on her approach. It was the return of the captain—conveniently unable to retreat to his flight deck—that gave her the solution to boarding the aircraft.

It had taken less than five minutes to liberate an airport security car from the Helsinki motor pool. Acquiring a uniform had been harder. Finding a real guard who was small enough that she wouldn't look ridiculous in his uniform had taken almost twenty minutes. She hoped that the guard woke up before he froze to death in just his long underwear—the one bit of attire she hadn't needed. If he didn't, that was his problem.

On her return, the captain was still there, trying to huddle out of the wind and not even pretending he was in charge. Perfect.

She parked her clearly marked vehicle close, but not too close. Visible, but in the shadows. Elayne planned her walk carefully. Casual, friendly. Not some sexy slink.

Just a cop on patrol...and just as bored as you. Bored enough to just hang out and watch a mundane loading process.

"*Hyvää iltaa,*" she wished him a good evening in Finnish.

"*Tak?*" Ukrainian.

She was fluent in Ukrainian, and very conversant in six other languages, but he'd know that her Ukrainian accent was too Russian. With the tensions there, she didn't want to arouse suspicions.

"Good evening?" she asked in intentionally awkward English.

"Ah! Good evening." He finally focused on her face and most of his shivering went away.

Elayne knew why she'd originally been recruited by the SVR. The Russian Foreign Intelligence Service needed beautiful spies, especially ones petite enough to appear completely unthreatening, even if she'd proven time and again that she could take down nine out of ten men courtesy of her Spetsnaz colonel father's years of tutelage.

But she'd also been raised by a submarine engineer

mother. With her own degree in aviation engineering—Elayne's original life's plan—her assets had proven attractive to the SVR, and more than just the physical. She'd quickly found her niche as a military aviation specialist for the foreign intelligence service.

It hadn't taken her very long to ascend to the operations directorate. A brief tussle for her between the S (illegal intelligence) and X (scientific) Directorates had been resolved by Zaslon quietly recruiting her while the others argued. No one questioned the most secret and elite black-ops team in the entire Russian Federation. Now, eight years as a Zaslon agent-saboteur, she drew a steady chain of challenging solo assignments.

Not that the Antonov captain looked to be particularly challenging.

"Good evening," he said in a much warmer tone as he stood straight and squared his shoulders.

"Slow loadings?" She nodded toward his plane.

"Damned slow. Made the mistake of going to the café down the road rather than hiding in my bunk."

"Tell that you did not the eating of Madame's meat soup?" She had watched him do precisely that.

At his expected groan, she laughed sympathetically.

"If you walk three more roads…streets?…there very good steak."

He groaned more dramatically, "I didn't need to know that." His English was almost as good as hers actually was. Better to let him think she was struggling to keep up with him.

She removed her hat. After all, Helsinki was tropical

compared to where she'd grown up at Polyarny submarine base, three hundred kilometers north of the Arctic Circle. Her long, white-blonde hair fell loose over her stolen parka's shoulders. Truth be told, she was missing the guard's long underwear at the moment as the Finnish night wind *was* quite bitter.

Elayne paid attention to the six helicopters being loaded. It gave the captain time to look his fill.

She was glad that it wasn't her job to hunt down the pilots who had betrayed the Motherland by defecting and delivering these to the West. She'd castrate them slowly, then make them cook and eat their own balls before she cauterized the excision point with a blowtorch.

There was a hard metal-on-metal bang from inside the Condor. By the lights inside the cargo bay, she could see that it was just one of the loaders cursing at a freezing cold pry bar he'd dropped on the deck while tightening a chain. No damage, but the sound had echoed and been reinforced so that it seemed to blast out into the darkness. Her own breath was clouding so thickly that it was blurring her view.

But not enough to hide what was in the cargo bay.

A Kamov "Helix" that looked to have all of its Airborne Early Warning system's electronics still intact. Two Kamov "Alligator" attack helos. One of the brand-new Kazan Ansat multi-role birds. A monstrous Mi-17 gunship that shouldn't fit inside any aircraft, at least nothing less than the Antonov. And the last was the true prize, an Mi-28NM "Havoc"—newly upgraded and with all of its armament intact. Castration was too kind for the bastard-pilot who'd stolen that aircraft.

It was an incredible intelligence haul.

"Sorry, Captain."

"What?"

Elayne remembered herself. "Sorry that you must stand out of sides in such colds."

And sorry for you that you were assigned to carry the wrong cargo. Not your fault, but that doesn't change the bad things coming your way.

"Would you like to warm up in my automotobile?" She made the offer.

"That would be most good. Thank you."

Very nice, she corrected him in her thoughts. Not challenging at all.

As she'd left the heater on high, they both soon shed their jackets as planned. He wasn't the handsomest man, but he clearly worked hard to stay in shape. Seducing him there in the shadows of her stolen but warm car was laughably easy.

And surprisingly good—once his hands warmed up.

He was a skilled lover, better than any she'd had in a long time. Best of all, if everything went as planned, there would be no loose ends to worry about—ever.

Fort Campbell, Kentucky (final approach)
1 hour ago
(11 p.m. Central Standard Time)

Dmitri Voskov lined up with the approach vector into

Fort Campbell and daydreamed of what wonders awaited him in Kentucky.

The load of Russian helicopters would go to the 160th Special Operations Aviation Regiment. SOAR was the US Army's secret helicopter regiment and no concern of his.

Kentucky though…

It wasn't the land of petite Scandinavian white-blondes, but he'd been in the American South enough to appreciate the seriously built gold-blondes as well—even when it was dyed.

No one would match the Helsinki Airport security officer who wore nothing under her uniform. That would be asking too much. But she'd left him with plenty to dream about. She'd also left him a phone number and first name—Valery. Valery, a female name in the West and a male name in Russia; it fit her strength well. She had the finest body he'd been invited to plunder since a fiery Irish redhead on a layover in Shannon, Ireland, three years before.

While finishing the tie-downs and double checks, Portnov had lowered the cockpit stairway and Dmitri had given Valery a tour upstairs.

Bunks near the back of the compartment—just ahead of the wings. Enough for the two loadmasters and the four-man flight crew to live in comfortably. The Antonov was their home most days of the year. A small lounge, bathroom, and a decent kitchen.

They'd tiptoed through as the rest of his flight crew were snoring away in their bunks. Normally, he'd be ticked that they'd been so comfortable while he'd been trapped outside, but he *had* just spent a very, very friendly hour steaming up a car's windows with an exceptionally flexible officer.

In the cockpit, he gave her the full tour and grabbed a couple of nice feels. He'd spent most of the evening wishing Portnov would hurry up. Standing in the cockpit with Valery, he wished the man would screw up and ground them here for a week.

"May I use bathing room?"

"You know the way. Don't worry about waking the other guys; you could drop a nuclear bomb and they would sleep through it."

On her return, Valery had asked in that charming mangled-English of hers as she closed the cockpit door, "Does these doors lock?"

He'd reached across her, latched it, and tried to take her right up against the surface.

Instead, she'd guided him to the pilot's chair. Sliding it to the back of the stops, there was just room for her to straddle him once she stripped.

Over Valery's bare shoulder and out the windshield, he'd caught Portnov looking up in surprise from the ground four stories below, then grinning.

Plenty to grin about here.

The only thing more amazing than her hair, face, and breasts had been what she could do with her hips.

She would start a motion somewhere deep inside that built in a slow gyration to—

The radio hauled him back to the present. "Antonov, this is Campbell Army Airfield. You're cleared to land Runway 23. Winds light and variable. Barometer two-niner-niner-five."

"Roger, Tower. I have the ILS." Everything looked good.

Everything.

Including the updated schedule from the home office

that said they'd be back in Helsinki in just three weeks. The first moment he was on the ground, he'd text Valery with the good news.

He rode the big plane down the glide slope into the darkness. They'd flown west all night—a rough ride north of the Azores, but nothing unusual. Here in Kentucky, it was still before sunrise under crystal clear skies.

Dmitri barely needed the Instrument Landing System; the runway was properly lit and clear despite the busy American Army base wrapped around it.

Fort Campbell had plenty of runway, but he still placed the main gear on the pavement in the first five hundred feet. Nose gear down at a thousand.

It would be good to get out of the cockpit and stretch. He might not even go barhopping. Maybe he'd just hit his bunk, think about Valery, and count the days until they were back in Finland.

WHEN CAPTAIN DMITRI VOSKOV PULLED BACK TO ENGAGE THE thrust reversers on the four brand-new GE CF-6 engines, a hidden microswitch was engaged.

It had been placed by SVR Zaslon Major Elayne Kasprak as Dmitri had buried his face in her breasts—so skilled with his tongue that she'd almost missed the proper placement.

But the switch was in the correct location and was now pressed by the control lever.

The switch turned on a tiny transmitter that sent a signal to a receiver she'd placed fifty feet behind the cockpit. Elayne Kasprak had hidden it beneath the rearmost bunk while ducking out of the cockpit to supposedly use the bathroom.

The receiver was attached to a detonator.

The detonator had been rammed into the heart of a shaped charge of C-4 explosive. The device—called a Krakatoa and originally designed for the British SAS, which she'd picked up from a UK munitions plant to avoid it being traced back to her—was no bigger than a fat beer can. That had made it easy to hide in her security officer's parka coat.

The two kilos of C-4 plastique exploded.

The copper bullet formed by the device could punch a double-fist-sized hole through a warship's armor plate at twenty-five meters.

At two meters, it punched a half-meter-wide hole through the crew cabin's thin rear pressure wall and the central wing fuel tank close behind it.

As a by-blow, it also turned the bottom of Loadmaster Portnov's bunk into a thousand pieces of shrapnel. His body was shredded—along with the *Playboy Polska* magazine he'd picked up in Warsaw last week, and had been using as a visual aid while he imagined Dmitri's blonde going down on him.

The sound had been muffled by the sleeping room door —now blown off its hinges—and the closed cockpit security door. In the cockpit, twenty meters forward, it was no louder than a blown tire on the main gear.

"Shit!" Dmitri checked the indicators, but no red warning lights. Hopefully not a brake fire or a broken wheel axle. *Please let it just be the rubber.* An Antonov was a rare enough bird that they carried their own spares, but they couldn't carry everything. With twenty main gear tires and four nose

gear ones, and two stashed in the hold, he could lose one with few worries.

The central wing tank had been run mostly dry during flight. Now it was filled with a shallow pool of Jet A fuel and nitrogen that had been pumped in as the tank emptied to decrease the chance of fire.

The blast of the Krakatoa not only heated the remaining fuel above the ignition point, but the hole it created allowed oxygen to rush into the breached tank. A small windstorm sucked various detritus into the breached tank.

Four seconds after the initial detonation, their speed was down to a hundred knots. The massive plane wasn't pulling to either side, so Dmitri decided the problem might not be too terrible; probably just a flat tire rather than a frozen axle.

Two thousand feet of runway gone, eight thousand still clear ahead. Under normal operations, the Antonov would need only a thousand more feet before turning off onto a taxiway—for all their size, helicopters didn't weigh much, less than a third of the Condor's load capability though they had filled every square meter of deck space.

At five seconds, a fireball followed the stream of oxygen and flashed back through the original penetration in the tank and the cabin's rear bulkhead. Portnov's bunk had collapsed to partially block the hole. The blockage only lasted a few hundredths of a second against the monstrous pressure wave.

It ignited the entire crew cabin and killed the other loadmaster, filling his lungs with fire when he breathed in to scream.

Other than a sudden inward bulging of the closed cockpit door, the active flight crew, including Captain Dmitri

Voskov, remained unaware of what was happening behind them. The copilot had opened his small side window to smell the fresh Kentucky air—splendidly warm and lush in the mid-March night—so their ears didn't even pop at the sudden overpressure.

Seven seconds after the initial blast, the mounting explosion's pressure wave inside the fuel tank exceeded critical rupture.

Both of the central tanks' side seams failed at a hundred and thirty-seven percent of design maximum.

Steel shrapnel from the shredded central tank blew through the wing tanks to either side, spilling the three thousand remaining gallons of reserve Jet A fuel into the wing structure. From there, it cascaded down onto the runway through mechanical openings for flaps and landing gear.

At nine seconds past ignition of the Krakatoa, both wings exploded internally. Bits of fuel tank and wing covering were blown so high that the last of them didn't return to the ground until well after the rest of the plane was destroyed.

The flash lit the darkness. The emergency response teams, woken by the blast, were on the move before the control tower could even sound the alarm.

If the wings had broken free, the fuselage might have survived.

Still marginally attached, they kept spilling fuel and feeding the fire along either side of the plane, turning the fuselage into a furnace that was still being cooked from the inside by the burning of the fuel dumped from the central tank over the helicopters in the cargo bay.

Captain Dmitri Voskov's final act fully damned the aircraft.

He stood hard on the brakes for an emergency stop.

They worked. All twenty-four wheels locked hard, leaving ten-meter stripes of black rubber on the runway that would be visible for years.

The Antonov AN-124-200 Condor squatted in the middle of its own inferno and burned.

Directly below the cockpit and crew area, the armament on the Mil Mi-28NM Havoc helicopter heated past critical.

An Ataka-V anti-tank missile was the first to go. The blast ignited the three other missiles in the rack as well as the five smaller weapons in the S-13 rocket pod. These in turn triggered the Product 305 air-to-air missile that the West was very eager to inspect for the first time.

The navigator and flight engineer died instantly from the impact of the multi-headed explosion against the bottom of the crew section. No one heard the copilot's scream. Instinct had him reaching for escape through his small side window when the force of the explosion severed his arm against the sill.

The combined blast was sufficient to separate the already weakened connection between the crew section and the wing assemblies. As the sides of the hull blew outward, the cockpit and living quarters were blown upward as a unit.

Because its attachment at the nose held longer than at the wing, the rear end of the twenty-meter-long assembly arced skyward, trying to fly one last time before breaking free and landing on its back ahead of the fire.

The inverted cockpit assembly now lay on Runway 23 at

Fort Campbell, Kentucky, clear of the shattered fuselage and its raging heat.

Its escape from the fire didn't matter.

The final slam of the cockpit section onto the runway had killed the last survivor.

It snapped pilot Dmitri Voskov's neck as neatly as if Major Elayne Kasprak had done it herself.

She always got her man.

1

Spieden Island, Washington
10 p.m. Pacific Standard Time
Now

MIRANDA'S PHONE INTERRUPTED HER ATTEMPT TO MAKE THE others say, "Ewan McGregor."

It was Charades, but she didn't know who Ewan McGregor was.

When she'd asked Holly for help—it was guys versus girls—she'd whispered "Star Wars" as if that explained anything.

"Timer's still running," Mike called out as she stopped to answer the call.

Good. Maybe it would run out before she was done with the call. No, Mike was tipping the tiny hourglass onto its side to stop the running sand. It *was* only fair.

"Hello?"

"Where's your team?"

Miranda had always appreciated that General Drake Nason didn't waste his time on unnecessary niceties.

"Holly's on the couch, Mike is in my mother's armchair,"—Mike looked down at his seat as if that was somehow shocking—"and Jeremy's sitting on the floor by the coffee table."

Drake's soft laugh made no sense. "Okay. Where are *all* of you?"

"At my house."

"Where is *that,* Miranda?"

Oh. "I live on Spieden Island in the San Juan Islands of Washington State, United Sta—"

"Yes, I know that Washington State is in the US."

"—States. Okay, well that's where we are."

"How fast can you get to Kentucky?"

She didn't need to ask why. There was a major military airplane crash or he wouldn't have called.

In fact, though they'd met many times, it was only the second time that the Chairman of the Joint Chiefs of Staff had called her. The first, the CIA had been using a SWAT team to try and capture her during a crash investigation. She hoped that it would be less traumatic this time.

"We've had wine. Except for Holly, who's had beer. But she's not a pilot anyway, so I suppose that isn't of direct consequence. Neither Mike nor I can legally fly for another eight hours. So, we can be aloft at six a.m. My Sabrejet can make the crossing in three hours and the Mooney in twice that."

"I assume there's a runway on your island. I'll get a C-21 headed in your direction."

"It could land, but it couldn't take off again. My runway is eleven hundred feet too short for a Learjet's minimum takeoff roll." Its required forty-seven hundred feet was almost half the length of her entire island from rocky cliff to rocky cliff.

There was a long pause before he came back. "What's the side-to-side clearance?"

"Two hundred feet."

"Good." Another, briefer pause. "I'll have a Hercules C-130 out of Joint Base Lewis McChord there in twenty minutes."

"I wouldn't advise tha—"

"Just get ready." The Chairman of the Joint Chiefs of Staff knew that Miranda hated unfinished sentences.

"I wouldn't advise *that.* No sane pilot would land a C-130 in the dark at a grass strip airport with only thirty-five feet of clearance off either wing."

"We have the best combat pilots in the world, Miranda. Be ready."

And he was gone.

"They're going to send a C-130 Hercules to land on Spieden Island?" Mike was frowning. As the team's other pilot, he would understand the implications.

"That's so cool!" Jeremy sprang to his feet and rushed off to gather his gear.

Only as they were driving the golf cart through the chill drizzle from the house to the hangar did Miranda remember the problem.

"The deer!" The sharp pine smell of the Douglas fir trees

made her think of them curled up cozily in the field grass, already growing lush despite the cold spring.

"The deer?"

"The island has a herd of deer. They've been sleeping on the northwest end of the runway lately."

"No worries." Holly dropped the three of them at the hangar to gather the rest of the gear. She always drove when they were together—which seemed to irritate Mike Munroe every time.

Perhaps that was why she insisted?

Miranda was never very sure on what made people do things.

Then Holly raced off into the night beeping the cart's little horn as she went.

Good thinking.

Only as Holly was returning from the far end and the sound of four Allison T56 turboprop engines roared by close overhead did Miranda remember to turn on the runway lights.

Not quite such good thinking.

2

"I swear to God, I thought they were messin' with me, ma'am, when you turned on those lights. Telling me to land here? Look at me, I'm still shaking." The pilot said as they ascended the plane's rear cargo ramp.

He held out his left hand with the fingers spread wide and shook it like a leaf.

Then he raised a rock-steady right hand, "Thank God this is my flying hand."

"I thought it took two hands to fly a C-130?"

"I'm so good I only need one." He winked at her for some unfathomable reason.

Miranda tried to understand how someone could control both the wheel and the throttles simultaneously with only one hand.

Before she could ask, Holly had tugged her away from the pilot and led her up the ramp.

"What's with the yellow hats, you all on the same team?" he called out after them.

"Yes," Holly called back over her shoulder.

"No," Miranda stopped. "Well, we are, but the hats aren't relevant to that. The Matildas are the Australian women's national soccer team and—"

Holly towed her out of earshot as the pilot turned to Mike and repeated his line about how he'd made the landing one-handed.

If he was untrustworthy in his speech, was he also untrustworthy as a pilot?

Miranda considered the landing to have been good work, but turning around a plane with a hundred and thirty-two-foot wingspan between massive Douglas firs only two-hundred feet apart had been even more impressive to watch. The C-130 did have a published turning ability within a hundred and eighty feet; she'd just never seen it demonstrated before.

Her own jet had a wingspan of a mere thirty-seven feet and still it felt cramped to make a full turn. The Hercules transport was by far the largest plane to ever land on Spieden Island. It was a pity that it was so dark, it would have been nice to have a picture of that.

For now, she would trust the pilot of the Hercules, if not the man who was the pilot.

She sighed.

That particular incongruity was going to bother her for a long while.

Inside, the Hercules transport's cargo bay was nine feet high, ten wide, and long enough to carry three Humvees. The four of them and their packs took up very little of the space.

As soon as they were aloft, Holly scrounged up some

blankets and ear plugs from the loadmasters. "Get shut-eye while you can."

It was good advice. Miranda had stayed up far past her bedtime to play a game she didn't understand.

And the game wasn't over. She could picture the little glass timer still lying on its side by Mike's armchair. The game was merely suspended.

A niggling piece of her brain wanted to suggest they go back and finish it first, so that it would be complete and she wouldn't be thinking about it until they did. But Holly tossed a folded blanket on the steel deck, shoved two more into her hands, and pushed Miranda down onto the first one as the plane reached its cruise altitude and headed east.

Holly lay down close beside her. The guys were up forward looking over the pilots' shoulders and asking questions about the plane—Mike about the piloting and Jeremy about how absolutely everything on the plane worked.

Miranda lay back and pictured the game.

"Holly, who is Ewan McGregor?" They were close enough that she didn't have to shout too loudly over the engine's roar to be heard, despite the earplugs.

Holly didn't bother opening her eyes. "Actor. Best known for being a Jedi master. Fights with a light saber. Becomes the second greatest Jedi master ever, Obi-wan Kenobi. At least until Luke. Nah, Obi-wan is better than Luke. Ewan's way cuter, too. Though my brother was always a fan of Luke's. Wanted to be just like him..." Holly's voice trailed away strangely.

"There are so many things that I don't understand about

that explanation that I don't know where to begin." Luke, light saber, Obi-wan, that Holly had a brother…

"You don't watch movies."

"Not space movies. And most of the action movies are so technically inaccurate that I simply can't bring myself to continue when I do start one." Which in itself was decidedly irritating. All of the incomplete movie watchings in her life were a real annoyance. "They're just…*wrong.* Did you ever see a movie called *Airplane?*"

At that Holly opened her eyes and looked at her. "That's *s'posed* to be a laugh, Miranda."

"Oh. Well, it's still wrong."

She thought about it a while.

Holly didn't say anything.

"*Air Force One* and *Flightplan* weren't much more accurate and those aren't comedies."

"Sure, but Harrison Ford and Jodi Foster sure kicked ass. He was seriously cute when he was younger. So was she for that matter—just not my type."

Miranda wondered what type of man was Holly's type. "Are you going to sleep with Mike?"

"Jesus, Miranda!" Holly jerked up to a sitting position as if she'd been electrocuted. She twisted around until she spotted Mike still standing behind the pilots' seats and released a hard puff of relief.

"What?"

"That's a hell of question."

"Why?"

Holly just sputtered.

Mike and Jeremy came back into the cargo bay and began spreading out their blankets. Miranda could hear them talking about flight characteristics and control systems. She liked that they'd been studying that. One never knew when such information would be useful during an investigation.

Holly probably already knew the plane from her deep military experience—the Australians had a number of the C-130s in their inventory.

"You still haven't answered the question." Miranda didn't like unanswered questions any better than incomplete sentences or unfinished games. They were all starting to pile up on her and were cluttering her mind.

"What question?" Jeremy chimed in.

"I just wanted to know if—"

"Nick off, all of you." Holly made a show of jamming in her earplugs before lying on her side facing the hull.

Miranda knew Holly was right. Getting some sleep *was* a good idea. Tomorrow would start in less than five hours and it was bound to be a busy day.

3

Holly could always sleep on a flight.

Any flight.

Loud engines.

Cold steel decking.

Crammed up against a pile of combat gear.

No problem.

Her years as an operator for the Australian SASR had taught her that. Special operations meant never knowing when you'd get sleep next, so sack out while you could.

The habit had followed her just fine to the Australian Transportation Safety Bureau when she'd had to leave the Special Air Service Regiment abruptly. And still when she'd opted for a year's exchange program with the NTSB because getting completely out of Australia had suddenly seemed like a really nifty idea. Not hard for anything to seem that way when your life had been totally flushed down the shitter.

But could she sleep here?

Now?

Mike?

No way!

First, she'd seen his taste in women—witnessed it on too many investigations over the six months that the team had been together.

Mike wasn't a blonde hound or a tall-and-willowy dog. He was plain and simple just a complete female hound dog.

The 737 stewardess. The captain of a UPS cargo jet. One of the eyewitness passengers from that broken Bombardier commuter jet *and* one of the air traffic controllers from the same crash—after the passenger had bought a bus ticket home, but still.

Not that she'd ever actually caught him in a hotel with one, but he sure eased up to them like an old dog, despite being a young dog.

The man was as deep as a puddle on smooth tarmac. and too...pretty.

Lousy excuse.

She liked the pretty ones. Better them than the Spec Ops operators whose egos were even more built up than their muscle tone. beyond imagining. Like, *of course* she'd want them because she was the lone Sheila on the team.

They'd learned fast quite how wrong they were.

It had gotten better toward the end, but not much. An enlightened Australian elite warrior was roughly as evolved about women as Captain Kirk in the original *Star Trek* series —on a good day.

The "pretty" ones were still nice to look at, and their egos were far more manageable.

Besides, she liked Mike Munroe, as much as she liked

any man. His Mr. Suave wasn't just in his looks. He was sharp, funny...

And she was losing her mind.

No way on earth was she that desperate.

Not that she wasn't up for a pleasant tumble now and then, but she'd rather swim with a great white shark than be another notch on Mike's brag shelf.

If anyone other than Miranda had asked, Holly could laugh it off.

But Miranda wasn't some shit-for-brains. She just saw the world in a different way. Strange and incomprehensible ways that allowed her to walk straight into the center of an airplane crash, point at some insignificant fact that no one else saw, and eventually prove it to be the solution's key.

So what was she seeing that Holly had missed?

That question was a game that Holly used to play whether doing survival training in the Outback, rock-and-ice practice up in the Snowy Mountains of New South Wales, or on assignment as Libya ate itself alive during Gaddafi's downfall. By constantly asking what was she missing, she saw so much more than most people.

Libya had been a fine time.

Muammar al-Gaddafi had finally pushed both the West and his own people too far. To give the rebels a fighting chance, NATO had sent in jets to bomb military installations. The attacks were so visible that the protests from other Western governments against them had been almost as loud as the bombs themselves.

So, they'd sent in the black ops warriors instead.

No one knew how many elite teams were on the ground, not even the teams themselves. Hers had almost taken on a squadron of French GIGN in Sabha before they figured out they were on the same side. Neither team imagined that anyone else would probe so far in-country.

Once they'd decided not to kill each other, they'd had a good time disabling, and occasionally destroying, the old MiG-25 Foxbat interceptor jets that had been based there. Gaddafi's Air Force had started out much larger than the rebels'…and ended up much smaller thanks to their efforts. They'd worked four of Gaddafi's six air bases. The rebels had controlled the other two.

There'd also been a French dragoon who she'd done a lot more than talk explosives with.

But she'd just been a young nipper back then. Now Libya was nine years in her past and her world had changed.

Her job was no longer about some game of survival—identifying and taking out military threats before they took out something themselves.

The daily challenge now was the slow-and-steady of analyzing wreckage and unraveling what had happened to it.

Crash investigator was the "new" her. Even after a year with the ATSB and six months more with Miranda at the NTSB, it still hadn't fully replaced the "old" her. Or had it? Could that be what she'd become?

Holly tucked aside the edge of the scratchy wool Air Force blanket and rested her forehead against the cold steel clarity of the C-130's cargo deck.

This was real.

The humming vibration was familiar.

Despite the two previous times that Miranda and their team were called to military air-crash investigations, it was her first time flying aboard a military plane in over a year.

All too familiar.

Like she was back home, in so many ways.

The accents were American and her teammates were crash investigators rather than black ops warriors.

But it was home.

Except she could never go back home.

It was a kindness that Command had merely let Holly fade away. Nobody wanted the embarrassment of court-martialing one of the nation's most elite warriors. They said it wasn't her fault, but she knew better.

Frankly, if she'd been in command, Holly would have taken herself off into the Outback and put a round through her thick skull.

4

"This one is ugly, Miranda."

One of the pilots had woken her twenty minutes from landing to take the secure radio call from the Chairman of the Joint Chiefs of Staff. CJCS General Drake Nason didn't sound as if this was one of his teases.

"Okay."

The sun was just rising out beyond the windshield of the C-130 Hercules. The rolling fields and the wooded hills of Kentucky were still deep enough in shadow to all look the same.

"I need to know what happened and I need to know it fast."

"Drake you know—"

"—that you can't guarantee results, duration of the investigation, or any of that."

Miranda considered her distaste for incomplete sentences. Was it acceptable when someone else had completed her sentence correctly for her?

Yes, she supposed that it was. Therefore, she allowed Drake's interruption to stand.

But was it now his sentence or was it still hers? Was it her turn to speak next?

Drake resolved the question for her by continuing. "Just hurry, Miranda. Call me if you need anything. I placed a Major Swift in charge of protecting the crash site—I trust him implicitly and you may safely do so as well. Shit this thing's a mess. I'd rather that no one knew about it."

"Then why did you ask for this team?"

"Because, Miranda, I'm guessing that without them you're of much less use to me. Sorry. That was more blunt than I intended."

"Meaning that I'm unreliable." She didn't mind blunt; it was far easier to follow than implication or suggestion. But to be called unreli—

"No! Shit!" Drake groaned. "It came out wrong. Not unreliable. Maybe *unpredictable?* More... I don't know. I've seen how you function with your team—and without. You're...better...with them. You and your people are doing things that no military crash team can match. I need that Team Chase magic on this one."

"Team Chase?" How would the others react to not having their names included?

"I need to know if it was a crash or an attack on US soil. And I need to know *fast.*"

That was language she finally understood. "I'll tell the others."

As she handed the headset back to the engineer, the pilots slowed the engines for the long descent from their cruising altitude.

Holly was awake and sitting in one of the fold-down web seats that lined either side of the cargo bay. She'd chosen a seat as far as possible from where the two guys still slept.

Miranda went and sat by Holly.

"Something nasty, boss?"

"That was Drake. He chose the adjective 'ugly.' He's placing a major rush on the cause: accident or attack?"

Holly whistled tunelessly for a moment as if just passing the time. "Sounds like fun. Did he tell you anything else?"

"We're to liaison with a Major Swift."

"I meant about the crash?"

Miranda could only shake her head. "You said that it 'Sounds like fun.' You always have a strange idea of what's entertaining, Holly. I can never seem to predetermine what you'll find amusing."

"That's okay, following your thoughts isn't exactly a cakewalk either. I've been thinking about that..." Holly glanced toward where Mike and Jeremy still slept before continuing softly, "...open issue."

"Which one? The Ewan McGregor one or whether you were planning to—"

"The second one. What? Are you still worried about the first one?"

"Mike laid the timer on its side. The matter is held in suspension pending completion of that step of the game."

"Well, we could just play out the last bit of it between now and when we land if that would make you feel better."

"No, we can't. The timer is still in Washington. We're in Kentucky." If she'd thought to bring it, would she have been able to keep it level so that the amount of remaining time didn't change? Probably not. Better that it remained where it was.

"It's just a game, Miranda. It doesn't really matter."

"Is that supposed to make me feel better about not completing my assigned task? Can the pilot really land a C-130 with only one hand? Is all of the teasing you and Mike do just a game?"

"The first? Mellow out. The second? No, he was joking. And—"

"Or is it a prelude to sexual relations? Or have there already been sexual relations between you of which I'm unaware and this is part of an aftermath pattern? I don't understand how to judge that and assess—"

"Whoa! Whoa! Whoa! I have not slept with Mike and I don't plan on *ever* doing the old two-step with that boyo."

"But—"

"No, Miranda. I don't want to know what you observed that made you ask that question."

"What question?" Jeremy had come up without either of them noticing.

"Nothing," Holly almost shouted. "Girl stuff."

Then she grabbed Miranda's hand and hooked their pinkie fingers together.

"Girl talk only," Holly looked so seriously into Miranda's eyes that she couldn't look anywhere else.

Holly spoke so softly that Miranda had to pull an earplug to be sure she heard properly. The engine and propeller noise had abated somewhat for landing or she wouldn't have heard Holly's next words even without the ear plugs.

"Pinkie swear. Girls only."

Miranda had never done a pinkie swear before.

Not ever.

"Okay. Pinkie swear. Girls only."

At Holly's nod, Miranda felt as if she'd done something right.

"Do we need to pinkie swear about the security on the crash investigation?" It seemed to fit but she was unfamiliar with the detailed rules governing pinkie swears versus other levels of secrecy classifications.

"No," Holly kept their fingers hooked. "Pinkie swears are way more powerful than security clearances."

"Oh. Okay. We should probably wake Mike."

"I'll do it." Holly let go and pushed to her feet before Jeremy could even turn his head.

She strode up the length of the cargo deck. Holly looked as if she was going to kick Mike in the ass—hard. Instead she glanced back at Miranda, appeared to sigh, and then kicked the bottom of Mike's boot with enough force to have him yelp in surprise.

"What was that for?" he looked around wildly, blinking hard to clear away sleep.

"You deserved it."

"Why?"

"Just... Trust me, you did! Now get your act together, for once. We're landing soon, you total wanker."

5

Elayne Kasprak enjoyed the First-Class American Airlines direct flight to JFK. International customs never caused her problems, except the Swedes, who appeared to be impervious to all of her usual I'm-so-cute-and-innocent tactics for easing through borders. She could almost like them for that.

Delta Business to Nashville was also surprisingly pleasant.

Zaslon, unlike US Special Operations, pampered its operators whenever it could. Their near unlimited budget wasn't restricted to just weapons and training, but also offered comfortable travel and fine hotels—when it wasn't out of character.

The SUV that she rented as Valery Tomaka in Nashville for the hour drive to Fort Campbell was a little flashy for her role, but she trusted American drivers even less than Russian ones and preferred the added protection. Besides, the Porsche Cayenne was hella fun to drive. The gas mileage sucked like most SUVs, but gas here in the United States cost about the same as it did in Russia, despite having double the mean income. Really cheap.

Americans were *so* spoiled.

Not her worry.

Her worry was passing herself off as the Antonov factory rep long enough to ascertain that no useful intelligence was recoverable from the crash. It wasn't often that she had the opportunity to review her demolition handiwork and looked forward to that.

Normally, she'd have used a timer and blown them out of the sky over the Atlantic. But Command had wanted to rub it in the Americans' faces that they almost had the six Russian helicopters—until they suddenly didn't.

She'd timed her trip well.

When the Antonov had finally left Helsinki, she'd already been halfway to New York. The layover in JFK and driving up from Nashville had placed her just eight hours after the crash.

So, her cover story couldn't be that she'd come from overseas. And she hadn't looked up what technical conferences might have placed her already in the US. March was too early for the big US airshows.

"I was meeting with a client in..." she practiced on a massive furniture truck in the next lane as she blew by it on Route 24.

Houston would be NASA's Space Center...no.

Washington, DC? No, that would imply more than she wished to.

Florida? Too boring. And it would imply too little.

San Antonio? Yes! It was nicknamed Military City for a reason.

She wouldn't need the heavy-handed English she'd required with Voskov. Russian-inflected with minor syntactical errors would be more than sufficient.

"I was meeting with a client in San Antonio. No, I can't say which one."

No contractions.

"No, I can not—make it two distinct words—say with which one. *Da.* That is better," she told the next truck with a giant Chick-fil-A sign on the side.

Fast-food fried chicken versus the slow-braised beef tenderloin with finger potatoes and fresh baby asparagus served with a split of California merlot during her transatlantic first-class flight. Tough choice.

She hated fast food with a passion—America's most heinous export. She only ate it when some of Zaslon team she was temporarily inserted with, usually for training, insisted they "Go eat American" at a Moscow McDonalds or some other similar slimehole.

San Antonio. It was good. Such a story would imply that she had security clearances without having to reveal what they weren't.

And she had a forged Antonov ID just in case she'd needed it to get on the plane last night. Whoops! Except that was in the name of Elayne Kasprak.

So she was Elayne. The only one who knew her as Valery should be very dead at the moment. Actually, if the Antonov's pilot was still alive, her presence would be inexplicable, but she had confidence in her work. He wouldn't be.

She punched scan on the radio until she found a local news station.

The Top story took less than three minutes to cycle through: *Major crash at Campbell Army Airfield. No survivors.*

Perfect.

Elayne turned off the radio and stowed Valery Tomaka back in a safe corner of her mind for some future mission.

"You are now Elayne Kasprak, Antonov engineer. You have just come from meetings— What? Oh, sorry, I can not say what meetings, in your San Anne Tonio."

Yes, that would work well.

She hadn't had occasion to try an American military commissary, but their reputation was good. Maybe this time.

6

Miranda watched the pilots carefully as their C-130 Hercules transport neared the shorter Runway 18. It crossed the main runway at one end of Campbell Army Airfield.

But the copilot was in control for the landing, and he used two hands. She didn't get to see if the pilot used two hands or not.

Disappointed, she turned to watch out one of the three small round windows.

Wisps of smoke still wove lazily upward, lit by the first rays of sunlight. Every Striker fire truck from the entire base must be gathered around the massive wreckage in the center of the main runway.

It was too obscured by the smoke and spray foam to readily identify.

"That's a right mess," Holly said close by her shoulder.

Mike and Jeremy were each at one of the other two windows.

"Thanks, Miranda," Holly continued in a whisper. "I'm so not up for explaining your question to those two."

It was one of those situations where there were two separate conversations going on. Miranda could now recognize when this was occurring, but it still flummoxed her on how to handle it.

"What I'm trying to understand about relationships in general is—"

"For us to talk about later. When there aren't any boys around."

"Is..." Now she was stuck with an unfinished sentence on top of an unfinished game as well as a one- or two-handed pilot. Things were piling up.

Fine. She would focus on the wreck. That's how she would handle all of these broken pieces. Focus on the one thing she was good at to the exclusion of all else in her life.

"I don't like seeing it all at once." She preferred to approach a wreck in stages from the outermost sphere of environment, moving to the innermost of systems and data recorders. Then interviews last of all to corroborate her findings. With a logical framework, she could develop a more accurate and holistic platform from which to build information architectures upon which to test original causes.

"Don't think of it as information gathered too soon. Think of it as an overview to aid in choosing next actions."

Miranda turned to face Holly, and to look away from the wreck. "You're suggesting that I pre-construct a, if you will, meta-sphere with a tentative structure that I reshape as the investigation progresses."

"Wow! You should definitely be yarning with Jeremy on that one. He'll be sorry he missed that."

"I didn't! That's an utterly awesome—" Jeremy dropped into the seat next to them and snapped on a seatbelt just moments before the wheels hit the runway, "—way to think about it. Then any hypotheses can be tested against a dynamic three-dimensional space."

"Dynamic, yet hypothetical," Miranda didn't like it. "Hypotheses are dangerous by predisposing our minds to certain conclusions."

"Right but—"

"Down to stun, buddy," Mike clapped a hand on Jeremy's shoulder. "Don't mess with the magic."

"What magic?"

Mike reached across Jeremy to tap Miranda's forehead in what appeared to be a friendly fashion.

Miranda tried to blink away the feeling of foreignness where Mike had tapped her. When that didn't work, she scrubbed at it with her hand and it seemed to come off.

"Magic?" Jeremy squinted at her forehead as if trying to see something there.

She had to rub her forehead again after all his staring. "I don't feel very magic. Oh, wait. That's what Drake was asking for."

"You spoke with General Nason?" Mike leaned on Jeremy's shoulder as if he was a signpost. The plane had slowed from its landing and was taxiing across the airport.

"Yes, that's why we woke you. Drake has declared this to be a matter of national security. He's very concerned that it might have been an attack. He has asked for," Miranda took a deep breath, unsure how the others would react, "Team Chase magic."

"Whoo-hoo!" Jeremy raised his hand in a high five.

"Team Chase!" Mike and Holly called out in unison and took turns slapping Jeremy's palm and each other's.

"It doesn't bother any of you that he didn't include your names in the team?"

Mike shook his head and smiled.

Jeremy slapped his hand over his heart, "It's an honor."

"Team Chase it is," Holly whispered in her ear.

Miranda would never understand people.

7

HOLLY COULDN'T SEEM TO CATCH HER BREATH.

Team Chase.

Fuck!

She hadn't been part of a team since...

Since...

The end of her decade as an operator for the Australian Special Air Service Regiment.

One infinitesimal moment in time, one tiny decision, and she'd gone from being on a SASR team she trusted to the extremes of life-and-death to...

Nothing.

To be on a team again was incomprehensible. Beyond pear-shaped and right over into FUBAR—effed up beyond all recovery.

She should hit the ground and run the other way. For all of their sakes.

But for six months, these three wonderful people had

welcomed her. They'd given her a sense of belonging that she missed like a piece of her body.

Without even noticing, she'd slid back into patterns and modes that she swore she'd never risk again. She'd lost an entire team once, even more than that once before. When she left SASR, Holly had sworn off being anything but independent ever again.

But now...*Team* Chase?

This was wrong in so many ways that she didn't know what to do. But that didn't make it any less true.

Habits were deeply ingrained; they were how a soldier stayed alive when the situation went sideways. By rote, Holly shrugged on her NTSB vest, shouldered her field kit, and tugged down on the brim of her Matildas baseball cap.

Third time was the charm, right?

After all, she'd survived the first two disasters, even if no one else had.

That was one promise she made here and now. No one on this team would ever be at risk—other than herself.

Like a, God help her, *team,* they trooped through the cargo bay together as the rear ramp of the C-130 Hercules began to lower.

Despite herself, she began noticing the details.

The March air spilling into the gap was crisp but not cold. Probably over ten degrees—forty-five in this last bastion of Fahrenheit temperatures—and already smelling of spring in ways that were still a month away on Miranda's private island.

Rather than taxiing to the hangar, the C-130 Hercules had taxied onto the main runway and carried them close to the crash, before doing one of those tight turns. The lowering ramp revealed the wreck in stages.

The first thing to see was the farthest away, the tall vertical tail rose perfectly straight six stories into the sky. Painted white with a blue swoosh on the side of it.

"An Antonov AN-124 Condor." She knew she was right without even seeing the rest of the plane.

"Really?" Jeremy was pushing up on his toes to see more, but Miranda's nod confirmed Holly's identification.

As the ramp lowered more, it revealed nothing else that belonged to the monstrous plane.

Nothing of the upper fuselage in front of the wings remained.

The wings themselves were broken off and lying to either side of the fuselage. The hull itself had been flattened. Yet somehow that banner of a tail had remained upright.

A gentle, sunrise breeze flickered by, just strong enough to riffle her hair across her neck. Then it brushed by a little stronger as if pushing aside the last of the night.

It also brushed the giant tail.

Which wavered.

One way.

The other.

Then it began to topple to the right.

There were shouts among the fire crews that were still gathered around the wreck. In moments, they were jumping out of Striker firefighting engines and sprinting to get away from the fifty-foot wide, six-story-tall tumbling tailfin.

It looked as if everyone got clear, but two of the big airport fire engines were probably write-offs as the tail crashed down on top of them.

The bang as it slammed onto the runway seemed to gather and boom around the inside of their parked Hercules, forcing them all to cover their ears.

With that piece gone, the plane was a much squatter affair. The main part of the hull had been blown outward as if someone had filleted its backbone and peeled it open to lie flat, except for the pieces that had been blown completely aside.

In front of the plane lay a massive block of metal that seemed as if it should make sense, but it didn't.

"Well, at least the cockpit section remained structurally intact," Miranda said to no one in particular as they all moved down the Hercules' ramp and headed towards the wreck. "There should be some good information there."

"The cockpit? Where is it?" Thankfully Mike asked the question so that she didn't have to.

Then Holly saw it.

The entire cockpit section had been flipped onto its back in front of the plane. It was the craziest thing she'd ever seen.

"This crash separated further aft than the C-5B Galaxy that crashed in Dover in 2006," Jeremy pointed. "See, the entire crew module remained intact. Of course this one was separated from the lower section of the fuselage. The Dover C-5 broke vertically across the boundary between avionics and crew quarters when they crashed two thousand feet short of the runway. This appears to be the entire section from the cockpit to the aft bulkhead. We gotta check this out."

Jeremy raced off.

Holly was about to follow. Should have followed. Should

have controlled Jeremy into following Miranda's meticulous approach to crashes.

But she couldn't.

Miranda, apparently caught up in the swirl of Jeremy's wake, also moved ahead.

"Who's the ghost?" Mike stood at casual ease beside her.

Holly stood just one step from the runway, both feet still barely on the C-130's ramp. Perched before the fall. The cliff.

"You've obviously just seen one. Even for a 'hot blonde Sheila with a sexy accent from Down Under'," he teased her with a broad Strine accent. "Seriously, Holly. Never seen you so pale. What's up?"

Unable to think of how to explain her ghosts—besides, she'd rather be eaten by a dingo in the middle of the Great Victoria Desert than try—Holly did the only thing she could think of.

She hit him.

Not in his pretty face—but hard.

8

"WHAT THE *HELL* IS WRONG WITH YOU, WOMAN?" MIKE shouted from behind them.

Miranda turned just in time to almost be plowed to the ground by Holly who was head down and moving fast.

What was wrong with *her?* Miranda should start a list about herself—but never did because she was half afraid that if she started she'd never be able to finish no matter how long it was.

Mike had both arms wrapped around his ribcage.

Then she understood that Holly was the target of his question.

If she understood their expressions correctly, they definitely weren't sleeping together. Or if they had been, they weren't anymore.

Miranda wanted to ask, but recalled the pinkie swear just in time.

Mike was still back at the helicopter ramp, doubled over now.

Jeremy was well ahead.

She and Holly stood in a void between them.

But an Air Force officer was walking up to them.

The pinkie swear had included the phrase, "Girl talk only." Did that preclude asking why Holly had struck Mike due to the presence of an unknown male?

She was fairly certain that it did. But did that additionally prevent her from inquiring whether or not the stranger's presence did indeed invoke that implied but unstated aspect of a pinkie swear? Pinkie swears should be like planes; they should come with a manual.

Her doubt was set aside—along with the unfinished game, the unanswered status of Holly's relationship with Mike, and the pilot's one-handed flying abilities—for the moment. Assuming her head didn't simply split in two before any of those were answered.

"Ms. Chase, I assume." The officer's greeting was cheery. "Hope you're not having any trouble with your people." He winked at Holly for reasons that passed understanding.

"Not a bit," Holly replied, then pointed at her. "But she's the one you want."

He stood five-ten, half a foot taller than Miranda herself, and had short, wavy hair that was halfway between her brown and Holly's blonde. Fatigues, a light jacket, and major's oak leaves on the collar points.

"My apologies. Didn't expect the NTSB's Number One investigator to stand half a foot down. I'm Major Jonathan Swift, but everyone calls me Gull."

"From *Jonathan Livingston Seagull,* I assume," Mike came up, though he was still rubbing his ribs as he introduced himself.

"No," Miranda shook her head. "It would be because Jonathan Swift wrote *Gulliver's Travels.* Actually, that's what it's commonly called, but the proper title is *Travels into Several Remote Nations of the World. In Four Parts.* I found your book very confusing."

"Not my doing," Major Swift held up his hands. "Mom found out we're very remotely related so named me for him. They rousted me for the crash four hours ago. Two hours ago Chairman of the Joint Chiefs of Staff General Nason did everything short of ordering me to polish your boots as my first priority."

"I'm Miranda Chase. Investigator-in-Charge for the NTSB." Introductions had already happened, but an investigation required that she state who she was. Not NTSB rules, but Miranda rules. It sounded odd this time. Apparently Major Gull thought so as well.

Major Swift? Gull? If General Nason wanted her to call him Drake...

"Jon, I'm ready to start."

He waved her toward the wreck.

She turned her back on him and the wreck, and looked up to observe the sky. The sunrise was now fully above the trees and she could already feel the coming warmth of the day on her face.

Jeremy rushed up. "Wind light and variable. I asked the tower and it was at the time of the crash as well. No report of microbursts. The terrain is flat with no significant hills or obstacles in the flight path. The runway was dry, no rain or ice on the surface. Overnight low was just thirty-nine degrees. Humidity low at forty-five percent."

"Thank you." That defined her outer layers of interest. "Let's do a perimeter walk to define the debris area."

Yet she continued scanning the field. Fort Campbell was a new one for her and it was unlike any other she'd ever been to. The hangars and runway configuration were typical enough. Yet something was bothering her and she wouldn't be able to focus until she understood what it was.

A flight of five pitch-black MH-6M Little Bird helicopters lifted in unison.

That's when she picked it out. Most airports were dedicated to airplanes—helicopters were incidental or simply not present.

Here the vast apron parking areas were populated with long rows of neatly aligned helicopters. Small Little Birds, Black Hawks, massive Chinook twin-rotor transports, and Apache attack helos. One whole section of the rotorcraft were painted in typical Army colors, but another were all painted in flat black—Night Stalkers' black.

By the time she turned to the wreck, Jeremy waved a fistful of orange flags on thin wire stakes he'd pulled from his pack. "They won't work on the runway, but we can lay them down in the right places and replace them with cones later if we need to."

Miranda walked slowly forward, looking for the leading edge of the debris.

"Why you in particular?" Mike asked Jon as they followed close behind her.

"I'm with the US Air Force Air Combat Command Accident Investigation Board. Now there's a mouthful. Normally you'd have a colonel heading an investigation, but it wasn't one of our airframes, so you only get a lowly major."

"You don't seem very bothered about having us treading on your turf."

"Are you kidding? I've been waiting years to work with Miranda Chase. She's something of a legend, you know. All the way back to..."

Miranda blocked them out when she spotted a sheared 12 mm bolt lying on the pavement. She pointed, and Jeremy lay a flag beside it.

She looked up and had to stumble backward. Jagged shards of metal, which hung on the back of the cockpit module's rear bulkhead, stood out mere inches from her face. The surface stretched a story high and twice as wide. It was curiously devoid of features.

She flickered a flashlight into the large hole. The only one in the rear bulkhead, but there wasn't much to see from outside. A few bits of white, but mostly scorched debris.

Beyond this bulkhead lay the crew compartments. To this side would have been the wing structure and central fuel tanks. Other than control connections—now little more than sheared steel wires and electrical cables—there was only one other significant penetration of the surface. A small access door bent beyond any possibility of opening.

The structural connections along the hull edge, now lying at her feet, were badly deformed by the accident.

"Jeremy?"

"Here!"

"I want both a still and video record of everything. Start right here. The rest of us will do the perimeter walk."

"Team Chase! I'm on it!" He pulled out his tablet and selected an image-mapping application. Each photograph would have its precise GPS position stored as a part of its metadata. "Want to give me a hand, Major Swift?"

"Jon. Sure." And Jeremy handed him a compact video camera.

"Holly? Mike? Let's go."

Usually Miranda took the outside end of the line so that she could assure herself that nothing lay further afield, but this time Holly and Mike lined up on either side of her.

Miranda was about to ask Holly to switch positions with her but Holly shook her head—short and sharp.

Miranda guessed that meant she was supposed to stay where she was. She didn't like it, but Holly was often right about things that Miranda didn't perceive at first, so she stayed in the middle as they began the walk.

9

Elayne's ID as an Antonov engineer let her slip through Fort Campbell's security. She knew it was standard for a specialist from the manufacturer to be at any major crash investigation. Apparently the gate guards knew the same thing.

Normally, of course, they'd be there to make sure that the minimum of blame was attached to their aircraft, but she didn't give a damn about that. She simply needed to verify the extent of the destruction, and make sure that the investigation didn't point any blame toward Russia.

Her role also earned her an armed escort, with her rental left at the gate.

Fine with her.

She did her best to kick back and act casual, but it was hard. It was the first time she'd been on a US military base, at least inside the US.

Aviano Airbase in Italy had been a delightful storehouse of interesting information. It was amazing how dense guys were. Her Italian wasn't even particularly good, but her clothes and her cleavage had been the top of Milan-casual and opened many interesting doors. A very successful intelligence gathering mission for her superiors, including numerous selfies with the over-friendly pilot, which showed very interesting equipment in the backgrounds.

Fort Campbell's Morgan Road—better paved than most roads in Russia—slid past whole sections of housing. What had to be officers' homes, bigger than anything she'd ever lived in, gave way to smaller homes that were still ridiculously luxurious. There wasn't a single one under two hundred square meters. Two thousand square feet sounded even larger—maybe that's why Americans kept the English measurement system.

Each house had a yard and at least a two-car garage. Each group of them had a playground for their families. What did they do with so much space?

A few turns and they were going past nondescript office buildings, training centers, and a gym. A Burger King commanded a major intersection.

A grove of thick trees to the right, a hospital to the left—good to know in case there actually was a survivor that the radio report hadn't known about. If there was, she'd have to find a way in there to make sure their survival was brief. Not impossible, now that she was inside the security perimeter, but not easy. It would probably include killing her escort driver, which wouldn't be much of a waste. If he was a typical specimen of "America's Finest," Russia had little to worry about—lean and gawky.

They drove past a helicopter parking area.

All black!

The 160th Special Operations Aviation Regiment (airborne). She must contrive a way to inspect these. Some of them were so specialized and rare that there were under twenty of them anywhere—and they were all for the Night Stalkers. If she could get aboard a DAP Hawk and take good pictures, they'd make her a *polkovnik*—jumping straight from major to colonel.

Even as she watched, a Black Hawk lifted clear of the field before shooting away to the south where she knew they had a large training range.

Then everything else dropped away.

Past the hospital, the view of the runway opened out before them.

They'd arrived at midfield, and dead ahead was the most magnificent wreck she'd ever seen.

Like a dissected frog, the plane was opened up and spread out with all of its insides showing. The twisted, melted masses of the helicopters—which took her a moment to even identify as such—were among the highest points remaining.

She'd make sure that everything, and everyone, was accounted for, but she could already see that her work here was done.

Most of the people she could see were close by the wreck, still dressed in firefighting outfits.

Most, but not all.

A small group of three people were well away from the aircraft. They were walking parallel to it rather than toward it. Every twenty steps or so they did a curious sideways shift, sometimes inward, sometimes outward.

Locating the debris perimeter.

The site investigation team.

"Take me over to them," she ordered the geek. They'd have the most information on personnel and salvageable information.

Without even asking a question, he drove in their direction.

10

MIRANDA APPEARED TO BE OBLIVIOUS TO THE APPROACHING vehicle.

After more than an hour staring at the ground for every stray nut and bolt, Holly was feeling a little oblivious herself.

The vehicle was coming far too close for Holly's comfort. Most of the explosion's force had been dissipated upward, but enough had been lateral to scatter pieces far and wide.

They were following a distinct bulge in the shape of the debris field that was wider than at any other point.

The white Ford Explorer, with a bright-green Fort Campbell Military Police decal, showed no signs of stopping short of the possible debris area. Holly finally gave up any pretense of searching the ground and starting walking toward the vehicle to stop it with her palm facing out.

"Holly? Where are you going?" Miranda called after her.

She'd learned that Miranda would flounder with such an unexplained change, but she didn't have time to explain.

Instead, she needed something to occupy Miranda's attention for the moment.

Still, the car kept heading toward them.

"Why is there such a big bulge in the debris field here, Miranda? Wider than a billabong." She hated to do it. Forcing Miranda's focus to shift from inspection to conjecture would be hard for her to recover from.

Nothing but silence behind her. It had worked, she just hoped it wouldn't take her too long to recover.

Holly accelerated her pace until she finally came to a standstill directly in front of the vehicle's path.

She could see bits of debris to either side. Inconsequential bits, but the field did reach this far. Probably more that the vehicle was driving over.

Miranda would be upset.

Holly was *livid.*

The MP jerked to halt close enough that she could bang the hood, so she did. Hard enough to dent the metal.

"Hey!" the driver shouted.

"Back it up!"

The driver climbed out of the car with a hand on his sidearm but was looking at the hood of his car. "Why did you do that? I have to report that, you know."

She got right up in his face. "I. Said. To. Back. Up. You fuck knuckle. What part of that didn't you understand?" Fury beyond any reason roiled in her gut.

The patrolman jerked out his sidearm.

She double slapped his wrist. Her left hand took control of his weapon as her right broke his wrist. She then unleashed a right elbow into his solar plexus. Rather than letting him collapse, she jammed his gun up under his chin hard enough to have him rising on his toes to ease the pressure despite wheezing for breath.

The passenger door swung open.

Holly shifted her grip. Her right fingers, wrapped around his windpipe, kept him on his toes as she aimed the Beretta M9 pistol at his fellow patrol officer with her left.

The small woman, with white-blonde hair and civilian clothes, slapped for a weapon.

It took all of Holly's training to not put a round through her forehead.

She was unarmed—and froze in place with her hand slapped against her hip.

The patrolman gurgled as Holly kept him suspended by his windpipe. She let him go and he collapsed to the ground. A slap on the small of his back as he went down revealed no backup piece. She kicked his ankle and he grunted as her boot connected with steel.

Keeping the M9 aimed at the woman's face, Holly knelt down and found a Colt M1911 inside his right ankle by feel—ridiculous monster for a backup, heavier and half the number of rounds of his official issue. She slipped it into her waistband.

"Real slow. Hands on the hood."

The woman was exceptionally careful to make no extraneous movements as she complied.

Holly edged over to the door and glanced in. Everything in the car was oriented for the driver—laptop computer, shotgun holder, even a lone coffee cup rather than two.

Shifting the other way around the hood, Holly moved until she had a clear view of the woman, but didn't approach her. The SASR had trained her not to make that typical mistake of letting herself get within grappling range. A lesson the groaning cop probably still hadn't learned.

Designer boots. Skinny jeans that had never seen a Gap. A silk blouse and a leather jacket tailored tightly enough to reveal any but the slimmest weapon. It didn't.

"What's going on here?" Major Swift sounded as if he'd come on the run; actually, some part of her had heard him doing just that but not cataloged him as a threat.

"Jesus, Holly," Mike was close behind him though he'd started out closer than Swift.

A quick glance revealed Miranda was with him.

She began speaking directly to Holly immediately on arrival. "Based on the wings having broken free, and as they are presently lying along either side of the fuselage, it implies that the expanded debris field was most likely due to an explosion occurring in the forward section of the plane."

The white-blonde made some move that drew Holly's attention fully back to her. But her position was unchanged —other than her gaze had shifted from Holly's weapon to Miranda.

"Further, as you've asked me to create a meta-sphere of potential for testing conjecture, I would estimate that the explosion was centered under the aft third of the cockpit section. This *would* shear it from the wing box assembly and blow it upward. For that to occur with sufficient force to flip the entire cockpit section end-for-end, it would have to be an explosive in the thirty-to-fifty kilo range, I think. That's taking into consideration the hull surviving intact long enough to maximize explosive overpressure. Perhaps a hundred kilos, but that doesn't fit the damage profiles we've seen on the debris so far.

Perhaps less if something else had already weakened the structure. But thirty-to-fifty is a good first-level approximation."

Then Miranda looked from Holly's arms to the gun in her hand to the unknown woman leaning against the car hood as if noticing it for the first time.

"What's going on here?"

"Precisely my question," Major Swift was kneeling by his downed patrolman.

"That...no-hoper," Holly resisted the urge to kick him just as hard as she'd punched Mike, "drove into an uninspected debris area despite my signaling him to stop. Then he drew on me when I stopped him."

The anger hadn't abated. It had been churning there in her gut just as it had when Mike had attacked with his question.

"He did *what?*" Miranda immediately circled the vehicle, repeatedly squatting to look underneath the vehicle. She crossed within a foot of the unknown woman putting herself in easy range as a hostage. Miranda had all the survival instincts of...Holly couldn't come up with a decent analogy. No animal walked knowingly into danger, yet Miranda had done that several times over the last six months. And now she was simply being oblivious.

Apparently satisfied that there was nothing under the vehicle, she began backtracking along its line of arrival, looking for damaged evidence.

Holly forced herself to reassess.

"I may have bunged his Ford's hood a bit first," she had to admit.

"I didn't stop," the patrolman croaked after Major Swift

helped him sit up, "because I didn't see you. I almost ran you over."

"I was right in front of you. What the hell were you looking at?"

He glanced behind her as he cradled his wrist. "I didn't even know we had a crash. I just came on shift and they told me to escort Ms. Kasprak to the airfield. Then I saw that."

The blonde looked chagrined. Apparently *she* was used to being the center of any male's attention.

"And who are you?" Holly reset the weapon's safety but didn't lower it just yet.

"Elayne Kasprak. Antonov engineer. That. It is one of our planes and I was sent to assist in inspection of it." Her English was heavily Russian and only a little awkward.

"You arrived quickly." Holly handed the weapon back to the patrolman.

He reached out with his broken wrist and yelped. Holly took pity on him and tucked the M9 back in his holster for him.

"I was in your Military City, San Anne Tonio? Meeting with clients. Yes. We have only one hull loss since 1996 and that, it is not our fault—they shelled our poor plane on the ground at Libya airport in June 2019. We're very upset over this new loss and wish to help solve it quickly for our reputation."

Holly untucked the Colt M1911 from her belt and shoved it back into the patrolman's ankle holster as Major Swift helped him to his feet and led him to the back seat of the car.

"You might find a better driver next time."

"Not my choosings. May I lift my hands now?"

Holly nodded and half a second later Mike slimed in with his hand extended.

"Welcome, Elayne. Mike Munroe, NTSB. Sorry for the greeting. We're glad of any help; this one's a mess."

So predictable.

As the Major drove the car and the patrolman toward the nearby clinic, Miranda returned to look under where the tires had been at rest.

"Nothing important. It's okay."

So *totally* predictable.

11

SHE SHOULD NEVER, *EVER* HAVE SLAPPED FOR HER WEAPON. Elayne hadn't been expecting to face a soldier on an accident team, but she should have. It was a military team.

And fast!

Hopefully, like didn't recognize like. Of course, Elayne had been given more to observe. The takedown of the patrolman hadn't been textbook; it had been reflex. That was a very deep level of training. Ex-Special Forces. Perhaps even ex-Special Operations?

Yes, she must be very careful not to reveal more of herself to the team's enforcer.

And here was the perfect distraction.

"Mike Munroe. A pleasure to be meeting you." She shook his hand with a warm gentle grip that men liked, but not so light that they'd think she wouldn't be fun in bed.

She made a point of looking him in the eyes, a pleasant if unremarkable brown. But his face was so handsome they were of little consequence.

"What has your team learned so far?" Elayne asked him. The blonde woman was clearly his team's security officer and could be ignored.

"We were just finishing up the edge patrol of the debris field. The fire crews appear to have extinguished the last of the fires, so we'll be moving to inspect the wreck now. How long have you been working for Antonov?" She let Mike lead her away from the others.

"Not for so very long." She must remember to keep her English rough. And her answer must give her an excuse for not knowing more about the Antonov than she did. "I was flight...specialist. Yes?"

"Flight attendant?"

"Yes!"

And she could tell that this Mike knew just exactly what reputation most flight attendants had—whether or not they deserved it.

"I work for Aeroflot while I make my engineering degree. I leave when they invade Ukraine and take Crimea from us. At Antonov, I use my new degree, my flight experience, and my very good skills with customers for Antonov cargo operations. I also help negotiate new parts. We can no longer use Russian parts and must make new contracts with Americans and British for what we do not make ourselves."

"So, now you're here to make sure that it wasn't a problem with your plane."

"*Nyet!* Never! Our planes are so very good. Not their fault."

"If you say so, I'll believe you. Shall we go see your innocent plane?"

"No," a brunette no taller than Elayne herself stopped

beside them for a moment. "I'd like to map the major debris first."

"But they need to reopen the runway as soon as possible." Suddenly Mike appeared to be the submissive one, not the team leader Elayne had been trying to attach to.

"I don't think that should have an effect our course of action," the brunette was adamant.

"Will the possibility of a speedy result best be served by mapping the debris field or by an initial inspection of the hull?" Mike sounded as if he had no opinion and was waiting for the brunette.

Elayne was trying to figure out what was happening. Who was this little woman? She should be a librarian or a schoolteacher for little children. She—

"An interesting question with numerous open variables. We don't know the relevant details, Mike. There's—"

"Something strange about this aircraft," a young Asian man interrupted.

"Very good, Jeremy. That is precisely the point I was about to make."

The young man looked as if he'd just been patted on the head like a dog.

"However, Mike's point is not without merit."

"Mike said something useful? That's news," the blonde enforcer joined them and her tone was quite dismissive.

Elayne's head was spinning. Who *was* in charge here? Her normal tactics included attaching herself to the team leader—male or female. That always afforded her both the purest information flow as well as being best placed to strategically mistrack any plans that weren't to Elayne's advantage.

"Let's consider," the small brunette spoke and no one interrupted.

"Consider what?" Elayne asked into the silence.

"Try using your ears, and keeping your gob shut," the enforcer snarled at her.

"Nice one, Holly," Mike shifted closer to her, but Elayne was no longer sure if she *wanted* him close. But she'd already blown the join-with-the-leader gambit. This Mike was now her designated access point into this investigation.

Or maybe Mike *was* the leader and this Holly person was a complete bitch even to her team leader?

"Major Swift *has* already twice inquired how long it will be before he can begin clearing the runway." Again, it was the brunette leading the conversation.

"Do we even have a body count yet?" Mike asked.

"Six," Elayne spoke and then wished she hadn't. She knew because she'd screwed one and been introduced to five others—while her shirt was still unbuttoned enough to reveal that she wore no bra. Voskov had apparently liked bragging to his crew. It had been useful to have them focusing somewhere other than her face while she catalogued each of them for herself. "Unless there is a stowing person."

"Stowaway," Mike offered.

"A stowaway. Yes. We, Antonov Cargo, fly with flight crew of four and two of loadmasters," or had it only been this flight? What *was* Antonov's standard practice? Didn't matter. She knew there were six on this crew as a fact.

"Major Swift's team of medics were only able to locate five bodies."

Elayne felt the blood drain out of her head.

None of the crew would be likely to remember her face, except Voskov who she'd screwed twice less than eighteen hours ago. She looked again at the plane.

He *must* be dead.

12

Holly pulled Miranda aside, leading her back toward where they'd nearly finished mapping the edge of the debris field. She knew how much that incompleteness would be frustrating Miranda. They stopped right where the dirt met the edge of the runway pavement.

Jeremy plunged back to photographing every detail about the wreck.

The Elayne woman started to follow them.

As much as she hated to do it, Holly signaled to Mike to distract her.

Mike didn't even have the decency to hesitate before he swooped in and was once more chatting her up in that smooth way of his. Bastard. Sure the woman was stunning in an ever-so-cute, petite-blonde-in-designer-clothes way.

Yet Holly could never predict Mike.

He certainly acted like a total dog around women. But then she'd stumble on him sitting out by the pool of whatever motel they'd landed in near the site investigation.

Fully dressed, lying in a lounge chair, with a half-finished beer beside as he watched the stars—alone.

He'd certainly had plenty of opportunities. The brunette passenger from the 737 crash. He'd been like glue on her... checking on her in the hospital and then putting her on the bus home.

After that, he'd cozied up to the redheaded stewardess from the same damn flight.

And extensive interviews with a lot of useful observations would end up in his reports.

Holly could never quite determine that he'd slept with them, but she'd be shocked if he hadn't. Her trust of him definitely didn't run even skin deep, no matter how useful he was.

Even now, was he calculating how to get Ms. Designer Blonde out of her knickers? Probably.

He could get anyone to take him anywhere.

She'd seen him do it.

Schmooze his way into some place where he had no right to be, make everyone his friend until they were begging him to stay, then...she didn't want to know what.

She'd tracked him down in air traffic control centers, airplane cockpits, off yucking it up with a group of hard-worn, rough-as-hell mechanics who thought he was God's gift just like the women.

Not that she'd been staked out and watching or anything.

Mike wasn't worth the time.

She was just protecting Miranda. That's *all* she was doing. *Sure thing, Holly. Tell that one at the pub and see how far it flies.*

Holly tried to lead Miranda back to where they'd been standing when she'd spotted the approaching vehicle.

But Miranda was showing no signs of a desire to complete the unfinished Debris Field Sphere of her typical investigation pattern.

That's when she remembered that Miranda had said... she couldn't quite recall what...while Holly was keeping a gun on the Antonov woman and holding the boy in blue upright by his windpipe.

"You said something."

"I've said many things. But you keep not wanting to answer them."

"Sorry," Holly inspected the ground, the wreck, and wished she could think of somewhere else to look. Jeremy, photographing something along the far edge of the right wing wasn't particularly interesting. Even a flight of helicopters returning from some practice flight wasn't going to work as a sufficient distraction, because she knew exactly what was coming.

Give it up, Holly. She braced herself.

"Okay. Fire away, Miranda."

"First, can the pilot really fly a C-130 Hercules one-handed?"

Or not.

Six months ago, Holly would have been confused. Three months ago, she would have laughed in Miranda's face for making that her first question. Now she knew that it was best to just answer.

"No, he was just bragging."

"Bragging that he could or that he couldn't?"

There were times Holly wished she saw the world as

such a simple, yes-or-no place. "Bragging that he could and making a joke at the same time. He can't. You need four hands—two people," before Miranda could ask about multi-armed humans, "to fly a C-130. You know that."

"I do. But he said... Okay. I get it now. Though I don't see why it's funny."

"That's not you. It was a pretty lame joke."

"Oh. Okay. Are you sleeping with Mike?"

"No!" Even knowing it was coming, she wasn't ready for the question. Holly just couldn't imagine why this kept coming up when it was so...*wrong.* "No. Not now. Not ever: past, present, or future."

"Why not?"

"Why do you think?"

Holly could see her struggling and felt awful for answering a question with a question. Miranda never did well with those.

"Look at them, Miranda."

They both turned. Mike and Elayne were now arm-in-arm, strolling toward the wreck.

"Any bets on how long it takes him to get her in bed? The answer is: not long. I won't be another notch on his belt. I want my lovers to at least pretend I'm human. What made you ask that anyway?"

Miranda looked away and kicked at the edge of the runway's pavement for a moment. "I wondered if your verbal sparring was some sort of mating ritual."

"So not. His type really irritates me is all. Oh, that's why you asked what my type is?"

Miranda just nodded without looking up.

"You wondering what your type is?"

She nodded again. "If I even have one at all," she told one of the lights marking the runway's edge. "I'm not an idiot, Holly. I know how much I don't fit in…anywhere. I can't ever seem to—"

"Miranda, I'm not going to let you finish that sentence no matter how much you want to. We all have a type. Even you. You're different, sure, even by my utterly whacked Australian standards. But you've absolutely got a type. Your type is going to be smart as hell and understand just how special you are."

"Really?" Miranda's voice was so soft, and so afraid, that Holly could only answer it with a hard hug. Miranda gave her a brief pat on the back, which was the most response she'd ever given.

And then they separated.

"The other thing I said was…"

Holly couldn't remember what else except the dumb-ass game timer.

"Based on the wings having broken free, and as they are presently lying along either side of the fuselage, it implies that the expanded debris field was most likely due to an explosion occurring in the forward section of the plane."

"Word for word," Holly knew as she turned to inspect the plane herself.

She let her eye follow the line of orange flags. There *was* a distinct forward bulge of the debris field, starting from where they stood, swinging out to where she'd stopped the Security Forces patrol car, and the final curve of it tailing back toward the nose of the fuselage.

Nothing lay forward of the fuselage except the flipped-over cockpit and crew quarters section itself.

"Thirty-to-fifty kilos you said?"

Miranda, never one to repeat herself unless specifically asked, simply nodded.

"Say the size of a couple missiles on a helicopter?"

Miranda did one of her look-into-space things for under thirty seconds before replying. "Not as the primary explosion—insufficient energy and the force vectors are wrong. But certainly as a secondary one."

Holly nodded. "We need to inspect the hull next. The debris field can wait."

"Okay. If you say so. But what about the rest of the perimeter walk?"

Holly scanned the tiny bits of AN-124 Antonov Condor scattered far and wide over this end of the airport. It would be a long and tedious task.

"Tell Mike and his hot blonde to do it."

"Okay," and Miranda went over to do precisely that.

Holly headed for the wreck itself. Maybe if she just screwed Mike, Miranda would leave it alone.

13

Elayne stood at the beginning edge with a fistful of orange flags. Over at the wreck, which she still hadn't gotten close enough to, everyone except her and Mike was gathered.

"Why are you stuck with this job? Can you not assign it to someone else?"

"Nope. Once Miranda assigns a task, that's pretty much it."

"Why her?" She and Miranda were the same height, but that's where all similarities ended. This Miranda was dressed like a fieldworker. She did nothing to take care of herself. No makeup, her hair looked as if it hadn't even been brushed at all today. She needed highlights, a new wardrobe, and lessons in how not to look drab just standing still.

"It's her team. That's Miranda Chase, the NTSB's best investigator. I guarantee that she'll figure out what happened to your plane."

Which was the last thing Elayne wanted. She'd heard

Miranda's report that she'd looked at the shape of the debris field and concluded that there'd been an explosion on board. Even if no one else had heard, it was the last line of investigation that this team should be allowed to pursue.

And she was powerless to stop it.

Maybe if they hurried through the current task, she could return to the aircraft in time. She jammed a flag's wire stem next to a piece of debris by her feet and hurried toward the next one.

"No, wait. That won't do, Ms. Kasprak."

"Why not?" She didn't mean to snap at him, but she was in a hurry.

"We're still identifying the outermost edge of the debris perimeter. We'll then sweep the area again for relevant pieces. For now, we'll walk side by side, but five paces apart. I can promise you that somehow Miranda will know if we miss so much as a wingnut or stray coffee cup." Mike's smile was a charming one.

Out of options, Elayne cast one last look at the others as they delved into the center of the wreckage where the Mi-28NM Havoc had once been tied down. Out of reach for now.

This was going to take longer than she planned, but she had to be sure that nothing important remained and she had a role to play until she was.

"Tell me about her," she addressed Mike as the edge of the debris led them away from the plane.

Mike seemed only too happy to do so.

Elayne listened with one ear. She promised herself—if that drab little woman discovered anything of importance, Elayne wouldn't hesitate to break her neck.

14

"Why here?" Major Jon Swift had caught up with them as they reached the center of the wreckage.

Miranda considered if there was any deeper meaning to this being the center. They were actually in the forward third of the fuselage, but because the crew section had been flipped forward, it was roughly the geographic center of the wreck from the tail to the far end of the flipped crew section.

No. No relevance.

"Observe the burn marks on the cargo deck." Everyone looked down at where she pointed.

The burn marks had formed a near perfect bullseye. The center of the area was punched downward like a shallow crater. Scorch marks radiated outward in all directions from that point.

"The center of the blast," Holly was the only one looking out at the debris field. Even Jeremy didn't see the correlation of the expanded debris field pointing directly to this spot.

"You found it," Jon whispered. "You've been here, what,

under three hours? Most of that was walking the debris perimeter. And you found the point of origin in five hundred meters of wreckage."

"Not necessarily. All we know is that an explosion happened here." Miranda began scanning for further evidence.

Jon came to stand close beside her. His patient silence made her explain what she was looking at.

"Look at the side panels of the fuselage." They lay on the ground, still attached at the cargo deck level, but otherwise lying out flat to leave the deck open to the sky. "They've certainly been blown outward to either side from this point. The weapons mounted on this helicopter exploded and destroyed the airplane."

The panels lay on the runway to either side of the aircraft and did indeed demonstrate curvature consistent with an interior blast.

She moved to the edge of the cargo deck to look down at one. "That's odd."

"What's odd?" Jon followed her.

She waited, but he must not see it. She would have liked the confirmation, as the pattern was subtle.

Then he held his hands out in front of him, as if to look through them. He held one with the fingers spread as widely as possible and his palm toward where the blast had punched a starburst pattern of marks into the hull plates.

He spread his other hand wide, and began turning it one way and then the other as if dissatisfied with its positioning.

She reached out and took his probing hand in hers. She pushed the fingers together so that they were all pointing the same way. She then shifted it so that it was below his splayed hand and pointing toward what had been the top of the fuselage.

"You're right," he breathed softly. "I see that now. But I don't understand what I'm looking at."

"The explosion created a radial burn pattern as represented by this hand," she tapped the back of his splayed fingers. "But there was a fire first. We can just see the upward burn marks of a fire. A hot one. That's what this hand is mimicking."

He looked at her from uncomfortably close by. Why was it uncomfortable? They'd been this close a half dozen times over the last few hours. Because he was looking directly at her from so close?

Would a woman, a *normal* woman... Would Holly look him straight in the eye?

Yes.

But Miranda couldn't quite bring herself to do that. Instead she turned back to gaze at the long panel section that had once connected the cargo deck to the base of the crew module.

Would a fire weaken the hull's connection to the crew module? Not significantly. At least not very quickly. Not as fast as it would cause the helicopter's explosives to detonate.

An explosion here should have blown the side outward, then the crew module would have collapsed down into the fuselage rather than being flipped end-over-end out of the way.

"What are you thinking?" Jon still squatted beside her.

"That there are other forces at work here."

"No argument from me."

She didn't know how to interpret his tone.

15

"Are you seeing this?" Holly whispered to Jeremy.

"Seeing what?"

She should have known better than to ask him. They were halfway down the cargo bay, inspecting each of the destroyed helicopters as they went.

Jeremy proceeded to answer the wrong question. "Every single helo shows the same pattern. There was heavy fire damage, then each airframe was subjected to a high-pressure blast event originating near the front of the aircraft." He lined up five separate parts—chunks of shredded metal—on the cargo deck.

"That's the nose section of a Kamov Ka-52 Alligator." She'd know it anywhere—one of those had nearly killed her in Syria.

Jeremy made a note to that effect, then photographed the parts lying together. "Am I seeing it? They all exhibit the same burn pattern, before they were torn apart by the blast. Fire, then explosion. Yes, I'm seeing that."

"No, Jeremy, are you seeing... Never mind. You're right. Well done." But she couldn't stop looking forward to where Miranda and Major Swift were kneeling side by side and practically playing pat-a-cake together.

How fast had Miranda integrated their brief Q-and-A talk? No time for Holly to give her warnings or maybe some guidelines. What trouble had Holly unwittingly sent her into?

What trouble had she unwittingly let her prior team fall into so that—

"Well, we've got the perimeter staked," Mike came up and reported with little Ms. I'm-Acting-So-Cute by his side. "What's with her skipping the debris field?"

"You know our Miranda," Holly managed against a dry throat. No longer sure that she did.

"Not when I see her so cozy with Jon. They make a cute couple."

Holly managed not to groan at the load of doubt weighing her down. "Look, Mike, whatever's going on up there...shit, I don't know. How about you grab a couple of hard hats and see if you two can go back and locate the black box? Maybe start getting eyewitness jabber from some of the fire crews before they all leave."

Many of the engines were indeed gone. But several were gathered around the area where the tail section had collapsed on top of two of the Striker fire trucks.

"Sure. Come on, Elayne. Oh, there's one crash investigation I've got to tell you about."

Holly kept an ear out as they moved away. Mike had damn well better remember what was classified and what wasn't. Both of their prior investigations for the military had indeed required their entire team's top-secret clearance. And Holly, at least, still remembered how fast Elayne had slapped for the gun she didn't have.

"There was this Beech King Air that somehow landed—"

Civilian. Unclassified.

Holly tuned him out. Sure, that investigation would make a good story. In fact, she'd be sorry to miss his rendition of it; Mike was a skilled storyteller, making it easy to laugh.

A laugh would be really good right now.

Then she glanced forward in time to see Major Swift helping Miranda to climb onto the back of the inverted crew section.

Did Miranda even have a clue?

16

GREGOR FEDEROV CHOSE THE LOCATION TO PLACE HIS CALL carefully.

Tantsy Bobor was just the place he needed. He liked the name because it required knowing English slang to get it. No Russian would waste his time checking out a non-descript place called the Dancing Beaver—faded lettering on a battered, unpainted door between a butcher and a shoe store, that led down into a basement.

Kiska, pizda, manda? Kitty, pussy, quim? Any of those names and the place would be thick with loud drunks. But those were Russian words for a woman's best part. Beaver was *American* slang.

The owners knew the kind of people they wanted when they'd named it.

Many people at the factory for Progress Rocket Space Centre in Samara were bilingual. It helped in the study of stolen American designs. The clientele at the Tantsy Bobor were still loud, drunk Russians—but they were smart, well-paid, loud, drunk Russians.

Members only, too.

And the décor was well done. The fittings were modern. The bar selection and kitchen both top notch. The central stage was brightly lit, but the table area was dim enough that he could safely ignore that asshole from optics without offending him as Gregor passed his table. Thumping Russian rock and roll added to the imagined privacy by making conversation impossible beyond a few meters.

And the caliber of the waitresses and floor show was incredible. Even the leather-strap-clad She-Hulk former-Olympian weightlifter who tended bar was a treat to look at.

He chose a corner table that put his back to two walls so that no one could look over his shoulder.

Vesna, his favorite, with black hair down to her exceptional ass and skin so pale she looked like an angel, came up and took his order in nothing but her high heels, thong, and her hair brushed forward. She shimmied to the throbbing beat of the hard-pumping music as she offered to join him.

"Later? For now, a vodka and an American burger. Very rare."

She left him after rubbing a hand slow and hard over his jean's crotch, knowing it would make him ache for her. Watching her walk away, the view interrupted by only the thin line of her black G-string, was one of the great pleasures of the Tantsy Bobor.

The owners also offered free, high-bandwidth Wi-Fi, protected with a very robust VPN.

Most guys who surfed here streamed porn. Which

seemed ridiculous as he watched Avelina start getting it on with Ludmilla on the raised platform at the center of the place.

If they were faking it, they were incredibly good at it.

Then Marta joined them, too wild for his personal taste but so fun to watch. things really started rocking.

They made a whole show of putting on a pair of double-ended strap-ons, lubricating them, and eventually taking Avelina front-and-back simultaneously. Definitely not pretend. She clung and groaned as they set upon her. He hadn't seen them do that before, and he watched long enough that he missed Vesna delivering his meal.

Gregor thought about calling her back to take care of his throbbing ache as the stage show escalated, but he had other matters to attend to first.

He pulled out his phone, plugged in a set of earbuds, then used the protection of the Tantsy Bobor's VPN to launch the Onion browser into the Dark Web. There he picked up an anonymous dialer that made him look as if he was in Malaysia, before keying in a number from memory.

"Monster!"

"Beastmaster!"

They'd agreed to never use each other's names, despite the precautions.

Clarissa Reese had tagged him with Monster the first time he'd revealed the scale of the endowment that nature had blessed him with for pleasing women.

He'd tagged her as Beastmaster for the creative things she'd thought to do while taming the Monster. Even the exquisitely skilled Vesna couldn't match what the tall American blonde could do to his body.

"It has been too long."

"It has," he sighed. They'd both been much younger when he'd managed to rent a cozy, but very private, summer dacha along the Black Sea. They'd made very full use of their week.

Everything from coating each other in slippery oils (something she called a Mazola Roller) to bondage to eating meals off each other's bodies; it was a time he dreamed of often and expected they would never repeat. Since then, nothing but phone sex. *Glorious* phone sex, but still, he kept hoping.

"What are you watching, Monster? I can hear the music."

He tapped the icon to select the camera on the phone's back and held it up for her.

Gregor watched Clarissa's smile grow as Avelina peaked and thrashed with the power of her orgasm. Ludmilla and Marta locked lips over Avelina's shoulder and kept going as they continued seeking their own releases against the woman pinned between them.

"Oh, you naughty boy."

"Gives me ideas, Beastmaster."

And she looked just a little sad. "I'm sorry, Monster. Life has intervened."

He'd known it was over, even if he hadn't wanted to really admit it. But now the time he'd known was coming had arrived. It was just as well; meeting a CIA agent for sex, even the best sex of his life, was too risky. But at least he still had the memories. Besides, Vesna was an artist and would take care of his fantasies—or at least most of them.

He kept the phone on the escalating show and enjoyed watching Clarissa's breathing quicken.

He didn't mind, too much, that it was over. "I have a present for you, Beastmaster. Just for old time's sake. Worth it just to see you again."

"Make it quick. I have a *lunch* meeting soon." And her tone said exactly what kind of a lunch meeting. Or maybe she was just teasing him?

He flipped the image so that she could see him again.

"Spoilsport. It was just getting good."

"The newest Persona surveillance satellite is done, and being packaged for a Vostochny launch."

Clarissa's blue eyes were suddenly very intent. Her face took on that look of perfect concentration that she always had the moment before exploding into orgasm. He tapped the screen capture so that he'd always have that image. Then he encrypted it and sent it to his Dark Web storage locker so that not even the FSB would be able to find it.

"That is *so* interesting, Monster."

"I thought you might like it. It's the same family as the Kosmos 2506, but with upgraded optics. We can't match your resolution of ten centimeters per pixel..." He left a pause in case she wanted to boast about what the Americans could actually resolve now. No, so he continued as if he hadn't paused at all. "but we're down to twice that. Thirty percent improvement."

Vesna was headed back his way. Once again, he tapped the camera icon to give Clarissa a view.

"Oh my, have her do a turn, Monster."

He signaled her and Vesna did a languid spin to the music, making her long hair swirl much the way Clarissa's always did when she let it down. Oh! That explained why he'd always been so partial to Vesna despite the coloring difference from the Beastmaster. Both were remarkably beautiful women, with absolutely *amazing* hair.

"She's lovely," Clarissa agreed. "I have no time for phone sex, so I'll give you just a quick little gift. Next time you have her, imagine that we're both there. A little virtual *ménage.*"

That *was* a nice image.

"Oh, here's lunch," and Clarissa flipped *her* camera.

No, she wasn't teasing about the type of lunch she'd be having...stud male. A tall, handsome man, about his own age and wearing a three-piece suit, was stepping through her office door. No question about what kind of meal he was expecting as he made a point of locking the door behind him.

"Think about the same from me," Gregor offered. "Two men to tame the Beastmaster." Not that he'd be willing to lie next to another man, even with her in the middle.

"Always a pleasure," she said it formally, which was fine. She had company. He knew she meant the words, not the tone. So, their future was to be relegated to occasional phone sex—at least he hoped *that* wasn't off the table. Clarissa offered exceptional phone sex and he always looked forward to it.

He hung up, pocketed his phone, and opened an arm for Vesna to slide in beside him. He stroked her lovely hair as she planted a nuzzle and kiss on his neck and a palm between his legs.

Should he imagine Vesna and Clarissa going down on him together?

Perhaps have the blonde Avelina fill in the role?

He looked to the stage and watched her reach a second shuddering peak. Her breasts were nice, if a bit small, but her hair was all wrong—deeply gold-blonde and cut severely straight at the jaw, almost boyish.

No, just the two of them: him and Vesna. Then he'd imagine the Monster and the Beastmaster together as a team, both going down on Vesna. Oh yes. *That* was good. Maybe he could get Clarissa to phone in and they'd both wear headphones. He and Clarissa had always made love in Russian, which was good because Vesna had only the poorest English.

He'd have to save that fantasy for later, though.

For now, Vesna undid his pants and lay her head in his lap. When he looked, the trio on stage had shifted. Now Avelina was taking a kneeling Marta from behind with long, powerful strokes of her own strap-on while Ludmilla strutted about, enticing the crowd to cheer them on.

The stage lights revealed sheens of sweat on all their bodies. They were as heated as he was.

Vesna was taming the Monster like never before, as he finger-brushed her lovely black hair in long, liquid strokes.

All the while, Gregor imagined himself and the American Beastmaster, with flowing hair the color of sunshine, at their cozy summer dacha swimming naked in the Black Sea.

17

CLARISSA ROSE FROM HER CHAIR AND MOVED TO MEET CLARK. In some ways, he was now a better lover than Gregor Federov had ever been.

He didn't have nearly the natural equipment that Gregor had, but it had made Gregor a very single-focus man—where could he place his self-declared Monster and how many times? His stamina had been remarkable, which had been a nice compensation, but his imagination had been lacking. And he was very Russian, so didn't take hints or even outright suggestions very well.

She'd have been just as happy to never hear from him again. But due to that one bit of information on the Persona satellite, she'd definitely have to keep stringing him along. Too bad he had insisted on verbal communication only. No documentation, images, or transmissions of anything else that he could be caught with, which meant no detailed design plans.

But his payment was easy. A man with no country one way or the other—his price for information was merely anything that entertained his Monster.

Clark was a staunch American patriot, who also had a different focus. Just like any hetero-male, he enjoyed nothing so much as being inside a woman. But he was also fascinated by the rest of her body. At first, it had just been her breasts, but *he* was open to suggestion. She'd taught him that there was so much more to be had if it was properly appreciated. And he *definitely* had imagination about where to go once told where to begin.

"How are you settling in?" Clark's voice was pleasantly deep, enough to make her gut clench in a nice way. Nice, too, that he asked.

It was her first day in Clark's old office.

She hadn't done much yet to make it hers. Perhaps she wouldn't.

People would see the continuity of the Director of the Central Intelligence Agency's office embodied in the broad cherrywood desk, the dark leather chairs, and the view toward the Potomac and Washington, DC. It was a very masculine room. It might be a sensible play for the youngest-ever Director (by a couple decades), and only the second-ever female, to keep that look and feel.

"I'm doing fine," she straightened his tie though it didn't need it.

Clark always liked the gesture, finding it affectionate. It was the last thing she did for him on any morning after they'd spent the night together. As essential as the parting kiss and the pat on her ass.

"How about you, *Mr. Vice President Clark Winston?*" Her plan had worked beautifully. The former D/CIA was a popular man, well-liked by both the President and Congress. His replacement for the disgraced VP had been almost automatic...once she'd arranged to have it suggested to President Cole.

Clark's own recommendation had carried most of the weight in her own selection and approval.

Though she hadn't held the Bible for Clark's swearing-in ceremony, she'd made sure she was front row and at his side for every photograph before and after. She'd taken a note from prior Second Ladies at such events and dressed in a demure yet elegant sky-blue two-piece with a single strand of pearls. Time to start making her own mark. Dowdy, but on point for the American public.

"I can't complain for a second. I just moved into the VP Mansion this morning. I can't wait to show it to you...every room." His gentle stroke of her breast and the slow circles he drew with his thumb through the wool of her Altuzarra double-breasted blazer told her exactly what he hoped to do in each room.

The Queen Anne Victorian at One Observatory Circle had eight rooms on the ground floor alone—if you counted the garage, which she didn't, and the pantry, which she just might. Though maybe Clark wasn't ready for that yet.

But their first time together in the mansion would be in the Vice President's bedroom.

Actually, that would be for her ego.

For his?

Perhaps one of the landings of the central staircase? "Oh,

I just can't wait until we're upstairs to have you. I'm simply so proud of you."

As if he'd ever have gotten there without her.

Yes. It was always good to remind a powerful man just how powerful he was.

The stairs were carpeted and the stately historic space could use a little lively sex in it.

"I can't wait." She trapped his hand against her breast as she kissed him.

"Can you leave early? Take the afternoon off?" He made a partial move toward the door, but she kept him in place by his hand.

"Tonight's soon enough." There was too much work to be done. For one, she had to think of what best to do with Gregor's tidbit of information. However, there was something she wanted to do as her first "official" act as the D/CIA. For herself.

She turned slowly. His pinned hand drew him toward her, reeling him in as she turned. When he pressed up against the back of her, she could feel his arousal.

His free hand slid around her waist rather than grabbing her other breast. Clark really was a decent man; she'd have to be careful to always remember that.

Together they looked out the one-way glass. No one could see into the D/CIA's windows.

Her windows.

This view was what mattered. This view and the two of them together just taking it in.

Okay, *she* looked out. Clark was too preoccupied with nuzzling her neck.

But she wanted to stand like this for a moment and just

let it all in. So many pieces of her future were coming together today.

The Director of the Central Intelligence Agency's office was now hers.

That Persona satellite dropping into her lap on the first day was a wonderful start. She'd been informed of it because of calculated choices in the past that simply bore fruit today, but she'd take it as a good sign of things to come anyway.

She hadn't fucked Gregor for his massive penis; she'd done it on the off chance that one of the senior design engineers at the Progress factory would call her some day with precisely this kind of information. Though she had no complaints about servicing that delectable piece of man-flesh when she'd had the opportunity.

Clark was now in place as the Vice President.

Her own entry onto the public stage had begun with the Senate's quick approval and Clark's swearing-in.

She must decide soon when Clark could propose to her. Perhaps tonight on the stairs. Perhaps in the Vice-Presidential bed. Now that they were both Senate confirmed, it *was* time to move to the next step.

Clark.

Yes, he was exactly where she wanted him.

And she was clearly where he wanted her as he used the arm about her waist to press more firmly against her from behind.

Many of her plans required keeping him happy, but that wasn't a burden at all. Sex, which had always been just that, was actually becoming good with him. *Very* good. That was an interesting change she hadn't noticed happening. She'd never particularly looked *forward* to sex before—just enjoyed it when it did happen.

Clark offered more.

Clarissa guided his hand down from her breast, down, until he was cupping her through her skirt, then leaned forward to brace both of her hands on her desk.

He no longer needed more guidance than that.

Clark had needed only minimal tutoring, and had her well-aroused before he even lifted up her skirt. Next he took the time to appreciate the results of all the work she did on the elliptical.

Yes, she would add at least that to her new office, maybe do some steps during her phone calls and do some reading there. A private bathroom with shower was one of the Director's many perks.

Clark also deeply enjoyed that she wore no underwear—something she'd always done at the office specifically for him.

With strong and skilled fingers, he showed his appreciation and soon had her body *very* highly charged. He was so good at that now that she had to hang her head just to breathe as she strained to press harder against his hands.

Ready for what came next.

So ready.

She looked once more out *her* windows.

No reflection in the glass. Not on this side. Not at midday.

The perfect faceless lover continued coaxing her up. Past speech. Finally past even the ability to groan.

At long last he undid his pants, slipped into her from behind, and found his favorite rhythm.

Even as he did, Clarissa let herself imagine that, after President Cole's second term, the distant sunlit buildings of Washington, DC, would be hers.

There was the true power.

Hers and Clark's...but hers.

18

"Just as I suspected," Miranda pointed down.

Jon let himself admire the firm certainty of her fine fingers for a moment before looking where she indicated.

Exactly as she'd predicted, the bottom of the inverted crew section they'd just climbed onto had two distinct burn patterns on it. The scorch pattern of a raging fire and the blast overlay of a hard explosion that had buckled the floor into the shape of a long, shallow crater. It would have been a smooth dome shape when the section was still attached to the plane. Now it looked like a broad crater exposed to the midday sun, absorbing it due to all of the char on the surface.

Miranda laced those expressive fingers of hers together and held them up in an inverted cup shape.

"See how that would even further refocus the explosion's energy into a lifting force. That curvature was the missing element to explain the force necessary to break loose this section and flip it over despite its size. Also, as it bowed in," she pointed to the far edge of the structure, "it would have ripped the connections of the rear bulkhead to the central wingbox, weakening its attachment to the rest of the structure. That explains the distorted metal we saw along the edges."

Jon decided not to point out that, despite his three years as a crash investigator, he hadn't seen it at all until she'd pointed it out.

"I don't see any hull penetrations except for where the stair entered in the middle." The stair itself dangled by a single bolt, but the hatch was open.

Miranda moved directly toward the entry, climbing over girder after girder that had once supported the floor but now pointed toward the sky.

Jon could only follow in bemusement. It might have taken him days to understand the burn patterns without her assistance. And how much math had she run in her head to determine that there'd been an extra, unexplained force component to the destruction?

It had taken Miranda the duration of an eyeblink.

He'd been a crash inspector ever since he'd shattered his hip due to a shifting load aboard his C-5 Galaxy jet transport. He'd been the off-shift pilot on a long haul and he'd gone below to stretch his legs. When it came time to land, he'd strapped into a cargo bay seat...and had been attacked by a busted pallet of MREs. He could walk fine now, but maybe one shattered hip in a lifetime was enough.

The AIB had been the answer.

He kept current doing ferry flights and the like, when there was no crash to investigate. No longer combat-qualified—some combat maneuvers took constant practice

—he was still cleared for standard flight as copilot on the C-5. She was a well-behaved and gentle bird despite her size.

He'd been offered full re-ups, but he liked working for the AIB. Sometimes the crash sites were gruesome, but he'd probably saved others from a lot worse than a shattered hip and that was a hell of a nice payoff.

Miranda was so easily dismissed—he'd seen that blonde from Antonov doing just that. But he'd noticed that the others on the NTSB team worshipped her.

He now knew why.

She didn't have the slap-in-your-face beauty of the Antonov engineer, or the outdoorsy devil-may-care of the exuberantly healthy and fit Holly. Instead, she was...herself. Short and slender, but he wouldn't think to call her petite. Hair pulled back from her face without any care of how it looked, just because she needed it out of her way.

Miranda Chase made absolutely no airs about being anything other than exactly who she was.

There was a quietness and a focus to her.

Pure business, but also a kindness.

She hadn't just told him what the burn pattern meant. In the middle of a high-priority investigation, with pressures from everyone—including himself—to hurry, she'd taken the time to teach him how to see it. Without condescension. Without judgment.

Yes, her reputation was well deserved. Actually pretty damn understated. General Nason had said she was the best. Did he have any idea just how good that was?

Miranda awaited him at the open hatch and they looked down together.

"I'll go first," he volunteered. It was at least an eight-foot drop. He found a smooth edge that hadn't been damaged and lowered himself down, then dropped the last foot or so. No twinge in his hip. "Okay, you next."

Miranda was agile and was dangling by her hands a moment later.

He wrapped his hands around her waist. "I've got you."

She let go and he settled her on her feet. It took a conscious effort to release her.

His ex had been a solid woman, not heavy, just solid. An Army nurse he'd married before his shattered hip, who had moved on to women a few years after. They got together for drinks and a meal when their billets overlapped, which wasn't often. No animosity, and only the slightest lingering heat. He'd married her because he liked her so much; still did.

Compared to her, Miranda felt almost magical or mythic or one of those m-words. Maybe some crazy cross between the kindergarten teacher that every kid had a crush on and a supercomputer.

Jon felt slightly giddy in her presence and followed to see what she'd unravel next.

The ceiling of the crew compartment, now their floor, was a jumble of detritus.

Forward in the cockpit, the debris lay light enough for the ceiling to be well exposed. Manuals and checklists. A couple of plastic coffee mugs that didn't smell of alcohol, but Miranda bagged them anyway.

A few random items, the type of collectibles that pilots who served primarily in a single aircraft accumulated. A snow globe of the Australian Outback that had a red rock planted into the bottom sand and fine red dust when it was shaken. A Hawaiian hula skirt, leaving him to wonder what the woman who'd worn it onto the plane had been wearing when she left. But generally the cockpit was orderly.

Much of the glass had broken out of the windows.

"It doesn't appear to have been blown outward. Some of it landed inside the cockpit." Miranda shone a flashlight on a small pile of it spilled across the ceiling.

He looked up at the chairs.

Notes recorded where each of the four bodies had been removed by the search-and-rescue teams.

Jon read out the tags. Each had some version of "Beat to death by the crash." Snapped neck, complete blood loss due to severed arm, another snapped neck, and face caved in by hitting the engineer's console with immense force—he could still see the brown smear of dried blood there.

"That's four of her six." Jon finished reading the details of the last one.

"Who said six?"

"Elayne Kasprak. She said there were six crewmembers on this flight."

Miranda just looked at him blankly.

"The cute little blonde?"

Still nothing.

"The Antonov representative?"

"Oh. Okay."

Apparently that was the only thing Miranda had decided that she needed to know about the woman and hadn't retained anything else about her.

Gods but she was funny.

19

Mike and Elayne were having problems reaching the voice and data black boxes through the tangle of wreckage, so Holly sent Jeremy to help.

With the three of them safely occupied back at the tail, Holly clambered out of the wreck and hurried forward to where the crew section lay on the runway.

The smashed-out windshield was at eye level. She arrived just in time to see Miranda and Major Swift moving out of the cockpit toward the plane's crew quarters. His hand on the small of her back as if guiding or steadying her.

Holly knew from experience that Miranda was very surefooted and didn't need either. But Swift was doing it anyway.

She found a spot clear of glass and vaulted up into the cockpit.

Landing with her back on both the circuit breaker panel and the sharp knobs of the radios, which would have been above the pilots' heads, hurt. She lay there for a moment, gazing up at the engine throttles of the control cluster wondering if she'd broken anything or if it was just pain.

The latter.

She rolled and clambered to her feet just as Miranda remarked, "The cockpit door is strongly bowed from rear to front—but evenly. And it still swings properly. Evidence that it was closed and latched during the explosion. The door held, supported by the frame all around. The pilots may not have even known about the disaster unfolding behind them."

"I see that," Swift was taking notes.

It suddenly all looked so innocent and Holly felt like a fool for worrying. What was so goddamn wrong with Miranda liking someone anyway? It wasn't as if he was coming onto Holly herself?

Swift acknowledged her presence with a friendly wave; Miranda didn't at all. Which was no surprise. She was in investigation mode.

Their dialog continued as they probed back into the crew section.

This was completely different.

Where the cockpit had been disorderly and a little bloody, there hadn't been any major damage. The instruments were mostly intact in the console, the crew seats and the carpet were still seat- and carpet-colored.

In the crew compartment, the air was so thick that she had to sneeze.

Carbon and...cooked meat. Probably human.

She sneezed again but couldn't quite clear the stench.

Everything was blackened. The soot—she scraped at it

with the toe of her boot to no effect—the *char* covered every surface.

"What a devo!" As they moved away from the front windshield, they had to rely completely on their flashlights.

"Dev-o?"

"Dev-o-station."

"Oh. Yep," Jon agreed. "It's the black pit. Like entering the Mines of Moria." Their flashlights seemed to illuminate nothing.

"Balrog, anybody?" Holly asked.

Jon laughed briefly. Miranda simply looked puzzled for a moment.

"Oh, Tolkien. Book One. *The Fellowship of the Ring.* Chapter Five. Is that an analogy for this space and the fall of Gandalf at the Bridge of Khazad-dûm? This space is hardly large enough to contain a hidden monster of fire and darkness."

"Forget I said anything."

"Okay," and that simply, Miranda apparently did.

So why couldn't she forget about her question to Holly about Mike? Worse, why couldn't Holly forget it herself?

"A lot of debris here," Swift read into a pocket recorder, though he appeared to be laughing at her.

She gave him the finger and he returned the gesture with an easy smile as he continued narrating.

Damn it! She didn't want to like him.

"The kitchen stayed surprisingly secure, but past that there are seat cushions, luggage, and so on. As there were four flight crew bodies up forward, we should find two loadmasters back here. The Antonov cargo bay is unpressurized during flight, so they should be here."

Holly moved past Miranda, past the lounge area, and back into the rearmost area where the bunks were.

A numbered yellow card was glaringly bright against the infinite black. She read the details.

"Severe burns. To the point of major flesh loss."

"That's one," apparently Major Swift wasn't squeamish, which earned him another point. "Where's the other?"

"The other what?" Miranda was squatting at the sole source of outside light, a half-meter hole in the rear bulkhead.

"The other body, Miranda," Holly said softly. "We're expecting to find two corpses somewhere in this space."

"Oh, it's right there. I saw it when we first arrived." She pointed behind her without bothering to turn to inspect it.

"Why didn't you say anything?" Jon moved up beside Holly. With the power of both of their flashlights, they were able to make out the smashed remains of a skeleton—bits of white bone showing through the char. The rescue teams had missed it.

Miranda didn't answer, so Holly did for her. Partly to see how he'd react, partly so that he didn't distract Miranda from whatever she was inspecting so carefully.

"She thinks of a crash in spheres, layers. Outside to in. Weather, terrain, outer edge of debris, the debris itself, and so on. Her final layer is people. Don't mix up the layers, it confuses her."

"But she skipped the debris field this time. How did she do that?"

He didn't ask *why*, but *how*.

Holly wished she could see more of Swift's face without

shining a flashlight directly into his eyes. He'd gotten it exactly right.

"Partly because you and Drake pushed. And partly because she and I talked it through and, for reasons I can't begin to understand, she decided to trust Mike."

"And you don't?"

Holly could really do without the hard questions.

20

Miranda waited to hear the answer.

But Holly didn't speak.

Was there a reason she didn't trust Mike?

Was it because of the sleeping together question? Or something else? She'd said something about the engineer from Antonov. Miranda had very little impression of that person. She would be a source of information when Miranda was ready for that—but she wasn't yet. Until then, Miranda had seen no point in further analysis of the engineer's information.

Closing her eyes to block out the damage that was before her, she tried to picture the woman.

Elayne.

Her own height.

Blonde?

Walking arm-in-arm with Mike.

Oh. That's what Holly had said about Mike. *Any bets on how long it takes him to get her in bed? The answer is: not long. I won't be another notch on his belt. I want my lovers to at least pretend I'm human. Maybe even special.*

Yes. Holly was very smart. Miranda wanted to feel special too.

A hand rested on her shoulder. She knew it was Holly's by the firmness of the contact.

"What have we got here, boss?"

Miranda opened her eyes and the jagged hole through the rear bulkhead was once again before her.

"This is point of origin."

"It's *what?* That can't be right." Jon pushed in beside Holly with none of the reserve she'd expect from an Air Force major.

"You don't believe me? What evidence do you have supporting an alternate point of origin?"

Holly smirked at Jon for reasons that were unclear. "Need evidence, mate. Not just some theory."

"There was an explosion of the armament at one of the helicopters." Jon stated it as if it was an answer unto itself.

Miranda had already been over this with him. Would she have to repeat herself?

"Hold it. That explosion was caused by a preceding fire."

Miranda nodded for him to continue.

"For that fire to be big enough, it wasn't electrical. It had to be fuel-driven."

Holly was watching him with an odd look on her face. As much as Miranda hated conjecture, she had little choice when attempting to interpret human expression. Perhaps...surprise?

"And for there to be a fuel fire, a major one, there had to be a major fuel leak—inside the plane. If it was from the wings, most of the heat would have been outside. It must have been a rupture in the central fuel tank. But what could cause that?"

Holly pointed at the hole; she understood, of course. "The tanks used to be right there. Notice which way the metal's bent—outward. I'd estimate..."

Miranda watched as Holly stared at the blackened ceiling, which had once been the deck, for less than five seconds.

"I'd estimate two kilos, four-to-five pounds of C-4 or Semtex might do this if it was a shaped charge. That's probably what happened to Mr. Bones over there. The charge would have been directly under his bunk."

"This is the point of origin," Miranda repeated. Holly smiled, somehow understanding that Miranda had meant it as a compliment and a conclusion at the same time.

"I'll be damned." Jon looked at his watch. "That's incredible."

Miranda was fairly sure that he didn't mean his watch was incredible as he had been wearing it since the moment she'd first seen him.

"Not quite there yet, mate," Holly corrected him.

Miranda couldn't think of what was missing.

Holly put on a pair of blue nitrile gloves and began sorting through the debris piled around the bones. She plucked a small clump of charred paper from the remains of a clenched hand. Holly riffled to the middle of it, revealing a few unburnt images. It took Miranda a moment to realize that it was a photograph of a naked pair of woman's breasts and just enough of her torso to show how outsized they were.

"Catching up on his technical reading," Holly said in an extra-thick Australian tone that Miranda had learned meant she was joking.

She appreciated the clear, tonal indicator and decided that it was also a better joke than the one-handed pilot's. Perhaps not worth a laugh, but funnier.

Holly continued her sorting through the detritus, then held up a small twist of wire attached to a bit of electronics. She made a "hmm" sound as she placed it in a small evidence bag.

"A Bluetooth or Wi-Fi receiver, maybe. Which poses the question—what total dingus set and triggered it? Unless Mr. Bones piled in the corner there was a suicide bomber, it was triggered to happen precisely on landing."

Right. Miranda was always forgetting about the people part. Holly was right; it was now time to move to the last sphere.

21

"YOU'RE KIDDING?" GENERAL DRAKE NASON, THE CHAIRMAN of the Joint Chiefs of Staff stopped what he was doing and looked over his desk at General Elizabeth Gray.

He'd learned about her sense of humor over the last few months. In private, "Lizzy" displayed a deep sense of humor. Her idea of a belly laugh was a bright smile—quickly covered with a hand. It was a quiet sense of humor, but it was definitely there.

But at work? There, "Elizabeth" had the sense of humor of a rock—a very *serious* rock. He supposed that it was appropriate for the head of the National Reconnaissance Office. Still, it was sometimes hard to reconcile the woman who shared his bed these last three months with the one who occasionally met him at his Pentagon office or in the White House Situation Room.

"You're not kidding." He hit the Do Not Disturb signal on his phone. His secretary would see that and stop all but the most urgent interruptions.

Elizabeth settled stiffly in the leather chair across his desk—neat, almost prim.

"You want me to steal a billion or so of Russian state hardware?"

She nodded. "Personally, I'd be happy with simply a full set of the specifications, but no one has been able to acquire those. Now we have a chance to possibly acquire the finished satellite itself. By the way, if it's similar to ours, it would be closer to three-point-five billion."

"We're talking dollars, not rubles? That's more than a Virginia-class nuclear missile submarine. Hell, we can buy a quarter of a brand-new aircraft carrier for that much. The Russians are going to notice that someone took it."

"Then make it so that no one notices."

Generally Drake liked when someone brought out-of-the-box ideas to his desk. This was a first from Elizabeth, and it was so far outside the norm that he didn't know what to do with it.

Slipping away with six helicopters delivered to the West by defectors was one thing. However...

The idea was starting to grow on him. Persona satellites weren't built cheaply or overnight. Removing a major spy satellite from Russia's lineup would be a significant setback both financially and in the ever-escalating intelligence wars.

"Where did you come up with this one?"

Her quick glance aside was all she needed to say.

President Cole had taken three months to choose a replacement for the disgraced Vice President. His choice of CIA Director Clark Winston had been readily approved by the Senate. He was an obvious choice; an old school traditionalist who'd managed to change with the times without getting his hands dirty. At least not in any way picked up by the Senate or the media. He was actually a bit of a media darling.

Winston's replacement at the CIA, on the other hand, was unbelievable.

Clarissa Reese had been the Director of Special Projects —one of the smallest and most shadowy departments of a very shadowy agency.

Not a chance she'd be approved.

At least not until surprisingly strong support arrived from the new head of the Senate Armed Services Committee and the Senate Select Committee on Intelligence. The two of them never agreed on anything—their mutual animosity was the stuff of legend—until suddenly they both agreed to make Clarissa Reese the youngest-ever Director of the Central Intelligence Agency.

Drake had to wonder what dirt she had on the two of them.

The D/CIA was usually a career spy in their sixties, not their thirties.

And they weren't usually a viper with the morals of...

"Wait a minute. Reese gave you a Persona satellite's location but didn't offer to steal it for you?"

Elizabeth nodded. "She said it was beyond their scope, but if there was any way in which they could be of assistance to please let her know."

"From anyone else in the world, I might even trust that. Do you think it's a trap of some sort?" Drake wouldn't put it past Clarissa. Of course, she had to have learned by now that if she harmed so much as a single hair on Elizabeth's head that Drake would kill her with his own bare hands.

Elizabeth merely shrugged.

"You want me to steal Russia's newest spy satellite so that you can look at it?"

"Drake," Elizabeth suddenly came to life, perched up on the edge of her seat. "We know that the Russians have made massive strides forward in their technology, and that it's not all by copying our KH-11 EECS birds. Our modern Enhanced Evolved Crystal System has as much relation to the design's origins that we gave to NASA for the Hubble as an Accuracy International MK 13 sniper rifle system has to the M1 that Marines carried onto the beaches at Normandy. The last intel we have about the Russian surveillance satellite capabilities are practically prehistoric. The Persona craft is their absolute cutting edge."

"Why is this one different?"

"Because, for the first time, we know where it is *before* they launch it into space. Once it's launched, we can't just sneak up and grab it without everyone, including the Russians, noticing. Right now they're in the final packaging stage at the Progress Rocket Space Centre in Samara in the west. It's scheduled to launch in five days from Vostochny Cosmodrome in the east. Their recent shift from Baikonur in Kazakhstan to their own Vostochny for their space launches means that they can't just throw it on a truck. They *have* to fly it."

Drake had to admit, that *was* interesting.

"How many people know about this?"

"You're number four. Clarissa, her agent on the ground, and the two of us."

"And you think the intel is reliable?"

"I retasked a pair of our satellites and got pictures of both ends of the route." She pulled up a pair of images on her tablet. "They definitely have something very busy going on in their final-assembly building at the factory. This is the building. Compare it to the rest of the plant."

There *were* ten times more vehicles around that particular structure.

"And they are setting up a launch at Vostochny." She pulled up an image that meant almost nothing to him.

He'd trust her interpretation as the boss of the National Reconnaissance Office.

"Back on the first image, look at that plane parked on their runway."

Drake squinted at it, then tried to suppress the chill he felt. It was *very* familiar; he'd been looking at the imagery of an utterly shattered one just six hours ago—strewn across the Fort Campbell runway.

"An AN-124 Antonov Condor." He could barely breathe as he whispered it.

"Yes," Elizabeth charged ahead. "The Russian Air Force has twelve in service as heavy lifters. They're launching something big, something that won't fit into your average transport."

"Satellite's aren't that big."

"It's almost fifty feet long and ten across. And that's before you count the protective fairing, which is almost double that. There's a surprising amount of hardware associated with launching a sat even on an otherwise assembled rocket."

"The launch could be anything. A weather sat. Or the ongoing expansion of GLONASS. Hell, we just upgraded half of our own GPS system, why can't they be doing the same?" Drake went for Devil's Advocate, but he wanted to believe.

"Unannounced. They haven't even put out air traffic control routing cautions for the launch yet, but the launch is already in pre-fueling. The only time they do that is for secret military payloads."

Drake wanted to believe, a lot.

He pulled up a map and tagged Samara and Vostochny.

"Six thousand kilometers." Then he zoomed back and felt a little ill. For half a moment he'd thought that perhaps the plane could be somehow hijacked as it crossed over the Arctic Ocean.

But Samara and Vostochny were far enough south that, even with the arc of the Great Circle route included, their best path for the entire flight ran through the very heart of Russia.

Inaccessible.

22

Elayne's favorite Saint Laurent jeans were dirty. Not just with dirt, but with soot and a grease stain she'd probably never get out. Even if she did, she'd know the stain was there.

Getting down and dirty in her fatigues and army boots wouldn't bother her for a second.

But she hadn't prepared properly for this role. Zaslon allowed her nice clothes, but they wouldn't be happy about replacing an eight-hundred-dollar pair of jeans because she hadn't planned ahead properly. They'd see it as a reflection on her mission planning abilities.

She shrugged it off.

The collapse of the Condor's tail had made the extraction of the black boxes a long and tedious process.

Jeremy Trahn had fussed and fussed about photographing and documenting everything properly before he'd given the fire crews permission to use the big crane to remove the collapsed tail section. Once aside, the crews had gathered to mourn over their crushed fire engines.

But Jeremy and Mike had burrowed into the exposed wreckage until they'd reached the black boxes. It always made her laugh that they were bright orange.

"Does the Antonov have a QAR?" Jeremy popped up in front of her like a Bouncing Betty landmine—like he was always about to explode in her face.

"A QAR?" Elayne knew it was a mistake as soon as she said it. Mike looked at her askance.

"A Quick Access Recorder," Jeremy didn't notice a thing, of course. "Not all planes have them, but it would certainly make our lives easier if this one does."

"I know..." Elayne thought fast, "...that some of our planes have them, but not all." She had no idea how to determine if this one did, or if any AN-124 Condor did. She knew how to sabotage a plane, not put one back together.

"Now that I have these," he hefted the bright orange flight data and cockpit voice recorders, each the size of a large lunchbox, "we can go look."

When she didn't move, Jeremy waved a hand toward the front of the plane. Oh, she was blocking the only cleared path out of the depths of the mangled tail section. Whatever a QAR was, it must be in the cockpit.

Good. She'd been trying to steer Mike there for the last two hours, completely unsuccessfully. Usually men were pushovers for her, but she wouldn't think about why Mike wasn't.

Only five bodies. *That's* what she needed to think about.

How was it possible?

No one should have survived...especially not Voskov. *Please* not Voskov.

She was careful not to look at Mike as she picked her way out.

This time almost earning a tear in her thousand-dollar ZILVER jacket.

23

"So it *was* sabotage," Jon asked as he helped her up from her squat.

Miranda nodded. "It is the only conclusion that fits the facts. I think it very unlikely that someone accidentally triggered two kilos of plastique aboard a cargo plane."

"Why here?"

"Where else would it be?"

"Over the mid-Atlantic where we'd never find anything?"

Miranda considered. She understood mechanics, not motivations. Why anyone would intentionally blow up a perfectly fine cargo plane was something she'd never, ever understand. Well, she could, but it was so horrible that she tried never to think about it.

"I can think of a handful of why." Holly was always good at that sort of thing.

Miranda would listen and try to learn.

"This was a load of Russian helicopters, presumably from Russian defectors."

Miranda hadn't noticed the make of the helos as it wasn't relevant. But now that Holly mentioned it, she considered the remains of airframes and configurations that she'd observed. "A Havoc, two Alligators, a Helix, and an Mi-17 gunship. And there was one I didn't recognize." Which worried her.

Jon shook his head. "No reason you would. The last bird on the manifest is a brand-new design called the Kazan Ansat."

"Multi-role, light helicopter. Mostly transport or medevac; the same role as a Bell 212. I'll have to look at that more carefully. I wish I could have seen it intact."

"Me too," Jon squeezed her arm in either sympathy or shared loss before removing his hand. She could still feel the tactile-echo of it.

Holly nodded. "So, I'd place a fair wager that Russia wasn't too pleased and sent someone to destroy the delivery before the Americans could get their hands on it."

"Again, why not destroy it in the mid-Atlantic?" Jon, like most people, seemed to find some comfort in repeating things.

Maybe Miranda should try that. "So, you, Holly. You're not sleeping with Mike because he's a jerk about women."

"Miranda! Pinkie swear! There's a guy present."

She looked at Jon. "Oh right. Sorry. I forgot." Maybe she wouldn't start repeating things she already knew.

Holly glared at Miranda, waiting for...something.

Oh, to see if she was going to repeat something else she shouldn't be. She shook her head.

Holly nodded carefully before continuing. "If I was the Russians—and don't anyone be saying this in front of that

Antonov woman, I don't trust her more'n a starving dingo—I'd have done it on landing just to thumb my nose at the Yanks. *You got this close, then we took it away. Right on American soil.*"

Jon nodded, "That fits. So something rigged to the gear or flaps?"

Holly tipped her head sideways as if thinking hard.

Miranda could hear her neck crack.

"No. The explosion was after touchdown. Mike did talk to the tower and rescue crews despite escorting Ms. Antonov around. The pilot never declared an emergency or any such. Landed clean. This explosion sequence: shaped charge, central tank rupture, fire, and explosion of the helicopter's armament would have happened quickly. All except the last within the first half second or so. No. It was..."

Then Holly walked away from them.

Miranda had to hurry to keep up with Holly's long legs and how easily she stepped over the deep debris. If she ever envied Holly of anything, it was having long legs.

Holly was standing on the cockpit ceiling when Miranda caught up with her. She was inspecting the control cluster, hanging from the now-overhead deck.

The throttles for the four CF-6 engines were pulled back and switched over to thrust reversers, which would slow the plane using the force of the engines themselves. It was an expected and appropriate maneuver for a pilot, but it also meant that he had died before the plane had fully slowed or the controls would have been back to the idle position.

Holly reached up, appeared to pluck something away with a quick pinch, and slipped it into a plastic bag.

"Hey, there you all are." Jeremy called in through the missing windshield. "Does this plane have a QAR?"

While he was looking up at the console, Holly immediately thrust whatever she'd found into a vest pocket.

"Not on this model, Jeremy." Miranda had to answer Jeremy's question first so that it didn't get in the way of asking Holly what she'd found.

The moment she turned back, Holly leaned close enough to whisper in Miranda's ear, "You didn't just see me do that. It's a top-secret-category pinkie swear."

Miranda didn't understand why, but she nodded.

Outside the missing windshield, Mike and Elayne came up beside Jeremy. At the same moment, Jon came in from the crew area.

"Ixnay," Holly said to Jon and waved a hand at the back of the plane.

He nodded.

Miranda nodded toward Holly's pocket.

"Not even him," she whispered.

Miranda nodded to show that she understood, but she didn't like keeping secrets from a fellow investigator.

"Just for now."

Okay, she could do that. For now.

24

"You want to steal a plane from the middle of Russia?" Drake waved helplessly at the projected flightpath through their heartland.

"No, *I* want to inspect their satellite. It's simply that the most likely opportunity to do so is by acquiring it while it's on a plane in the middle of Russia." Elizabeth offered one of her seraphic smiles that he'd learned were anything but. They both enjoyed word play, but this was too much.

"And who's going to fly it? And don't say you; you were a combat jet pilot, not a Russian cargo pilot."

"How about a Russian?"

"Is Clarissa's contact a pilot?"

"Engineer—design-type, not flight-type. And no, he doesn't have access to the information I need; he designed the communications system. He won't transmit plans, just verbal delivery of tidbits of information. I asked."

"So we need to come up with a plan on how to steal a Russian plane, *because* it's carrying a Russian satellite."

"Precisely."

Drake wished he slouched, but too many years in the military had made him unable to do it. Rangers didn't slouch, even ones who'd left the door-kicking to younger men three decades ago. How was he supposed to tell his girlfriend not "No," but "Hell no!"?

"No."

Elizabeth barely hesitated. "Don't we have people who do this kind of thing?"

"Steal three billion dollars of satellite? No."

"Well, we should."

"The closest we've got is the SOG, the CIA's Special Operations Group. And they're more about wetwork. Need someone assassinated, they're your people. You need a multi-billion-dollar satellite lifted in broad daylight...I haven't a clue."

Elizabeth's steady gaze said that even "Hell no!" wouldn't have worked.

"Let me work on it," though Drake didn't know what good that would do.

"Remember, only four people know about this at the moment." As if he needed the reminder.

"You know the old saying: *Three may keep a secret, if two of them are dead.* Old Ben Franklin knew what he was talking about."

"I choose me."

"As what?"

"The one who lives. I'm sorry, Drake. I love you, but if one of us is going down, I'm going to push you over the cliff ahead of me."

"Nice. Real nice." That would teach him to fall for a

warrior. Maybe he could slouch…just a little.

Of course, Elizabeth had just said that she loved him. Might not be worth going off a cliff first to hear that, but it might.

"Night Stalkers or Delta Force or one of those teams?" she asked without any awkwardly long pause awaiting his response to her offhand comment.

Seemingly offhand, Drake old boy. Remember, women are sneaky. Well, so were 75th Rangers—active duty or not.

"I can get them to grab it, but the Russians will know that we grabbed it. We need some way that they'll think it never happened."

"Maybe you could make the plane evaporate? Or crash, but not?"

That had Drake sitting bolt upright. "Now that *is* interesting. I knew there was a reason I loved you."

It didn't take her even a single beat to react.

The smile that lit her face was pure Lizzy without any hint of General Elizabeth Gray.

Score one for the Rangers.

25

MIRANDA'S CELL PHONE RANG LOUDLY IN THE ANTONOV AN-124 Condor's cockpit.

She, Jeremy, and Mike jumped in surprise.

The others didn't even blink. How did they do that? *Everything* surprised her, particularly loud noises.

"This is Miranda Chase."

"Hi, Miranda. This is Jill at NTSB. Is your team available for a launch?" It was the word that the National Transportation Safety Board used to send a team to an accident investigation.

"We're in the middle of one right now."

"Really? I don't have one on the books. Where are you?"

Miranda puzzled at that for a moment. Oh, Drake had called and mobilized Team Chase directly, without going through proper channels. She supposed that was the prerogative of the Chairman of the Joint Chiefs of Staff.

"We're at—"

Holly shook her head sharply.

"Where? I didn't catch that," Jill asked while Miranda mouthed, *What?* to Holly.

Holly whispered back, "Drake declared national security. Just say we're in Kentucky."

"Oh, good idea. Hi, Jill. We're in Kentucky."

"Well, that's perfect. We have a bit of a mess in Nashville, bad enough that the president of FedEx called us himself. I could haul Rafe back from vacation or pull Terence from teaching his classes at the Training Academy, but..."

"But what?" Miranda asked when Jill didn't finish the sentence.

"But it would really help if you could take this launch," Jill was laughing. She often did that during their conversations.

Miranda muted the phone this time. It was very hard to follow the two conversations at once. At least she could mute Jill and pretend that conversation wasn't happening for the moment.

"There's an incident in Nashville. They're asking us to mobilize."

"Go," Jon said before Holly had time to frown.

"But we aren't done here yet."

"You've mapped out the whole path of it. Beginning to end. I have an Air Force AIB team standing by. Let them have some glory. They can verify all the little details, not that you left many."

Miranda always liked doing all the little details.

"We'll brief them and you can on your way within the hour. Nashville is just an hour drive away. Better yet, I'll shake loose a helicopter for you."

Miranda looked at the others.

Mike just shrugged, but Holly nodded.

It didn't seem right, but it was the military's investigation, not the NTSB's. She'd been escalated off launches before, and only rarely with an AIB team for backup.

She unmuted the phone. "Jill, we'll be on-site in seventy-five minutes. Where are we needed?"

"West side taxiway at the Nashville Airport; you can't miss it. Some tool of a tech genius tried to park his brand-new seventy-million-dollar Bombardier Global 7500 luxury jet *inside* a fully loaded FedEx Boeing 767 plane. He survived, but he's pitching a major fit, as is FedEx. You know..."

"What?" Miranda wasn't sure what she was supposed to know. Jill never seemed to complete her thoughts. She was originally from Los Angeles. Was it a Los Angeles thing?

"Normal madness."

"I'm not mad at anyone."

Jill giggled. "Just go to Nashville, Miranda."

"Okay." Miranda hung up. "Jon, let's go brief your team."

He placed a call and simply said, "We're ready for you."

They all climbed back out through the missing windshield. Once more Jon went first and made sure she landed lightly on her feet. Did he hold on to her for an extra moment? If he did, she liked it. Even if he didn't, she liked it anyway.

"We only need the three of us for the debriefing," Holly waved to indicate Miranda, herself, and Jon. "Why don't you others do a quick scout through the debris field to see if anything unusual catches your eye?"

26

HOLLY WATCHED REACTIONS AS SHE MADE THE SUGGESTION. But she kept an especially careful eye on Elayne Kasprak as she did so.

Jeremy handed Jon the black box recorders and pulled out his tablet and camera, ready to go.

Mike rolled his eyes at her.

Elayne Kasprak looked actively distressed.

"What about my plane?"

"Oh, we know what brought it down."

Elayne's eyes went wide. Just for an instant—a flicker, then gone.

Not surprise.

Worry?

Fear?

"You can tell your boss that it wasn't the plane's fault. It appears that the loadmaster failed to safety some of the helicopter's armament properly. A hard landing apparently fired one of the missiles."

Miranda and Jon both looked at her in surprise, but they were behind Elayne, so it didn't matter, as long as Miranda kept quiet.

She *was* about to protest when Jon rested a hand on her arm to silence her. Smart. Holly couldn't help liking him.

"And did you find the sixth crew member?" Elayne's voice remained tight.

"Mr. Bones? Yeah. Rescue crew missed him because there's so little left of him."

"Oh, the poor man," but again her eyes belied her words.

Relieved.

Definitely relieved.

Holly hoped that her own feelings weren't so bleeding transparent. Maybe Elayne Kasprak didn't have her guard up. All the better. Holly hadn't missed that first slap Ms. Kasprak had made for a weapon, and now here were more anomalies in her behavior.

"Let's go."

Miranda and Jon headed toward a pair of SUVs that were pulling up. That must be the AIB team.

Elayne followed Jeremy into the debris field more readily than any other action she'd made all day.

Holly tugged Mike aside for a moment. Hopefully he wasn't too besotted to be sensible.

"Have you been keeping your eyes open?"

"Not stupid, Holly. You go pointing a gun at someone, I'm gonna trust your instincts. Something's wrong with her. I stuck close, but I can't figure out what's up."

"Huh. I assumed you'd be too busy trying for a little root fest to notice anything." How badly had she misjudged him?

"Root fest?"

"Looking for someone to go burying your root in, mate."

"God but you Aussies are crass. Sure, I wouldn't mind that for a second. She's incredibly hot."

Apparently not misjudged by much.

"Almost as hot as you. But you threatened to beat the shit out of me if I ever mentioned that, so I didn't just say it." And he hit her with one of those Mike Munroe killer smiles.

Well, she was made of sterner stuff than that.

Then he winked.

He was teasing her? If so, was it about his hopes of bedding Elayne or...

Shit! He was messing with her mind—successfully. That could *not* be allowed to happen.

She punched him and sent him off cursing to go pant after the perky Elayne. If that's what he was actually doing. Mike was the one guy she'd never been able to read.

Then at the last second she had a thought...

"Hey, Mike?"

"Yeah?"

"See if you can grab a set of her fingerprints. Both index fingers at least."

"With what? I don't carry a fingerprint kit."

"Maybe a piece of debris that she picks up. Bag it carefully."

"Woman doesn't like getting her hands dirty. Thought she was going to have a stroke when she got some lube grease on her fancy jeans. But I'll try." He gave her a casual two-finger-to-the-forehead salute before sauntering off.

Sauntering.

Too damn sure of himself by far.

But it was good that he'd been being suspicious of

Elayne rather than trying to bed her. If he ever forgot to protect Miranda first, he was going to be getting a severe wake-up call that it was time to die.

Finally alone, Holly pulled the small bag out of her pocket and inspected the contents.

It was very small and quite clever. A sticky back, a tiny microswitch, and a small circuit board that she'd wager was the transmitter matching the remains of the receiver-trigger she'd found. It had also been nearly invisible.

Whoever had placed it and the explosive charge had been in both the bunk area and the cockpit.

Alone?

That would imply official clearance to be aboard.

Or maybe as someone's guest, planting both devices while their host was distracted.

Yes, Elayne Kasprak would be very good at distracting any male she wanted to—except, curiously, Mike. But if Elayne had been playing the sex card, she couldn't just pull on gloves before planting the devices.

The tiny transmitter was just big enough to retain a single fingerprint of whoever put it in place.

27

ELAYNE KNEW THAT SOMETHING WAS WRONG, BUT SHE couldn't figure out what.

All six crew dead, that was excellent news.

But she knew that the helicopters' armament shouldn't just *go off.* Any fool would know that. For all their flash, how incompetent was this team?

Holly wasn't incompetent.

She was dangerously competent. But perhaps only as a warrior and not as a crash investigator?

Until Elayne could be sure of her, she needed an excuse to stick with this team.

"Mike, my rental car was acting very strangely. Do you think I could get a lift back to Nashville Airport when you go? I'll just call the rental company to come get it."

"Sure, no problem. Maybe you'd like to stick around and see us kick ass on another investigation. I'm betting we'll be overnight in Nashville."

His eyes didn't drift down her body, but his smile most certainly did.

It *would* give her a chance to overhear if there was anything else they'd learned from the Antonov crash—not that she was really worried anymore. But that Holly woman *did* run this crew, no matter what the others thought, and she was hiding something. Elayne would like a chance to figure out what.

If that meant taking pretty boy Mike for a tumble, she saw no reason to complain.

"That sounds wonderful." No suggestive tones, but she didn't want to close the door either. "I should be getting back to San Antonio, but I could also catch any early flight tomorrow before my first meetings."

As she finished the sentence, Elayne realized that she'd let her accent slip too far into clear English.

"Yes, that could be most good," she chose Dmitri Voskov's mangled English. Mike didn't react at all; he hadn't noticed.

As they began walking the debris field, she jammed her hands in her jacket pockets and focused on protecting her clothes from more damage.

28

THEY GATHERED IN A CIRCLE AROUND THE HOOD OF ONE OF the Air Combat Command Accident Investigation Board's SUVs.

Miranda checked in with Holly. "I have to tell them."

"Yes, everything."

Miranda tried to figure out why she could speak now, but not before. But she suspected that the reason was under one of Holly's secrecy rules, and with Jon and his team all here, she couldn't ask.

So, she laid out the entire progress of the accident from the initial shaped-charge sabotage, the fuel fire, and the final explosion of the Russian helicopter's armament.

On a large aerial photograph, she marked each of the key points of evidence and details that needed additional follow-up.

It took her most of an hour to complete the summary with all of their questions. Smart questions, they were just as high caliber a team as she'd expect from the US Air Force.

"The only thing we didn't find was who did it and how they triggered it," Jon told his team.

Right. Miranda had somehow again forgotten that.

She could see mechanical systems so clearly—versus people-based systems, which always seemed to pass in a blur. Perhaps if she considered a person's actions as the next logical step in the chain of mechanical events…?

She liked that.

A lot.

Miranda tugged out her personal notebook and made a note to think of people's actions as a chain of mechanical actions. Could that extend to person-to-person interactions?

For example, was there an extensible reason that Major Jon Swift had held her waist multiple times in the last hour, beyond her short stature and their circuitous entering and exiting the crew section of the wreck?

But his actions weren't connected to other systems, so that wasn't helpful. Perhaps if—

"Actually," Holly reached into her vest pocket and pulled out two small, clear-plastic evidence bags, "we know how the initial explosion was triggered, and I have an idea who."

Everyone turned to her in surprise.

"Exhibit A." In the center of the car hood that had been their impromptu meeting table, Holly set the broken bit of electronics and wire that they'd found mixed in with the skeleton's bones.

She marked where it was found on the diagram of the crew quarters.

"Bluetooth receiver," one of the technicians inspected it carefully.

Holly set her second small bag beside the first, "Exhibit B."

"Transmitter with a microswitch. Where was this?"

Holly took one of the team's tablet computers and pulled up an image of the AN-124's control cluster. She picked up an electronic pen and drew it in at the base of one of the throttle levers.

"Sorry I removed it, but I was under a bit of time pressure and had to make sure it didn't go astray."

Miranda could see the logic of it. "The thrust reverser. There would be no need to engage it on takeoff or during the flight. But the thrust reversers would invariably be engaged at landing with any large jet."

Jon turned to the man who'd taken possession of the flight recorders. "You'll probably be able to find the event on the recorders—thrust reverser engagement to the sound of the initial explosion. They should be nearly simultaneous."

"All that leaves is who." Miranda was getting the hang of this. Someone had placed the trigger which had caused the explosion. In the opposite process direction that implied a human action. Yes. "Whoever had placed it there."

"Anyone have a fingerprint kit?" Holly asked.

No one did.

"Get this to a lab. I'm hoping to get a match."

"With whom?" Miranda asked.

"Classified. Top secret. Sorry." Then Holly changed the topic, taking on what Miranda interpreted as Aussie teasing tone. "So, Major Jon, do you have a *swift* helicopter hangin' 'round to zip us over Nashville Airport way?"

"I do," he smiled at her and pointed to one of the nearby parking areas where dozens of helicopters rested.

29

HOLLY HAD NEVER RIDDEN IN A HELICOPTER OF THE 160TH SOAR before. The regiment was the elite helicopter team of the entire US military. Five years of an exceptional flying record in the regular forces *might* garner a pilot an invitation to *try out* for their two-year advanced training program.

The Black Hawk that Major Swift led them toward was, oddly, pure black.

No big white Army star. Even warning signs, usually painted in shocking yellow or red to get attention, were a dark gray. Nothing to catch the light. The 160th's nickname was the Night Stalkers and they did fly mostly at night. Delivering SEALs and Delta Force teams where no one else could put them.

In broad daylight, they looked like dark, helicopter-shaped holes in the world.

Holly placed two fingers between her teeth to let out a shrill whistle.

When the others looked up from where they were still

prowling the wreckage, she waved them toward the waiting bird.

Because of where they each were, they all arrived at the helo at roughly the same moment.

Holly was about to reach for the handle of the cargo bay door. She may not have flown with the Night Stalkers but she'd flown plenty with Australia's 6th Aviation Regiment and knew her way around a Black Hawk.

Mike flashed her a signal and lagged back.

Holly slowed to match him.

Elayne Kasprak arrived at the door first, reached up, and slid it open easily before climbing up onto the cargo deck.

"What do you need, Mike? Get any fingerprints for me?" The others were making enough noise boarding that the two of them could talk safely.

"She didn't touch a single thing. Kept her fists rammed into her pockets like it was midwinter."

"*Bloody hell!*"

"Until that," he pointed at the cargo door handle.

It had been a perfect move. She wanted to kiss him. Or slap a high five. But Elayne might be watching, so she went with her third choice and punched his arm. Hard.

"Ow! God damn it, Holly. Aren't you ever happy?" He rubbed his arm as Jeremy and Miranda boarded.

"Right now," she grinned at him. "Totally ecstatic."

"Got a damn weird way of showing it."

"That's me, mate."

Mike shook his head and climbed aboard.

Major Swift was waiting to close the door.

Holly whispered as she came even with him. "Major,

don't touch the outside door handle. We need to test it for a matching set of prints to the radio trigger."

He raised his eyebrows in question but was otherwise rock steady.

A *lot* to like about him. Might have considered having a go at him herself if his eye hadn't landed on Miranda.

"And just so we're clear. One misstep with Miranda and you'll have *me* to deal with. Roger that?"

He saluted sharply. "Yes ma'am." His tone was dead serious but his eyes were laughing at her.

"Laugh away, Gull boy. It could be your last travels."

"Yes ma'am. I will be careful." And that sounded serious. But maybe not because of her threat.

She climbed aboard and ended up next to Mike. She made a point of landing in her web seat with an elbow to his ribs, but she was feeling good so she didn't drive it home.

"You're crazy, you know that, right?"

"First thing you ever said to me. Doesn't make it any less true." Then she leaned forward enough to look at Elayne on his far side. "Isn't he just so sweet?"

"I think he's very cute."

Mike grimaced. Cute was the last thing that a guy like Mike wanted to be called.

Major Swift climbed aboard as well, which she hadn't expected, and closed the cargo door from the inside. He winked at her, then ended up between Jeremy and Miranda. How had she missed that seat being open?

In under two minutes the pilots had the engines up to speed and wheels off the ground.

If only she had some control on where all of this was flying.

30

"CONGRATULATIONS, MR. VICE PRESIDENT." DRAKE ROSE TO his feet and shook Clark Winston's hand as he entered the White House Situation Room.

"Thanks, Drake. And please, call me Clark."

"Yes sir, Mr. Vice President."

Clark smiled. "That means I'm now stuck calling you General Nason." He took his seat to the right of the President's chair.

"No sir. Protocol of respect only goes upstream. You're the Vice Commander-in-Chief. You can call anyone except President Cole anything you want."

"He's already insisted on Roy," Clark waved him toward his own right. "Vice Commander-in-Chief. I try not to think about that one."

"Still surprising to be in the job?"

"I was confirmed and sworn in Friday; this is Saturday afternoon. Give me a break."

"Nope. It's the hot seat now."

Clark scoffed at him, then turned to Elizabeth waiting quietly across the table. "Hello, General Gray. No chance of getting a 'Clark' out of you, is there?"

"No sir, Mr. Vice President."

He groaned dramatically, but appeared to be enjoying himself.

President Cole arrived in mid-discussion with his Chief of Staff, Nora Farber. She'd been his adjutant when he retired from the Green Berets and followed him straight into the Senate, then the White House. She'd been his right hand for almost two decades. There was a lot of speculation as to whether Cole could even tie a tie without her assistance...at least until someone pissed off Cole enough for the former Green Beret to surface.

He was already signaling for them all to stay seated even as he kept talking.

"Right. Get that and ram it down President Montoya's throat."

"Sir?"

"Do it nicely, but make sure he knows that he has no choice if he wants our continued trade agreement and naval protection."

"Yes sir," and Nora was gone.

"Anyone else coming?" President Roy Cole dropped into his chair.

"Not right now," Drake tapped the isolation switch, blocking even the Marines of the National Security Council who monitored the room to service any requests.

Roy Cole just raised his eyebrows in question.

"This is top-secret need-to-know information," he explained.

"Does that include his girlfriend?" Cole teased his new Vice President.

Drake hated politics. And having the VP, who he trusted, screwing the new Director of the CIA, who he wouldn't trust with a dull pencil, didn't help matters.

"While the D/CIA is the original source of this information, I'd like to keep this meeting compartmentalized for the time being."

Cole nodded.

Clark saw that and shrugged uncomfortably—the President had already agreed so there would be no point arguing.

Welcome to Day One on the job, buddy.

"D/CIA Clarissa Reese has a Russian source. Somewhere in the next forty-eight hours, the Russians will be transporting a Persona-class recon/surveillance satellite from the Progress factory in southwest Russia to their new cosmodrome in southeast Russia."

Drake waited to see their reactions. Two pros. He had their undivided attention, but that was all he could read. Good poker players.

"The compartmentalized portion of this conversation is that we've confirmed this is very likely to be accurate intelligence. General Gray and I would like to investigate possible scenarios to snatch the satellite."

"In the next forty-eight hours?" The President didn't even hesitate, cutting right to the core.

"All the warning we had, sir. This information is just three hours old."

For some reason that surprised Clark and had him checking his watch, then the time zone clocks on the wall.

No longer the D/CIA, many of his avenues of information would be cut off. Ah! Including from his lover, whom he must have seen in the last three hours to be so visibly bothered about not having been informed of this.

"Why?" The President stayed right on track.

Elizabeth spoke up and explained about the US's lack of intelligence regarding Russian satellite surveillance capabilities. Then he offered his own thoughts about not fully understanding the strategic ramifications of those new capabilities.

"Also set the Russians back on their asses," the President observed when they were done.

"Yes sir. They're on a similar launch cycle to us, one satellite in this category every four to six years."

"Won't that be a little obvious? Just grabbing the damn thing?"

"Our plan won't work if they ever find out about it," Drake was clear on that point.

"So..." Cole waved a hand to tell him to come to the point.

Drake took a deep breath and resisted looking to Elizabeth for support. It was her original suggestion, but he didn't want to put her in the line of fire if this went wrong. *He* was the one bringing the idea forward rather than burying it.

"Mr. President, I'd like to bring in that Chase woman and her team. I want them to assist us in staging a crash."

"How is crashing a satellite going to get it for you?"

"No sir. We were thinking of making it *appear* that the transport plane from Samara to Vostochny crashed. Crashed violently enough that they won't go looking for the pieces. Or they'll be fooled if they do."

"How in hell are you going to do that?"

"Not a clue. That's why we need them."

"This is that woman who attacked the White House in a Korean War Air Force jet?"

"Ha, ha, ha, sir." Drake still felt a chill when he recalled how close Miranda had come to dying on the National Mall when her plane was sabotaged.

"Gotta respect a woman with the guts to do that. Any thoughts, Clark?"

The new VP startled but also didn't hesitate. "I've only dealt with her the one time, sir, during the Casper drone incident. Her work there was beyond exemplary. And her parents have stars on our—on the CIA's Memorial Wall. They were exceptional agents, Mr. President."

Drake hadn't known that about Miranda. He saw that Lizzy had. Gave him some empathy for Clark; compartmentalized information in a relationship definitely sucked.

"Ms. Chase's team is one of the only ones in the NTSB entirely cleared top secret or better," Clark concluded.

The President pondered in silence for approximately thirty seconds.

Long enough for Drake to think back and wonder if that was something Cole always did on hard decisions. The timing when he'd made his own decision to bring this forward *did* feel familiar.

Battlefield tactics.

They'd both been out of the field for twenty years, but battlefield tactics still remained. Take the time to think things through, but not long enough for the enemy to start wondering what was happening.

"Do it. But only if we won't get caught with our hand in the cookie jar. I'm not having a war declared over this thing. Clear?"

"Clear, sir."

"Anything else for me, Drake?"

"You mean other than Afghanistan versus Pakistan, Saudi Arabia versus Iran, and China versus everybody."

"What is this? Playoff season? Get out of here. Clark, you stay."

Drake held the door for Elizabeth and was just easing it closed when he overheard the President.

"Clark, what are you going to do about Clarissa? Damned peculiar situation unless you make an honest woman out of her."

Drake's earlier chill became a shiver.

Make an honest woman out of Clarissa Reese? Was that even possible?

And that snake could be First Lady someday?

He liked Clark. But if it ever came down to it, he'd be voting for the other party as many times as he could get away with.

31

THE INCIDENT AT NASHVILLE WOULD HAVE BEEN LAUGHABLE IF there hadn't been so much upset.

The FedEx agent confronted Miranda as she cleared the edge of the Black Hawk's slowing rotor blades.

"I need immediate permission to unload those packages. I need to get them on a new flight. But they say that I can't unload them without your permission."

Before she could tell him that they'd be released when her inspection was complete, an older man with a ridiculous black toupee stormed up.

"That...that...that plane," he practically spit in her face. "It's all their fault. You're going to—"

Mike took him by the arm and tried to turn him aside. "Let's go look at what happened."

But the man wasn't having anything to do with that and spun free to continue spewing out his frustration.

Jeremy already had his instruments out and was measuring air temperature, humidity, and wind speed.

Where was Holly or Jon?

They were back at the helicopter talking to the flight crew.

The man came so close that he was practically standing on her toes. His cologne had striking power and made her eyes water.

He was still yelling. So fast and loud. She couldn't hear the words.

Too much.

Just when she thought she'd scream, someone moved past her.

"Let me help you, sir." The Antonov engineer took his arm.

Then she did something too fast to follow.

The man clutched his chest, gasped desperately, and dropped to his knees.

A second later, Holly and Jon had arrived to either side of her.

"I'm so sorry, Miranda." "Are you okay?" Their words tumbled over each other.

She took in a breath.

The air was still too thick with cologne.

Miranda backed up a step, then another.

She tried again and felt she could breathe—almost.

Normal sounds returned. The last descending whine of the Black Hawk's twin T-700 turboshaft engines. A Boeing jet by the sound of the engines—she glanced over, yes a 737 —was taking off along Runway 2C. An Airbus was nearly silent as it landed on Runway 2R at the far side of the airport.

"I'm okay." She hoped that her single answer covered both of their questions. *I'm so sorry, Miranda,* didn't really count as a question anyway. Yes, one answer was enough. Which was good as she didn't feel up to making a second one.

"Have you ever seen anything like it, Miranda?" Jeremy pointed. "I mean I once saw a pickup truck—small one, a Nissan Frontier—brake suddenly. The Corvette that had been right on his tail didn't react fast enough. As the Nissan nosed down, the rear bumper raised and the Corvette drove right underneath. Ended up going down the road another fifty yards with the pickup perched right on top of the car. But this? It's amazing."

Jon anchored her in place with a hand on her shoulder. As if he was holding her once more down upon the ground, which had become so unstable for a moment.

Finally able to breathe properly, Miranda looked around.

Nashville was changing, with a lot of new construction. But the three parallel runways and a fourth crossing one were the same as always. The FedEx facility was a small affair, presently including just four jets. Their main hub at Memphis, just four hundred miles away, typically had over a hundred at a time, all in some state of transition.

Their jets never remained still for long.

Except this one.

Jeremy's description was apt, except the smaller, lower plane hadn't rear-ended the bigger one.

The Boeing 767-300F freighter was sitting across the taxiway for Runway 2 Left.

Literally sitting.

A Bombardier Global 7500 had slid under the front of the 767 from the side, striking just behind the forward landing gear. It had lifted the 767's nose until its tail sat directly on the ground.

It was a good thing that the Bombardier had swept wings and rear engines mounted by the tail. It was so far under the bigger jet that the 767's landing gear would have ripped off straight wings. Leaking fuel and an explosion would have been nearly inevitable.

"Jeremy. We'll need the loading charts for the 767 as well as both plane's recorders. Gather any information that we'll need to make a calculation of the impact force necessary to place the Bombardier so far under the 767. They're both modern aircraft, so they probably have QARs as well. Make sure that you gather those too."

He hurried off.

As he'd already measured the environmental conditions, and there was no debris field, she moved forward to inspect the length of the skid marks. Both planes were exhibiting them.

The Bombardier's were long and black, indicating hard, late braking. Hard enough that all of the tires should exhibit a flat spot. Gentle braking and hard maneuvering might have avoided the calamity. Though, by the length of the skid marks, perhaps not.

The far more massive 767's marks were very short, but they were sideways. No indication that the jet had been in motion when it was struck on the taxiway.

"I'll sue you. All of you." The pilot, still on his knees in pain, had finally recovered enough to start shouting again.

"Just try," Elayne's snarl was nasty. "I am no pansy-assed American dog. I am *bull.* You don't stop whining and I kick your goose-ass as all the way to M…" Then she glanced around at everyone else watching and seemed to stumble for a moment. "All the way to Kiev."

Miranda appreciated Elayne dealing with him.

Pansy-assed? That sounded nice and pretty…if a little odd.

32

Holly knew Russian fluently. Enough for her to know that, even in English, Elayne Kasprak's accent was Russian, not Ukrainian.

Kick your ass all the way to Moscow?

Not so much an engineer with Antonov, are you, girlfriend?

Holly upped her bet with herself that if they recovered a fingerprint from the transmitter on the crashed Condor, it would be Elayne Kasprak's.

Then ...what the hell was she doing here?

Checking up on her own handiwork? That took a certain arrogance that even the Australian SASR didn't have. But the Russians? Maybe.

She glanced back to see the crew of the Black Hawk finishing with lifting the fingerprints. As she'd suggested, they were making a show of doing maintenance on the door so that it wouldn't be obvious.

One of the crew hit a button on his phone, then turned to glance at her, offering a microscopic nod.

Prints found and sent.

Elayne had her back to them as she was walking the toupee pilot over to a baggage conveyor that had been near the crash. Once there, she shoved him down to sit on the bumper.

The way the man winced and drew his knees together, the sweet-little-blonde Elayne had just offered to cut off his balls if he moved. He did indeed stay in place as Elayne rejoined the team.

Everyone was standing around inspecting the juncture of the two planes. Except Miranda, of course. She was slowly walking the perimeter of the two aircraft, probably making sure there wasn't any debris before she looked at the two planes looming above her.

Holly caught up with her near the tail section. "I'll walk with you."

Miranda nodded her thanks.

Even with two of them, they moved slowly, zig-zagging their way across the bare pavement.

"You like him, don't you?"

Miranda didn't look up as they circled around behind the 767's tail. It was strange to have such a close-up view, resting on the ground but still intact and undamaged. Though it would take some careful inspection before it flew again.

"Miranda?"

"Yes," her tone said that she was answering the first question, not the second one. "I think I do."

"Major Swift isn't setting off any alarms for me. But…" But what? Like Holly'd had such great luck with love herself. "Just take it slow."

"How do I calibrate a timeline for interpersonal relationships when I hardly know what they are?"

Holly laughed and Miranda looked up, hurt.

"No, sorry," Holly apologized. It took her a moment to get her laugh back under control.

"That's universal, Miranda. None of us has a bleeding clue what relationships are or how they work. We know we want to be with others, but what that means…?" She shrugged. "We have to rediscover that every single time."

"Like you and Mike."

"I wish you'd stop coming back to that."

Miranda stared at the ground, but clearly wasn't scanning for any debris.

"But, since you mention it, it seems that Mike isn't the hundred percent troll I'd judged him to be."

"What's his percentage of trollishness now?" Miranda wasn't much for jokes, but it sounded like one.

"Ninety percent."

Her flat statement earned the laugh Holly had been hoping for.

"The other ten percent is pure vile goblin."

Miranda actually considered Holly's tease. "No. The other ten percent is gnome."

"Like a garden gnome?" Holly liked that.

"Yes, they're cute and rather sweet."

"They're ghastly." But that was now two women calling Mike "cute." That implied a niceness factor that she'd somehow overlooked. Or maybe ignored?

Miranda appeared to have another question.

At which moment both of their phones rang.

Holly answered hers—blocked number.

"Harper here."

"We got answers from the lab," the man on the other end of the line didn't waste time with names. "The prints on the transmitter and the helicopter's cargo bay door handle match."

"I knew it!"

"There's more and, according to my records on you, you're cleared for it—which is weird as shit for a civilian, even with your background. But I'm looking right at your clearance, so here you go. Elizaveta Egorova's last registered fingerprint was over a decade ago. She was a flight attendant for Aeroflot. Not a thing since. We have one questionable report of an SVR agent of that name being killed ten years ago."

"Do you have a picture?"

"Check your phone."

Holly pulled it away for a moment. Elayne / Elizaveta had one of those ageless faces that didn't seem to change with time. Her hair had been a short bob, but there was no question it was the same woman. "It's her. Different name. Same face."

"If we trust her passport scan, she was born within the closed administrative area of Polyarny, Murmansk Oblast, Russia. Present age is thirty-three. Mother a torpedo guidance system design engineer. Father Spetsnaz Colonel. All we've got."

"Okay. Thanks. Tight lid on this. No one who doesn't already know."

"That would be me, you, and this computer."

"Thanks. Keep it that way."

"You *know* what she is?" It wasn't a question about Elayne, but rather about Holly's background.

"Yeah. I do."

"Okay. Be careful." And the guy was gone. No name. No organization. No way to call him back.

A spook.

A military spook if he understood the implications of Elayne's history the same way she did. The Intelligence Support Activity? Had she just had a call from the spookiest team of the entire US military? That ramped up her fears. For that fingerprint to ramp up to that level so fast was a very, very bad sign.

Someone had gone to a lot of trouble to cover Elayne Kasprak's tracks.

Shit! Even Special Operations types still had their names. Her own name was still hers. Elizaveta Egorova / Elayne Kasprak / Ms. Whatever had "died."

That only happened in teams like the CIA's Special Operations Group, Israel's Mossad Kidon assassination squad, or—Zaslon.

It took Holly three tries to slip her phone into her back pocket. She'd drawn against a Zaslon agent-saboteur-assassin and lived to tell the tale. Even though Elayne had been unarmed, that was a good trick.

Shit on a popsicle stick!

33

"I'M IN NASHVILLE ON ANOTHER INCIDENT NOW—NON-military. I should have called as soon as we solved the Antonov at Fort Campbell. I'm sorry that I forgot." Miranda really did feel bad about that.

Drake grumbled for a moment, then stopped. "Wait. You solved it? You landed in Fort Campbell, like, seven hours ago?"

Miranda checked her watch. "Six hours and forty-nine minutes."

"And you solved the crash?"

"Yes."

"In six hours and forty-nine minutes?"

"No."

"No? But you just said—"

She waited for Drake to finish his sentence.

But he didn't.

Then she waited for the loud buzz of a FedEx Cessna 208B turboprop racing into the sky on the nearby Runway

2L. A smaller aircraft, it must be making local deliveries, probably within the state. Finally it rotated and was gone aloft. Once more, only the background noise of jets on more distant runways filled the air.

"We did it in four hours and twenty-nine minutes," she told Drake. "Then we handed it over to an AIB team and proceeded—"

"Under *five* hours?"

"—to Nashville. We're currently investigating a collision on a taxiway with a 767 cargo plane."

"Miranda. Would you please tell me what you found?"

"I haven't done my investigation yet. A private Bombardier Global 7500 apparently rammed a fully loaded FedEx Boeing 767-300F as it was preparing to taxi for takeoff."

"I'm not talking about Nashville. I'm talking about Fort Campbell." He sounded rather upset. "What did you find *there?*"

"Um. Hold a minute." She muted the phone over his squawk of protest.

Holly had finished her phone call.

"Is it okay to tell Drake what's going on?"

Holly looked around.

Miranda did as well but couldn't figure out why. *Oh!* Pinkie-swear privacy.

Holly nodded and Miranda unmuted the phone.

"Yes, Drake. I can tell you."

"Damned right! There was a question about that? Never mind. Well?" His thoughts seemed to be jumping about quite erratically today.

"The incident was initiated by—"

"Accident or attack?"

She tried again. "The incident was initiated by a hidden microswitch behind the thrust reverser controls. It transmitted a signal to a shaped charge of approximately two kilos. This—"

"I don't need all of the details. Someone blew up the plane? Did I hear that right?"

Miranda had become better at incomplete sentences. But an incomplete report was so much worse.

Holly offered to take the phone, but Miranda shook her head.

"Drake…" Miranda took a deep breath. "Yes. The Antonov crew and the Antonov plane were not at fault—"

"Shit!"

"—based on initial findings."

She waited, but he didn't say anything else.

Miranda thought it best to wait as well. It seemed to be the only way to avoid being interrupted. While she did, she completed the report of the chain of events that had destroyed the AN-124 Condor under her breath. She felt better when she'd finished.

"Well," Drake finally spoke again. "We have a bigger problem."

"No. A Boeing 767 is not bigger than an Antonov AN-124-200. In fact, the Ruslan 150 can carry three times the load of a Boeing 767-300F."

"I need you back at Fort Campbell."

"But the 767—"

"I'll be landing at Fort Campbell in under thirty minutes. *We* will be in a meeting in thirty-one minutes. Do you have transport or do I need to arrange that?"

"But—"

"Miranda. Is Holly there?"

Resigned, she handed over her phone.

Holly looked around and put it on speaker. Another plane was taking off on Runway 2C—the fifth in the seventeen minutes since they'd landed. An Airbus A320 with the CFM rather than the IAE engines by the acceleration profile down the runway. Yes, the narrowed nacelle shape around the engine exhaust confirmed that.

Once the noise died down, Holly spoke.

"Holly Harper here, sir. I would really prefer it if you'd let Miranda complete her sentences in the future, sir."

Even to Miranda's ear she sounded angry. Or at least sharply irritated.

"I don't give a shit. I need—"

Holly hung up the phone.

"You just hung up on the Chairman of the Joint Chiefs of Staff?"

"He was being a jerk."

The phone rang again, but Holly wasn't answering it.

"He said that something else has come up and he needs us back at Fort Campbell immediately. He's meeting us there."

"Okay."

Miranda could never ignore a ringing phone. It felt as if her skin was crawling off her body with each successive ring.

Holly finally answered the call.

She started speaking immediately. "We're on our way. Now mellow the fuck out, mate." Holly hung up again, returned Miranda's phone, and smiled.

No question but Holly was enjoying herself as she started leading them back the way they'd come.

"But…" And Miranda didn't know how to continue. "What about this wreck?"

"Do you really want to spend the day arguing with this idiot? The Night Stalkers pilot had a little chat with the tower. Apparently the goober landed on the taxiway rather than the runway in his pretty new jet—arguing with his own copilot on an open mic so that the tower couldn't call them to abort. Frankly, just tell them to arrest him and let's go."

"But I haven't done a proper investigation." That made an incomplete sentence, an incomplete game of Charades, or even an incomplete incident report appear completely trivial.

"Miranda, how about this? You never even really properly started this investigation. So, maybe you can let go of it?"

Miranda considered. She *hadn't* really started properly. The offensive man with his noxious cologne had confronted her before she could introduce herself. She'd never even declared her role at this site.

So, if she didn't have a declared role as an investigator-in-charge for the NTSB, could she imagine that she hadn't yet taken on that role?

As they circled around from behind the tail section, they could once again hear the tycoon shouting at someone.

"Yes." Miranda decided. "Get the others, Holly."

Her phone rang in her hand and she almost jumped out of her shoes. It was Drake again.

"Miranda, do *not* answer that."

"Are you sure?" It was bothering her not to answer it, but

it wasn't creeping her out. Not completely.

"I'm sure. We'll see him in half an hour, he needs to just chill. Kick his uptight ass straight to voicemail. I don't care how many times he calls."

Miranda nodded her understanding. Holly knew so much more about people.

She wished she could be more like Holly.

More confident.

More sure that she knew what she was doing.

For a moment, Miranda pretended she was Holly Harper. She simply tucked her phone in her pocket and walked away toward the helicopter that had brought them.

Behind her, Holly laughed aloud and called out a hearty, "Goodonya."

Good on you. Well done, Miranda translated from Australian for herself and just kept walking tall. Well, kept walking five-foot-four, but that had to count for something.

The helo's crew were sitting on the other side of the aircraft in the sun. They were playing a fierce game of Dungeons and Dragons *Dragonfire.* That was new just a couple of years ago and she'd never played it.

But it reminded her of happier times when she used to play D&D with her parents most evenings to learn strategy —after she was done with her homework, of course.

She let them complete the current play, then the roll after that before she spoke up.

"I'm sorry to interrupt. We're ready to go back." She could hear the tech baron with the bad toupee's protests redouble as Holly called off the team. "Very ready."

They marked their places, closed up the game, and began preparing their helicopter for immediate departure.

34

HOLLY CALLED THE TEAM OVER. "WE'RE OUT OF HERE."

"But—" the FedEx guy looked incredibly upset.

"You have my permission to get those packages off the plane and get them moving again." She had absolutely no authority here, but she didn't see any reason for that to stop her.

"Oh, thank God. What about my plane?"

"Have the police arrest this asshole for being an asshole."

"What the *hell?*" Mr. Toupee sounded ready to pitch a fit. She didn't remember him having a black eye, but it was swelling up impressively.

Holly rested her hand on his shoulder and pinched the upper pectoral.

He gasped, then squeaked. Bonus pack: he also stopped talking.

"It's not nice to interrupt a lady when she's speaking." She didn't let go despite assorted whimpers. "Throw him in jail and ask the judge to set the bail at the value of your cargo jet plus the delay cost and the replacement flight."

"The tower has the recordings to back it up," Mike agreed.

Holly nodded her thanks that he was at least somewhat focused on his job before she continued, "An NTSB team will file an initial finding… Do you have enough information to do that, Jeremy, or do we call Jill to send another team?"

He looked at her in surprise, then down at his tablet, then back up at her. "Um, yeah. I've copied both QARs onto my computer. The tower is sending me flight and voice data. No one's questioning what happened. Well, except the owner of the Global 7500. I can't believe that he'd do that to a brand-new seventy-million-dollar plane. I'd like to inspect the plane more carefully, but only because I've never seen one before. There are only fifteen of them so far. We know what happened here. I was even able to interview the 7500's copilot—after she punched the owner and quit, but before she left the site. I've got measurements and—"

"Congratulations. You're about to file your first NTSB report. Miranda will check it for you, but it's yours."

"Oh my God! Really? I can't believe it. I mean this one is so simple, but I've always wanted to—"

"To present yourself in a calm and dignified manner."

"Oh, right." Jeremy grimaced, then looked down at his tablet clutched tightly in both hands as if he couldn't contain his excitement any other way.

Holly let go of Mr. Toupee, who sagged—straight into the arms of the two airport police who'd been hovering nearby. They read him his rights as they handcuffed him and led him to their squad car.

A news reporter, who'd somehow talked his way through airport security, was having a great day. Mr. Toupee was going to have a very bad one when his board saw the news he was creating—hissy-fit GIF had probably already gone viral. This crash was particularly photogenic and Mr. Toupee captured in all his rage was most definitely not. Or maybe his board would love the publicity; who could tell with corporations.

Holly ignored them and turned to Elayne / Elizaveta.

"Ms. Kasprak, I'm sorry that we won't be able to spend more time with you. Thank you for your assistance with the regrettable loss of the Antonov AN-124 Condor. Please make sure that Mike has your contact information—"

Mike held up his phone and nodded to show that he already did. *Total* dog. He'd just regained his hundred percent troll rating—not one speck of cute garden gnome anywhere in sight.

"We'll make sure that your company receives a report of our investigation and any on-going information gathered by the AIB team. Again, we've made an initial determination that your plane is not at fault. We may never know exactly what happened, especially if it was human error in the handling of the helicopters. But I assume the plane was insured and you will be found not at fault."

"Um, thank you. Where are you going so soon?" Again that fleeting expression, this time definitely triumph.

Nailed your skinny ass! But Holly kept her own smirk to herself.

"We've been called to another matter. Civilian, but more pressing than this foolishness. I'm sure someone here at

FedEx will be glad to run you over to the passenger terminal."

Holly shook Elizaveta's / Elayne's hand and felt the calluses.

Inside the first joint of the forefinger.

Deep in the webbing between thumb and forefinger.

A slight one at the base of the palm.

Holly used to have those—shooter's calluses.

The trigger finger. The repeated kick of the gun against the webbing. The repeated hard kick of the butt of the gun against the palm.

But they weren't just some average shooter's calluses. They were very distinct against her own, now softer hand.

No one shot as many rounds as the most elite units of Special Operations Forces. America's tiny Delta Force shot more rounds in training than the entire Marine Corps. SEAL Team 6 far outgunned all of the other Navy SEAL teams combined.

And their hands showed it.

Zaslon would be the same, far more practiced than the rest of Spetsnaz.

Elizaveta Egorova / Elayne Kasprak wasn't some cute blonde. She was exactly what Holly had feared she might be.

"Mike, Jeremy, let's go."

Then she turned and walked away—managing not to wipe her palm against her jeans as she did.

It had been over a year since she been that close to death in a living-breathing form. Closer than she'd thought she'd ever be again after leaving the SASR.

Actually, all her years in the SASR, she'd never been so close—close enough to shake death's hand.

She'd killed people, but always at a distance. And most of her tasks had been executing bridges, planes, vehicles, and other targets in need of her explosives specialty.

Only once before in her life had she been close enough to hold death's hand. That time she'd lost everything except her own life.

Given the choice, she'd rather have lost it—if she could have saved the other.

35

"GODDAMN THEM BOTH!" DRAKE FINALLY GAVE UP AND slammed his phone down on the small table of the C-38 Gulfstream G100 business jet.

"You *know* what Miranda's like," Elizabeth didn't show the least bit of sympathy. "Antagonizing her won't help a bit. What's really bothering you?"

"I told her it was of the utmost urgency, then she doesn't call me back when she solved the crash."

"You know that's *not* what's making you angry."

And *that* was the problem with sleeping with someone. They got to know you too well, could read you too easily.

With Patty, that hadn't been a problem. She'd been a sweet, gentle soul who he'd started dating in high school. She'd been a housewife and active in the church that she believed in much more than he did. Around her, he'd been able to leave work at work, usually, and done his very best to be a good husband and father when he was home. Five years gone and he still missed her like a piece of him had left and never come back.

Elizabeth, however, was part of his civilian life *and* his professional one. And she was a very different person from Patty. No one became a general without being smart and driven, and never taking anyone else's shit—just as she wasn't right now, sitting across from him so calmly.

"Yes, I *know* how Miranda Chase is." He yanked his seatbelt tight as the plane began its descent. It was too tight, but he'd be damned if he was going to ease it.

Elizabeth still waited.

"And yes, I know that's not what's making me angry. Though I'm going to have a word or two with that Holly Harper for hanging up on me."

Elizabeth laughed aloud, atypical enough even aside from being in "General" mode. "Oh, please let me be there to see that."

"See what?" But then he pictured it himself and didn't like the image.

"You. Taking on a former Australian SASR operative, who's defending her boss. A civilian, I remind you, with nothing to lose in our world. Are we taking any bets on which of you will be on the ground first?"

"Rangers lead the way," he quoted his old unit's motto.

"So, you'll be going down nose-first? As I said, I really want to watch this. Do you mind if I post it on social media?"

"Damn your smile." It was a great smile...even when it was laughing at him.

Elizabeth didn't need to say anything else to put him in his place.

The military pilot of the C-38 VIP transport was making

a fast descent. Fine. Couldn't get him on the ground soon enough.

"What's really making you angry, Drake?"

"I knew it!" He pounded a fist on the table, making his phone jump. "Russia has been ramping up the rhetoric for years. I *knew* that it wasn't a crash. Who crashes after making a clean landing on a dry field? No one. The goddamn Russians have driven us right back into the Cold War. I was feeling bad about actively stealing one of their satellites. I'm completely over that now. You know what happened thirty years ago?"

Elizabeth nodded, because of course she knew her history. He was preaching to the choir but couldn't stop himself.

"I was stationed in Berlin when the Wall came down. I was right there. The parties, the sheer joy was like nothing you've ever seen. Families, separated for decades, stepped through the gaps ducking as if still expecting to be shot in the back. But they came through anyway, and were welcomed with open arms. You never saw anything like it. And what now?"

Elizabeth simply sat and waited.

"Now, the Cold War is back. Russia allying with China. We do nothing. They snatch the Crimea and we say, 'Hey, don't do that.' Now they're blowing up planes on *our* soil and we're talking about stealing a multi-billion-dollar satellite."

"And so you take it out on Miranda Chase after flying over an hour to ask her for a favor?"

Drake slumped in his chair. Or he would have if his seatbelt wasn't so tight.

"You know she's going to hate it? Faking a crash? She'll say it's completely wrong."

Drake nodded, then sighed.

Yes, he knew that.

The problem was that she was right and he had to convince her anyway.

36

Holly really had to rearrange where she sat, not that there were all that many choices in the back of a Black Hawk. The main part of the cargo bay was eight feet square and half that high. Webbed jump seats had been rigged in the middle, two groups of three back-to-back.

To one side Miranda, Jeremy, and Major Jon Swift were hunched over the information from the Nashville Airport mishap. Listening to tower recordings and viewing the data from the Quick Access Recorder as well as the numerous photos Jeremy had taken.

She could hear Jon giving useful input from his own accident investigation experience. All the more reason for Miranda to like him. One saving grace, Jeremy and his tablet had ended up in the middle seat between the two of them.

To the other side of the seating...she and Mike.

The roar of the Black Hawk flying back to Fort Campbell was an odd background. It was soothing in its familiarity from a hundred missions and a thousand training flights. It was also an unnerving reminder of a past she'd been doing her best to never think about.

And she needed a subject change right now.

Holly switched their two headsets onto a private channel. "What do you know about your blonde?"

Mike grimaced because, of course, he was bummed at losing his shot at bedding her.

A brief image of Mike tangled up with Ms. Petite Wholesome-but-deadly really didn't help her mood.

"Really, really glad to be rid of her."

Holly twisted to look at him, but he didn't appear to be joking. Instead his head was back against the webbing and his eyes were closed.

"There was something really wrong with her. Don't know why I thought she was attractive for even a second."

"Because she was a hot as hell blonde?"

"Usually I can see past that. Not with her. How did I miss all the signs?"

As he appeared to be talking to himself, she kept her mouth shut. Not the Mike she'd been expecting at all.

He shook himself as if he was a dog trying to shed his winter coat.

Or maybe as if he was a little disgusted with himself? What did that mean?

"What do you know about her?" Mike sounded tired, tired to the very core. So rather than some caustic remark about how she wasn't the sort to go about "knowing" women in any biblical sense, she answered.

"Insanely dangerous. Russian foreign agent of the worst kind—a group called Zaslon. She's the one who downed the

Antonov. Probably fucked one of the pilots to get onboard and plant the explosives."

Mike just nodded. "Wouldn't surprise me for a second."

Surprised the hell out of Holly that Mike would feel that way.

"Her accent kept slipping. Her English was actually impeccable. And her reactions were all wrong. She didn't even know what a QAR was or where to go looking for it. Knew a great deal about planes, but almost nothing about the Condor itself. So I knew she wasn't working for Antonov. Bored where she should have been interested and vice versa. I did my best to make sure she thought we were all incompetent. You did a nice job of playing into that. Thanks."

He opened his eyes and turned to her. His deep browns were incredibly close. Even over the headset, his whisper barely carried above the noise of the racing Black Hawk.

"We *can't* tell Miranda or Jeremy." He grimaced before continuing, "Neither one can keep a secret for shit."

"Got it in one, Mike. I'm impressed."

"Not stupid, Hol. Couldn't survive on this team if I was. If Elayne Kasprak or whoever she is ever found out we even suspected, who knows what she'd do."

"Elizaveta Egorova, at least that's the name she was born with, would terminate their asses. Ours too."

"Great." Mike leaned his head back against the webbing once more. "Just great."

And now that Mike, of all people, had made her think about it, Holly didn't like having Elayne out there as an open question.

Holly knew all too well what it was like to keep looking

back over your shoulder waiting for the axe to fall. There was no way she could allow that to happen to Miranda.

"So what the hell spooked you?" Mike was watching her again.

"What are you talking about?"

"I'm talking about the ghost who bit your behind as we got off the C-130 Hercules transport this morning. I'm talking about your final handshake with Elayne. I've known you for six months and nothing gets past those thick defenses of yours. But something did—twice in one day."

Holly's throat cut off her breathing as if it was trying to throttle her.

"There. That." Then Mike's tone softened. "Seriously. If you need someone to talk to, I wouldn't mind if it was me."

"Why?"

"Why? Because you're the most capable and honorable woman I've ever met."

"You don't know shit!" Her shout was loud enough for Mike to wince as the intercom headset must have made his ears ring. The others behind them stopped what they were doing and turn to look her way through the webbing despite being on a different intercom channel.

"You don't know shit," she repeated much more softly after the others had turned back to their study of the FedEx mishap.

"Sure, Holly. Whatever you say." Mike's tone said that he was now as disgusted with her as he'd been with himself moments before. He closed his eyes and turned away.

She knew what ghosts had loomed up before her.

Holly didn't like Mike's disappointment—not in her. He was, oddly enough, the one she was closest to of their group.

Jeremy was just the overeager, incredibly competent geek. Always a happy little vegemite.

Miranda was...complicated.

She and Mike? They were the ones who had a clear vision of how the world worked and what was required to function in it.

Closest to Mike? Wasn't that the strangest twist since Crow stole fire from the seven Karatgurk women who then became the Pleiades star cluster. Except this wasn't some story of the Australian Dreamtime.

And Mike had just proven that he deserved better than she'd been giving.

The helo slowed and descended; they must be nearing Fort Campbell. A glance out the window and she saw they she hadn't been paying attention and they were almost down. They'd arrived in Fort Campbell at dawn, gone to Nashville by noon, and now the midafternoon sunlight was starting to stretch out the shadows of the ranks of parked helos back at Campbell.

She didn't want Mike to think badly of her, and *wasn't* going to think about why it mattered. It simply did.

Unable to face the piece of the past that Elayne Kasprak's hand had unearthed, Holly chose the other one.

"Team Chase."

Mike opened one eye. "*That's* what spooked you on the Hercules?"

"You've got *no* idea."

The helo's wheels hit the pavement.

Holly's knees were unsteady enough when she climbed down that Mike held her arm for a moment until she stabilized.

Rather than hitting him for it, she offered a nod of thanks.

It was all she could manage at the moment.

37

"No." It was just so completely wrong. Miranda could only shake her head. "I *save* airplanes. I study them to *avoid* crashes, not to *cause* them."

"No one will be hurt. It only needs to look like a crash." Drake was quite adamant. Or was it pleading?

Mike snickered in the background.

Miranda ignored him.

She studied Drake and Lizzy across the narrow aisle. They were meeting in the small C-38 Gulfstream G100 jet that Drake had flown to Fort Campbell.

The two of them sat in facing seats across a small table. She, Holly, and Mike sat on the couch opposite, their knees filling the aisle of the small airplane. Jeremy was in one of the rear seats diligently working on the Nashville report, hopefully using the framework they'd created during the flight.

At least analyzing multiple crash investigations wasn't an issue.

That stopped her cold for a moment.

"What?" Drake asked.

She ignored him.

Multiple crash investigations *weren't* an issue. They'd never bothered her. While waiting for metallurgy or Flight Recorder decoding, she'd always been able to work on some other matter.

Miranda turned to explain it to Holly, but Holly didn't look at her in turn. In fact, she hadn't said a word since the landing and sat there staring out the window between Drake and Lizzy. They were facing the process of cleaning up the Condor crash, though Miranda didn't understand why Holly would find that so all-consuming.

Mike was watching Holly, with what even she could tell was a worried look.

Perhaps it would be better if she waited to discuss how she could extend her previously unnoted mechanical multitasking capabilities into "soft" realms like incomplete conversational threads.

"Miranda?" Drake was asking about something.

About... *Oh!* "I am *not* comfortable with engineering a crash."

"Engineering a *simulated* crash."

"You want to steal a large transport jet. To avoid suspicion, you'll have to create a debris trail, which means creating a real crash."

"But we won't crash it. We want to retain its cargo. That's the whole point."

"I never said to crash the transport jet. But you need a crash of an identical aircraft. And you need to destroy it sufficiently that even detailed inspection couldn't identify the fake. That's airframe number, serial numbers on thousands of parts, even a wiring modification that was performed on one aircraft and not another."

"What if the destruction is so complete that there's no way to tell?" Mike put in, nudging Holly's elbow.

Miranda waited for Holly to say something. Or elbow Mike's ribs.

But she didn't respond.

The lack of response was even more confusing that having to pause for the expected interruption.

"I'd still be able to tell," she informed Mike. "Drake, no. Just...no."

The only person making a sound in the whole cabin was Jeremy, humming quietly to himself as he typed rapidly on the fold-out keyboard he sometimes used with his tablet.

The silence stretched until it was almost painful.

"Let's take a break," Mike suggested.

"But we just got back here."

"Let's take a break anyway. Miranda, go see how Jon is doing on the cleanup of the Condor. Holly, you're with me."

She was closest to the door, but didn't move until Mike pushed her a few times. She went surprisingly meekly.

Jeremy didn't even notice their departure.

Miranda wouldn't mind checking in with Jon.

Perhaps see what else the AIB team had discovered since their departure. Maybe he had new evidence emerging from the aircraft's disassembly.

"Hey!" Drake called out after them, but Lizzy shushed him.

38

THE SPRING AFTERNOON WAS WARM, COMFORTABLE, AND smelled of growing things. Low dogwoods offered bright pink and white blossoms along the airport perimeter road.

And it all left Holly feeling like mud along a stagnant billabong.

Holly leaned with her butt against the C-38's wing, facing the wreckage of the Condor.

In the few hours they'd been gone, Fort Campbell Army base had mobilized. A pair of Black Hawk helicopters, capable of lifting five tons at a time, were now above the site. The sparks of at least ten different welders were burning their way through the aircraft's remains. You couldn't just drag ninety tons of airplane and another forty-five tons of burned up helicopters aside to clear a runway—you had to remove it in manageable pieces.

Each section the welders sliced free was lofted on helicopter cargo lines within seconds. The Condor was disappearing with surprising speed. It was all the small debris that would be the real pest.

Already a double line had formed back at the plane's touchdown point.

A line of pickup trucks was moving ahead slowly as a team gathered all of the larger pieces remaining once the welders and Black Hawks had moved on. The heaviest debris was being plucked up by a Little Bird helicopter and whisked away to wherever the two Black Hawks were using as a dump site.

The Night Stalkers of the 160th SOAR were on the job and they were damned efficient.

Behind them, the long string of personnel was doing a classic FOD walk. Take a step, stop, scan for Foreign Object Debris. Another step, another look. Each person, no more than an arm's length from the next, had a trash bag. Not so much as a bolt that could be sucked up into a plane's engine would be left behind when they were done.

The plane's tail and the two destroyed Stryker fire engines were already gone. All of the burned helicopter remains and one of the wings had already been removed as well.

"What the hell, Holly?" Mike stepped right in front of her to block her view.

"What's your problem, Mike?"

"*You!*"

"No wucking furries with this Sheila."

"What?"

"No fucking worries, mate. Grab a clue. I'm fine."

"So not! Miranda's in there fighting for her life and you aren't doing shit about it? What the hell's wrong with you?"

"Why don't *you* do something?" Holly shoved him away, but he stepped right back in her face.

"I'm trying, but they don't listen to me the way they listen to you. Now answer the goddamn question: Why are you leaving Miranda hung out there on her own? They're gonna massacre her."

"She... What?"

"There but for the grace of God go I!" Mike cursed to the heavens.

"You a religious kinda boy, Mike?"

"Nothing Catholic school didn't permanently cure. Where you been, Holly?"

"Nowhere good," was the only answer she had for him.

"Spill it or I'm not letting you back in there."

Holly shook her head to clear it. A glance over her shoulder revealed Lizzy and Drake arguing inside the plane. Through another window, she could see Jeremy hard at work.

"Where's..." Then she spotted Miranda over by the wreck standing next to Major Jon Swift. "What's up with that anyway? Do you think they're—"

"No more evasions, Holly. Spill."

Christ! She was already letting Miranda down? Couldn't she ever be a part of a team without screwing everything up?

"Team Chase. I just..."

Now, Mike was suddenly all patience. He shifted from confronting her almost nose-to-nose to leaning against the wing beside her. He made the transition seem perfectly natural—right down to his shoulder just brushing hers. It was calming; perhaps all that let her continue.

"In the SASR—that's elite Australian warriors to you—

we were in a six-person squad. Then I—" she swallowed hard then just spit it out. "I lost my team. I'm the one who lived." Good thing she didn't have a hari-kari knife at the moment.

"What happened?" Mr. Sympathy. If this turned out to be manipulation, she'd kill him. But it didn't feel like it.

"We were tasked with taking out a bridge. Some Southeast Asian shithole. But we were supposed to drop it so that it looked like a structural failure—with the dictator's convoy on the span. A hundred meters down into a rocky gorge. No survivors kind of show."

"*That's* the sort of thing you used to do?"

She nodded. "I'm an explosives kind of Sheila. I make big things, like that," she nodded at the remains of the AN-124 Condor, "end up...looking like that."

"What happened?"

"I woke early and slipped out of camp. I was under the bridge," she could see it.

Just dusk. The thick smell of the jungle slapped her again, even here in a Kentucky spring afternoon. Thick with decay and wilderness. More biomass in ten square meters than in a thousand square where she'd grown up. Moving so stealthily that it didn't even disturb snoozing macaque monkeys.

"Just getting a start. Climbing under it to identify critical structural points. I could have easily brought that bridge down with five kilos of C-4, but I wanted it to be elegant. Just enough and no more—to minimize evidence that it was any type of an attack. Our job was for no one to know we'd ever been there. So I was taking some measurements and had about two-thirds of the charges placed."

She'd felt the approaching vehicles vibrating the steel before she heard them.

The dictator's convoy hadn't been due until dawn still ten hours away.

No heavy military engines—tanks or armored personnel carriers. This guy was a former army general and liked keeping his troops close.

But there were a lot of vehicles coming, fast ones. From the wrong direction, so it wasn't the dictator.

A squawk on her headset radio, "Hol?"

"Under bridge. You've got incoming."

"Roger. Stay put."

The convoy had halted just past the end of the bridge.

Inspection team? How paranoid was this guy?

Using her climbing straps, she'd hauled herself up into the deepest shadows right against the underside of the bridge deck. Then she'd made sure she had no dangling lines that might catch someone's attention.

She had her Thales F90CQB Close Quarters Battle rifle across her chest. After checking that the magazine was full and the strap was wrapped around her arm so that she couldn't drop it, she'd gone silent.

Another convoy from the other direction.

They halted close, but not too close.

Not friendly.

Or not *too* friendly.

Rather than a military escort...a transfer point along the drug export chain? Around here that meant opium or refined heroin.

"Just do your dirty and go away, guys. We don't care about you tonight."

But they hadn't listened.

"Those idiots," she told Mike, "a bunch of drug-running wankers, stumbled on our SASR team. Turned out it was a hundred to five. My guys took out over fifty while I was dangling there like an idiot monkey under the bridge unable to go help."

"Oh Christ. I can't imagine what that was like." Mike rested a hand on her shoulder, and she let it stay there for a few moments before shrugging it off.

She didn't want comfort.

She didn't *deserve* comfort.

"What did you do?"

"I slapped everything I had on the bottom of that bridge. When they rolled back over it, I fired off over thirty kilos of C-4. I didn't just drop the bridge span—I blew it back into the Stone Age. Whoever thought they were escaping after taking down my team wasn't left in big enough pieces for their mothers to identify them."

"Well, at least there's that."

"I hung there, under the remaining cliff-edge stump of that bridge, all night and all the next day. I watched them come and search the wreckage—bird's-eye view on that hundred-meter-down gorge. I saw them walk away with weapons, ones only my team would have been carrying. What if they were only wounded? Or captured? I killed my whole team, Mike."

"No, you don't know that."

"Command sent in a body squad. Recovered the corpses, but results were inconclusive on a couple of them about whether they were dead or only badly wounded before I blew them up. Let's just say that my commanders weren't real happy about it. I could have waited alone. I could have waited through the night, blown that bridge myself, and offed their bastard of a dictator. Instead I destroyed the last chances for any of my team. At least that's the consensus."

Mike's hand was back, as if he couldn't help himself being consoling.

She shrugged it off again, because she killed anyone she got close to.

"And then," Holly looked up at the darkening blue sky—dense with afternoon light so unlike the equatorial shit where she'd blown up her final bridge—because it was the only way to fight back the tears. "Then, I resigned so that they didn't have to figure out what to do with me. I ran as far as I could."

"All the way to the American NTSB."

"Right. That should have been far enough, shouldn't it?"

"Right up until Miranda said Team Chase," Mike nodded in understanding. "That's rough."

"No shit, Sherlock! Worst of all, I've exposed her to fucking Elayne Kasprak and I don't know how to undo it." Holly wanted to scream but managed to keep it inside.

"No, you didn't. They'd have met with or without you. You *saved* her from Elayne."

"How in all that's green is that even close to straight up?"

This time Mike punched her arm.

Someday she'd have to teach him to punch properly; he was lucky he didn't break a knuckle.

"Idiot, Holly. If you hadn't been there, Miranda still would have solved what happened. She'd have told Elayne. Then what would have happened?"

Holly pictured it. Miranda never would have left that

shadowed cockpit alive. She'd have "slipped and fallen" onto something horribly sharp and lethal, her body ending up close beside Mr. Bones.

"Yep!" Mike would have the same image in his head.

"Where did you learn how to be devious? Church school?"

"No. Well, a little. But no." He sighed unhappily and Holly was suddenly sorry she'd asked. "Long story."

"I'm in no rush."

"No, but they are." Mike nodded.

Miranda and Major Swift were coming in their direction at a fast clip.

Mike spoke quickly. "You're one of the main reasons Team Chase works, Holly. So no more goofing off on the job. Okay?"

Holly tried to think of how to thank Mike.

For being understanding.

For saying the right thing.

She did the only thing she could think of.

Holly punched Mike in the arm—hard.

"Goddamn it!"

39

"Jon has a hypothesis that I think you will find interesting. It is not the way I think; his brain works in ways that I don't fully comprehend or agree with."

He was always *so* glad to be talked about in the third person. Though maybe with Miranda he didn't mind.

They were crowded into the C-38's small cabin. Three of the team on the small couch. Jeremy, unsurprisingly, fiercely attacking a computer keyboard. An older, attractive Asian woman in very neat civilian attire sat at a small table across the aisle.

And the last person, with his back to him was...

"Holy shit! Sorry, sir!" Jon almost took out his neck on the cabin ceiling as he tried to snap to attention in a place where the ceiling was three inches too low. Then he smashed his elbow into the back of the divider as he attempted to salute.

"Jon? What the hell are you doing here?"

Miranda had said, *There's someone you need to explain that to,* when he'd come up with his idea.

She left out that it was the Chairman of the Joint Chiefs of Staff—Uncle Drake.

"This was supposed to be classified," Drake snarled at Miranda.

"General Nason," the Asian said in a soft, warning tone, and it stifled him instantly.

"I'm losing my mind here," he muttered and the woman patted his hand.

"Wow! How did you do that? No one could ever shut down my uncle."

She looked up at him with curiosity. "Uncle?"

"He's Mom's baby brother."

Uncle Drake had been more than stopped, he'd been squelched.

"Fascinating." The woman was watching him, not his uncle. "Tell me more. I'm his girlfriend, by the way, General Elizabeth Gray. Please call me Lizzy. You're the first of his family I've met other than his daughter."

"Major Jon Swift at your service," he decided against risking a salute again in the confined space. "His girlfriend? My uncle has a girlfriend?"

"I hope that's okay."

Jon didn't know how he felt about that. Their families hadn't been especially close—Dad based out of Coronado, California, and Uncle Drake in DC. But Aunt Patty had been...Aunt Patty—a thousand times more approachable than his uncle. In the five years since her death, they'd barely heard from Drake.

In reply to General Gray's question, he didn't know how he felt. So he shrugged.

"We'll give it some time. You had an idea?"

"Yes. But if this meeting is classified, perhaps I should depart."

"Drake," Miranda used his uncle's first name?

Weird!

"Is the reason that you said Major Swift was the only one I could trust no longer valid?"

"A little nepotism perhaps?" Holly jibed. "No offense, Jon."

"None taken." It was always easy to return Holly's smile. "And no, it wasn't. My uncle just knows that if I were to fail him in even the slightest way, my SEAL commander father would shred me limb from limb. It builds a certain kind of trustworthiness, I suppose."

"So, are you no longer his nephew or suddenly not susceptible to intimidation by your father or General Nason?" God but he loved the way Miranda asked questions. It made him look at everything as if it was fresh and new.

"No problem from my side. Ask him," Jon hooked his thumb at Uncle Drake.

"What's your goddamn idea?"

"Blow up a plane."

His uncle eyed him as if he'd lost his mind. He'd never dared tease Uncle Drake; the man was so goddamn brilliant about military and geopolitical conflicts. A simple question of some military tactic at a family gathering could cause him to unload a two-hour discourse on historically shifting strategies and the lessons applicable to...

Maybe dating another general *was* a good match for him.

"The whole point is that we want the plane's contents."

"I didn't say blow up *the* plane, I said blow up *a* plane. Switch the planes and then utterly destroy the decoy."

"This is a Russian plane whose flight path is completely over Russian soil. Not the Arctic, no oceans, nothing."

Jon shrugged. "Even better, convince them to blow it up."

"Did I mention that we wanted the plane's contents." Uncle Drake's tone was so droll it would have cowed him into silence under normal conditions. But with him having a girlfriend—still hard to imagine—and Miranda treating his fearsome uncle as an equal, he couldn't quite help himself.

"Duh! Switch planes and *then* have them blow it up." Had he just called Uncle Drake slow? No way. But he had.

Everyone just looked at him wide-eyed, except Miranda, who had understood right away.

Jon looked around for how to explain himself. "Miranda, stand up and hold out your hand. It's now an airplane flying at thirty-nine thousand feet."

"Which is my nose?"

"Your fingertips."

She twisted around and faced the other end of the cabin as she held up her hand, palm down.

"What are you doing?"

"Flight level three-nine-zero is for westbound traffic. I'm pointing the nose of my hypothetical aircraft west."

He noted the direction of the late afternoon sun slanting through the windows.

She was.

"Okay, flight level four-three-zero."

She glanced over her shoulder at him. "Lizzy had said

that the Russians would most likely be using an AN-124 Condor for transport."

"So you mentioned. Your point?"

Then he knew what she was going to say. They ended up speaking in unison.

"Service ceiling of thirty-nine thousand feet."

"Flight level three-seven-thousand feet, please."

She turned around and aimed her fingertips at him with her palm still down, lowering her hand slightly to represent the change in altitude as she made the turn. She made him want to laugh aloud. But with the way Holly was watching him... He decided that cautious professionalism was a far better choice.

"So, here you are, a fully loaded Antonov AN-1—"

"At only seven meters long and seven thousand kilos, the Antonov is far from fully-loaded with a Persona satellite. Even with the launch housings and other packaging, the Antonov will be far from fully loaded."

"You're right. Perhaps they have other items in the load or perhaps they are traveling well below capacity. Will a 'loaded Antonov AN-124' be a sufficient description?"

Holly eyed him carefully to make sure he wasn't teasing Miranda. Mike gave him a thumbs up.

Miranda did exactly as he'd hoped and simply nodded, holding her "plane" at the ready. He understood her desire for precision. In his decade flying the C-5 Galaxy, the biggest cargo jet of the US military, he'd been a fanatic about it and saw no reason to change.

"Please start flying east toward me." Then he patted the table between Lizzy and Uncle Drake. "This is minimum radar detection altitude, say two-hundred feet."

"My hand is too big," Miranda's exactness, of course.

"Your thumbnail?"

"First joint of thumb would be more accurate."

Damn but she was fast.

She held out her thumb, nail up, then tucked her other fingers so that they touched under her thumb knuckle. "It's too narrow, but I think we're close enough now."

"Okay, now dive down until your hand is below the table."

"But don't crash it?"

"But don't crash it. General Gray, you're our radar. If you can't see her hand, she's below the radar. Miranda, go."

Miranda slowed her engines, nosed down her thumb, and he'd wager that her rate of descent was proportional in scale as well.

"Wave your hand side to side as you descend. Okay, her plane is now making erratic moves as if it's in trouble."

She banked her hand back and forth as if fighting for control.

"Perhaps reporting a pressurization failure or something. Emergency descent."

She angled down steeply. The moment her thumb-plane ducked below the table, he took her hand in his and guided it to stay under the table. With his other hand, he made his own thumb plane climb back up above the surface of the table.

"Recovery from the problem. Reporting control of the aircraft once more. But we've switched transponder frequencies between the two planes, so to any radar tech, we're the same aircraft. Then we just convince them to shoot this one," he waggled his own hand, "out of the sky. If *they* shoot it down, they'll have no real reason to investigate. Perhaps they'll just write it off as a loss and look no further."

He realized that he was still holding Miranda's hand and let it go.

"Where do I go?" Miranda's thumb appeared to be tracking back and forth seeking a new heading.

"You can stop now, but the idea is you'd escape by staying below radar probably crossing the border in the dark through a lightly inhabited stretch of coastline. At night, they'll hopefully just assume it's some practice flight."

"And how do we do this without killing the crew of plane Number Two?" Drake was watching her hand as Miranda flew her "plane" back up from under the table, then finally spread her fingers out wide.

Jon grinned at his uncle. "Satellite-based remote piloting. No one aboard when it goes down. That's how we fly our drones around the world from Creech Air Force Base now anyway. That shouldn't be hard to work out."

"And where do we get another AN-124 to blow up?"

"Davis-Monthan Air Force Base." Baiting the Chairman of the Joint Chiefs, even just a little, was getting kind of fun. Maybe Uncle Drake wasn't only the focused super-soldier commander he remembered as a kid.

"We don't have any AN-124s in storage, Jon. You should know that."

"I do, Uncle. I also know that we have sixty-four C-5A Galaxy transport jets parked there that we're unlikely to ever want again. Despite that, several still have a Type 3000 status of 'Flying Hold,' which means we could basically fuel them and fly. To fit one with remote pilot capability wouldn't be hard. Remember, the Antonov AN-124 is largely based on the

C-5 Galaxy. If we can keep them from getting a good look at our decoy before they blow it up, we just might pull it off."

"And if we don't? If they find out we're stealing their satellite? That can't come back on us. Little thing about possibly starting a war."

Jon hadn't thought that far ahead.

Apparently Holly had. "If they catch on to the switcheroo, land it in South Korea or Japan and have the pilots 'jump ship.' Then the Russians can send someone to retrieve their plane and the satellite. Maybe Japan can gain some diplomatic traction in the process. The pilots 'defected' but could never be found. They'll have a wild goose chase searching for the defectors because they won't be missing any pilots, we'll be gone quiet as a wallaby in the night."

Uncle Drake stared at him without blinking for over thirty seconds, until his own eyes hurt from matching him.

Then he glanced at General Lizzy Gray, who nodded.

When he turned to Miranda, she spoke up.

"First, I still hate the idea. But we're no longer seeking to create a plane crash that is proof against investigators. That removes it from my area of expertise."

She re-formed her thumb plane and moved it about a few times, watching it as she continued.

"However, while the logic is reasonable, the logistics will be very complex. Preparation of the C-5 Galaxy will be the least of the issues. We can't just take over their Antonov remotely. We'll need our own people on board."

40

DRAKE BLEW OUT A HARD BREATH.

He hadn't seen that piece coming. Frankly, he'd been too busy being impressed at Jon's plan. He'd come up with that solution with a Miranda-like speed. He should have kept better track of his nephew's career.

"Okay, genius. How the hell are we supposed to do that?"

Jon just shrugged. Apparently he hadn't thought through that part either.

Holly slouched down on the small couch without falling into the narrow aisle. She rested her boots on his chair arm.

"Well, mates, let's start with who speaks Russian. Super fluently."

Miranda and Jon both raised their hands.

Mike waved his hand part way, with an "sort of" waggle.

"And Holly makes three," she continued. "Miranda, you'd be no help."

"Why not?"

"Because you're not trained for this and we don't want you ending up dead." Holly turned to Jon, "You spent ten years flying a C-5 Galaxy. Care to take a crack at flying an Antonov?"

"*What?*" Drake knew he was shouting again but couldn't seem to help himself. "You can't just send him into Russia to steal a plane."

"Oh, no, mate. I figure he'll need a bit of protection." She tapped her own chest.

"Holly! No!" Mike rested a hand on her arm as if he could restrain such a woman.

"It's okay, Mike." She patted his hand (rather than slapping it aside, which appeared to surprise him as much as it surprised Drake).

A mellowed-out Holly Harper didn't fit his mental picture of her at all.

She continued, "We're gonna keep this circle small enough to sit around a campfire. As you reminded me, this is the kind of thing I do."

Jon was nodding slowly. "Takes four to fly an AN-124."

"Grab a couple of boys from the 24th STS."

Drake agreed with her suggestion on that at least. The combat controllers of the Air Force's 24th Special Tactics Squadron were one of America's three special mission units along with Delta Force and SEAL Team Six. They could run a multi-asset air battle—after three days of ground fighting to get there—and then manage air traffic for an entire captured airport from a handheld radio. Also masters at infiltration, they were the most capable people in the Air Force. If anyone could get a team into the heart of Russia, it would be them—and Holly.

"I'm not convinced yet, but let's see what it will take to do."

"Jeremy," Holly called out.

"I'd look at tail numbers 69-0020 or 70-0448," Jeremy spoke without rising from his chair.

Drake had completely forgotten he was there. Apparently he was a step ahead of everyone, just like Miranda.

"They're the most recent additions to the inventory. They don't make it easy to see the actual status..." The rattle of more computer keys. "Ah! 69-0020 is a better bet. Remote piloting controls aren't too impossible a retrofit. We could fly it up to Boeing in Seattle for a paint job at Paine Field. That would also place it well on the way to Russia. They have this awesome paint shed and could easily make it match the blue-and-white pattern of a Russian Air Force AN-124. Even the red flag on the tail. You know the tail section is going to be a real problem: the AN-124 has a standard tail, but the C-5 has a high T-tail. Maybe at least a stealth coating so that it doesn't look *too* wrong on radar."

The kid was making Drake's head spin.

"Make sure the flight, or at least the intercept, takes place at night to hide that and the other differences," Jon nodded.

"And how do we arrange that?"

Holly shrugged. "No worries, mate. We'll be the flight crew. Have Lizzy track the satellite and the Russian plane for us. We'll do the switch out over eastern Siberia, just before Vostochny. Still a mess of details, but no big hassle."

"That's got to be the understatement of the year."

But Drake looked around the team.

He'd learned over the years that if you had the right

team, they could do anything. And he'd learned to trust his gut. As unlikely as it seemed, this *was* the right team.

Last, he looked at Lizzy. Her nod matched his assessment. He nodded back.

"I hold the right to abort, but... Do it."

41

"ARTURO?" MIRANDA PLACED THE CALL BECAUSE DRAKE WAS busy discussing details with Lizzy. Besides, she suspected that there was some social obligation she'd been shirking by not calling him before this. Now the call could serve two purposes which had seemed the most efficient use of time.

"Miranda! I haven't heard from you in months. Are you in the area?" His voice was clear over the phone despite the roar of a departing jet in the background. He must be on the flight line of Davis-Monthan Air Force Base.

Jeremy was still looking things up on his computer. "Definitely 69-0020," he mumbled to her.

"No, I'm...in Kentucky." Holly had said to keep her whereabouts private.

"Oh. When are you coming to see me again? I can come to you."

Miranda hadn't called about seeing him.

Though Colonel Campos had made it clear during the

Thunderbolt investigation that he very much wanted to see her again.

Socially.

She hadn't pursued that because it had unnerved her. She had liked the sound of a relationship. But she hadn't been sure she wanted it from Arturo.

Then she remembered Jon holding her hand briefly under the table when she'd been pretending it was an airplane for his demonstration. She was already more comfortable around Jon than she'd ever been around Arturo. Oh, she'd imagined seeing the Davis-Monthan commander again, but the time had never quite seemed right.

Perhaps it hadn't been the *time* that wasn't right but rather the person?

She looked around for Jon so that she could gauge her own reactions. Except he was no longer aboard. He'd gone somewhere to place a call. And—

She had to remind herself that this wasn't a social call.

"I need airframe number 69-0020 pulled from the AMARG boneyard at Davis-Monthan and prepared for immediate flight. I also want you to scavenge whatever equipment you need from stored drones or any other aircraft to make it flyable as a UAV."

Arturo called out to someone for information and was back on the line a moment later.

"You want me to set up a C-5 Galaxy as a UAV? We've never done anything like that. What are you talking about?"

"I'm sending Jeremy to you. He'll be there in three hours. I'd appreciate it if everything could be ready before he arrives. Oh, he'll need a flight crew and enough fuel to reach Seattle. This is—"

"Miranda! What the hell?" He was shouting at her. "I can't just do something like that. And turning a C-5 into a drone. It's never been done. It could take weeks or months."

"I need it in three hours."

"What the *fuck* are you talking about, woman? Are you even batshit crazier than I always thought you were?"

Miranda could feel her hand shaking but couldn't stop it.

She'd thought about inviting *him* to her home?

She knew her brain was broken. Didn't he understand that? Didn't anyone besides her understand that? Thinking was no problem, but every time she let her thoughts into the outside world, the world bit and swiped back at her.

It was all just so...wrong.

So—

So—

She couldn't seem to connect two thoughts.

Actually she never could. At the moment she couldn't seem to even connect one.

Holly slipped the phone from her nerveless fingers. She kept a firm grip on Miranda's shoulder as she handed the phone to Drake.

"Colonel Campos. This is CJCS General Drake Nason. By what I could overhear of your tone, you are damned close to losing your command for behavior unbecoming an officer. You have three hours. If Mr. Trahn arrives and that plane isn't ready for immediate departure, you'll have me and then your commanding officer coming after you at three hours and one minute. Trust me, I'll be the first and worst of your nightmares. If anyone asks any questions, shut them down. This is need-to-know classified and, Colonel, *you* don't need to know."

He paused.

"Damn straight you owe her an apology, man. But right now you're wasting my time. Get your ass moving."

He hung up her phone and handed it back.

Miranda couldn't seem to wrap her hand around it.

Holly took it and tucked it back in her vest pocket for her.

It was backwards. After three tries, Miranda finally regained sufficient motor control to extract it and turn it so that the glass faced inward. It offered the glass better protection and also came into her hand the right way 'round if a call came in.

"I'm sorry, Miranda," Drake touched her arm too lightly, but she forced herself to tolerate it and he withdrew before it became too distracting.

She could only manage a nod.

Jon stepped back on board. "Jeremy, I've got a plane coming for you. It should be here in just a few minutes."

Jeremy gathered his big pack, stopping where she'd finally collapsed back onto the couch.

"I just sent you the first draft of the report on the FedEx 767. Based on the QAR data as well as the length of skid marks and tire wear, we can also ascertain that he was forty-three knots above recommended approach speed. Once he landed on the taxiway, it was physically impossible for him to stop in time. The tower's flight-tracking data concurs."

"Good, Jeremy." She latched onto the information. This was her job. *This* was what she understood. "I'll look it over as soon as I can."

"Thanks for the chance, Miranda."

Miranda glanced over, but Holly was now having an intense whispered debate with Mike.

That meant it was up to Miranda to handle the situation. She touched her NTSB ID. Nothing else, just that. It let her confirm the importance of what she'd done in order to be here.

"Be careful, Jeremy. Remember what Drake said, 'Need to know.' We're trusting you to see through the mechanical process of this flight. But don't get on the plane after Seattle."

"I'll remember," Jeremy laughed.

Miranda figured out why it was funny fast enough to join in the laugh only a little late. She could almost imagine Jeremy getting on the doomed plane just to make sure everything was exactly in place. But he'd heard it as a joke—as a humorous reminder to be careful.

"I can fly everyone else back to Washington," Drake announced after Jeremy left. "A good jump-off point for our Russia-bound team. Miranda and Mike, I assume you'll be with me in DC."

"Yes." "No!"

Miranda turned to look at Mike.

"No! This is crazy. You can't just walk into the most paranoid country outside of North Korea and Eritrea."

"I've done it before," Holly was calm.

Mike collapsed back against the sofa.

"Spoken like a Spec Ops soldier. But are you sure, Holly? You've been out of the service a while." Drake seemed to echo Mike's concern. Yet he was supporting her in this?

Miranda didn't like the shouting. She didn't like the mission. And she didn't like Colonel Arturo Campos of Davis-Monthan Air Force Base.

What did that say about Major Jon Swift? Did he, too, secretly think that she was broken? He didn't seem to act that way, but she knew all too well her failings at judging people.

Holly scoffed. "If I don't have to grunt a full pack for three hundred klicks across the Great Victoria Desert, I'll be fine. If this devolves into a shooting situation, well, mate, we won't be coming back out of it."

"And you're okay with that?" Mike exploded once more.

She shrugged. "It's what I was trained for."

Miranda knew what *she* was trained for. Fixing planes. Or at least discovering why they were broken. She moved to the seat where Jeremy had been working. She booted up her laptop and in moments was focused on reviewing his report.

This she understood.

She barely noticed when the plane took off.

42

"Request permission to kill Colonel Arturo Campos." Holly felt half-hearted in making the request. What she really wanted to do was get her hands around his throat and shake some common sense into him—even if she had to shake him really hard.

She knew Miranda had liked Campos.

Holly had been torn between caution and hope, though she'd never been comfortable with him.

She'd been right beside Miranda on the couch during their phone conversation and could overhear Campos easily once he started yelling.

Now she was torn between fury and going to lockup for murder one.

"Sorry, request denied," Drake's voice was appropriately grim.

"How about if I accidentally tie him to a stake in front of a charging a water buffalo? Maybe have a 'roo, a big red, use him for a bit of kicking practice?"

"Don't tempt me. Okay. We've got an hour to make a plan. I've arranged for a pair of F/A-18F Super Hornet fighter jets to be waiting for you in DC with full external fuel tanks. They'll have you to Ramstein in Germany in under four hours. There you'll pick up two combat controllers. After that, I'm afraid that you'll be on conventional transport, but we'll hope that it gets you there in time. If not, you'll just turn around."

"You'll need a decent cover," Mike grunted. It wasn't a happy sound, but at least it was something.

That relieved Holly far more than she'd expected. He'd been really upset at her plans to go behind enemy lines once more.

"Do you have a death wish, Harper?" He'd demanded the moment she came up with the idea.

"Not particularly." He hadn't taken her attempt to brush him off at all well.

"God curse it, I'm serious."

"Worse ways to go meet the Big Shelia upstairs."

Being flippant hadn't got by him any better. Since that moment to this, all he'd offered her was stone silence.

There *were* worse ways to go. She pictured the remains of her team scattered at the bottom of the jagged ravine in a country she could never admit to being in. Or even Mr. Bones aboard the Condor. Right at the center of the primary ignition point, he'd been ended fast.

Or her brother.

Shit! She tamped that down hard.

Remember the mantra of Special Operations: *Focus on the mission!*

"Any plan has to get us all the way in. At least to the plane at Progress Rocket Space Centre in Samara."

"Antonov inspectors?" Jon suggested.

"How's your Ukrainian?"

Jon's grimace answered that; no better than her own.

"Representatives of NASA, wanting to inspect the next space capsule?"

"No," Drake shot that down. "I'm not going to get NASA or any other agency snarled up in the middle of this."

"We need to contact Clarissa Reese." Miranda was suddenly standing in the aisle.

"No way!" Mike shouted in unison with herself.

"No, Miranda," Holly shuddered. "Just...no."

"Who?" Mr. Jon the Gull wasn't being too swift on this one.

"Total, dangerous, conniving snake," Mike's description was far kinder than her own would have been.

"Sounds like just what we need, who is she?"

Holly barely managed to grind out between clenched teeth, "The Director of the CIA."

43

CLARISSA ROCKED BACK IN HER CHAIR. SHE NEEDED AN ottoman right here so that she could turn from her desk, put her feet up, and contemplate DC.

"Hell of a first day, Ms. Reese," she spoke to herself.

Installed in her office. Clark departing her office very happy after they'd shared some sex and split a turkey sandwich. Her first department head meeting had also gone well.

She'd borrowed a no-nonsense attitude from President Cole.

Clark, when he was still director, had always chatted with each director, making them think he was their best friend.

Not really her style.

Instead, she'd waited less than two seconds after their butts hit their chairs. "Let's go around the table. Two-minute précis of what's happening in your department. Then we'll circle back as needed."

Any uncertainty about her control had been banished when she cut off the Russian Directorate in mid-sentence about their President's latest manipulation of the Syrian disaster. Two minutes to the second.

In thirty minutes, she had a good handle on the hot topics for each area.

Another half hour refocusing open discussion for five minutes on each of six topics. She intentionally hadn't gotten back to Russia.

But then she remembered a bit of how Clark managed a team and kept the head of the Russian desk afterward.

"Sorry I was hard on you, Marvin, but I had to set an example. I really appreciate you taking it so well." He'd fumed through the entire rest of the meeting and was caught off guard by her praise. "Now, if you have time, I'd like to hear the rest of what they're up to." By the end of another thirty minutes one-on-one, Marvin was completely on her side. Or at least no longer hoping that she'd die pithed on a burning stake.

One down, at least partly, fourteen to go—most of whom were firmly convinced that her chair should have been theirs.

She was exhausted and just needed a few minutes of peace to gear up for Clark tonight. He wanted to show off his new home. She *wanted* to show that she truly appreciated *their* future home. But she'd pay good money to have a quiet bath with a good book and a glass of wine.

Of course, the reading that hit her tablet was daunting. And the three eyes-only reports that she really needed to have under her belt by first thing tomorrow were only the top-level cut of the pile.

For just this one second, there was peace.

The sunset was coming from behind her, highlighting the white marble of the Capitol Dome, the Washington Monument, and the top of the Lincoln Memorial in lush reds. Next month the cherry blossoms would be out around the Tidal Basin. She never tired of walking beneath them. She'd make a point of having Clark go with her—a good photo op for the media.

Yes. She'd better dig deep and find the energy tonight. It *was* time for Vice President Clark Winston to propose to her.

The jangle of her phone ruined the sunset calm.

Not her desk phone.

Personal cell, face down on the desk. Not all that many people had that number.

She hoped it wasn't Gregor Federov. She just wasn't in the mood to soothe his ego.

She groped around without turning from the view, locating her phone by feel near the last ring before voicemail.

"Reese here."

"Good evening, Director."

Even worse than Gregor.

She was actually surprised that General Drake Nason hadn't managed to block her promotion and Senate confirmation—one of the reasons she'd had Ramson and Clark push it to vote so fast. It had been a nail-biting forty-eight hours as she wasn't sure she had the votes lined up yet. She had, but the margin had been slim, and there were tromped-on toes she'd never be able to set right.

But, as her CIA first trainer had drilled into her, *if it works, fuck 'em!*

Drake hated her guts almost as much as she hated his.

"We need your assistance."

Clarissa was so surprised that she missed the transition from sunset red to evening darkness on the distant marble edifices.

"Wow, Drake. That must have been hard to say."

His silence was all she needed.

Desperate.

Chairman of the Joint Chiefs of Staff General Drake Nason was desperate.

She so *loved* desperate men.

44

THE 309TH AEROSPACE MAINTENANCE AND REGENERATION Group was in charge of the world's largest boneyard. Over three thousand aircraft were parked in the high Sonoran Desert just southeast of Tucson, Arizona.

The dry air was parching after an evening in the wet San Juan Islands of Washington State and a warm spring day in Kentucky and Tennessee. It was also hot and had Jeremy stripping off his jacket and NTSB vest as soon as he landed.

Colonel Campos had been waiting for him.

Jeremy had only been aboard a C-5 Galaxy once before—out on the baking tarmac at the Joint Base Lewis-McChord biannual air show last year with one too many corndogs roiling in his stomach. They'd had it parked there, along with its two smaller transport brethren: C-17 Globemaster, C-130 Hercules.

The show drew a hundred thousand people across two days. Massive lines of families, an undecipherable mix of military families and the merely curious, worked their way through each aircraft. All the while, the airshow constantly ripped apart the skies overhead.

He'd spent a long time chatting with a trio of loadmasters who'd been looking bored out of their skulls along one side of the fuselage while the tourists mostly ignored them. He'd learned a lot about the shortcomings of the plane—like that the deck plates were integral to the structure, so a damaged deck plate meant she couldn't fly without replacement, inspection, and certification.

He'd also learned that they were crazy proud of flying the nation's heaviest lifter. When he'd mentioned the 747-800F freighter, they'd scoffed. "Civilian, Little Dude. Won't see them loading up a pair of M1 Abrams main battle tanks and winging them over to the dustbowl. Six Apache helos, with all their gear and crew, tuck in this baby slicker'n snot."

Meanwhile, the gawkers, in a line typically ten people wide, shuffled up the rear ramp and out the nose. Not one in a thousand knew they'd just walked farther *inside* the plane than Wilbur and Orville Wright's first powered plane had flown *outside*.

Now it was just him and Colonel Campos.

The scale of the vast emptiness was a shock.

"What's Miranda up to?"

"Crash investigations," Jeremy answered carefully. He'd heard General Nason saying that Campos didn't need to know.

"No, I mean..." he trailed off, then tried again. "Is she seeing anyone?"

Jeremy shrugged.

Yesterday, he would have said no.

Today? He was less sure. While he'd been working on

the FedEx 767 report, he'd kept an eye on everyone else discussing the new mission. He'd done it by putting a window on his tablet that was linked to his carefully positioned cell phone's camera.

He hadn't missed Major Swift holding Miranda's hand under the table. Neither general could have seen it. Mike and Holly had been looking at each other at that moment, but *he'd* seen it. Could count the seconds before Major Swift let go with what might have been a friendly squeeze.

Jeremy was still kicking himself for not recording the stream so that he could reverse and be sure.

Had Miranda smiled? Her back was to him so he didn't know.

It meant that he also didn't know how to answer Colonel Campos' question, so he kept his mouth shut and focused on the task at hand.

The C-5's cargo bay was an echoing cavern.

Campos must have caught that Jeremy wasn't going to talk about Miranda. He changed the subject.

"What the hell are they going to be doing with my plane?"

Jeremy knew that this time he *wasn't* allowed to say, so he just shrugged. "I'm just here to make sure it gets to where it's going."

"Which is?"

"Seattle. That's where I get off. After that—" He shrugged again, hoping that Campos would take the hint.

He did, finally.

"We have a flight crew and three engineers on board. We put together the remote-pilot gear with spit, bubblegum, and duct tape. As a test, your flight will be run completely by the remote pilots out of the drone center at Creech Air Force Base. The flight crew will act as a safety to Seattle, but mostly they'll focus on fine tuning the remote-control system. It is absolutely not certified for flight in controlled airspace in any way."

Jeremy knew that the remote pilots were actually at Groom Lake—far higher security clearances required by everyone there than Creech. But someone had told Campos it was Creech to make it seem more normal as that's where most of the nation's smaller drones placed around the world were flown from.

The C-5 felt so much bigger than the AN-124 Condor that he'd spent the whole morning crawling around. It didn't matter that Jeremy knew the C-5 was slightly smaller.

Cavernous didn't begin to cover it.

It was—

"It's too empty."

"Seems weird, doesn't it."

"No, I mean that it's *too* empty. We need to fill it up. At least partly."

"Any suggestions?" Campos' tone was deeply condescending.

The same tone he'd used when he'd upset Miranda—Jeremy's phone mic had been plenty sensitive to pick out the conversation, after he applied a few enhancement filters on the fly.

But Jeremy didn't have time to deal with that now, not that he'd know how. He was pretty used to people dismissing him. At least people not on his team. Miranda and Mike never did, and Holly did only when she was protecting Miranda.

He pulled out his tablet and flipped through the three thousand planes stored at the 309th AMARG's boneyard.

"There, that. Let's get one of these." He turned the tablet to Campos. "Just the fuselage."

The colonel just glanced at it, then stared at Jeremy as if he'd lost his mind.

"Now!"

Campos startled, then yanked out his phone with a curse and was already issuing orders as he hurried down the ramp.

Jeremy would have to remember to tell Holly that pretending to be her worked wicked...at least when backed up by orders from a four-star general.

45

CLARISSA DEFINITELY LIKED THIS.

They'd come to her. Landed their helicopter in the green center of the executive parking lot on the northeast side of CIA headquarters. She'd been able to sit in her office and watch through the one-way glass as they landed three stories below her window.

The heavy thump of the rotors through the thick glass had been positively sexual. She was definitely going to unleash all of that on Clark tonight. He'd never know what hit him.

They were now seated in *her* office.

Excellent. An even better high.

Generals Nason and Gray—such an odd couple. The grizzled warrior past his prime and the new general in charge of the NRO. Clarissa reminded herself that the NRO's budget was roughly the same size as hers. And that it wasn't generally subject to Congressional approval like so much of hers was.

Miranda, Mike, Holly, and a Major Jon Swift whom she knew nothing about. She didn't like having a wild card in the room.

"Did you lose little Jeremy?" She winced inside.

Clark would never use such a condescending tone.

"Sorry, it's been a long first day." And now she was apologizing? She *was* tired.

"Jeremy is on a special assignment," Drake said heavily. At least he was the one taking control of the meeting. The less she had to deal with Miranda Chase, the happier she'd be.

"So, what can the CIA do for you?"

"We need to get four people from Ramstein Air Force Base to the Bezymyanka Airport as fast as possible."

"Bezymyanka?" What? Was he trying to test her? Only one reason they'd be headed to that airport, on the north side of Samara, Russia. Fat chance she'd be caught lacking. "And from there to the Progress Rocket Space Centre?"

If Drake was feeling put in his place, he didn't show it. Maybe he assumed that she would simply know that was the public airport in Samara, Russia.

She turned to stare out the window for a moment to think. So, her tip to General Lizzy Gray had led them somewhere interesting.

"You want them aboard the transport flight." They were actually going to try and grab the Persona spy satellite. That *would* be an amazing coup...if they could pull it off. "Do they kill the normal crew or merely incapacitate them?"

"We're not at war."

She turned back to Nason. "Your wars are different from

mine, Drake. Or perhaps not so different if we're talking about stealing a major military asset."

"We have no intention of killing anyone as a part of this operation. However, secrecy dictates would point toward not having any Russian crew aboard for the flight."

"They're going to know that we took it if you leave the crew behind, even sedated." Clarissa was still in favor of killing them. "It would help if I knew the whole plan."

"Need to know, Clarissa. I need four people, Ramstein to Samara."

"Film crew." It was an almost autonomic response.

Perhaps the greatest ever, publicized, CIA rescue had used just that as a cover. Actually, the work had been mostly Canadian, but the CIA had come up with the film part of the solution.

When the Iranians took the US embassy in Tehran in 1979, six diplomats walked out the back door and hid in the Canadian Ambassador's house. Six weeks later a pair of CIA agents landed in Tehran with fake passports. They assembled with the escapees as a Canadian film crew scouting a location for a fake science fiction film named Argo and flew out of Tehran together.

And when Hollywood had made an Oscar-winner about it, *Argo*—Hollywood did so love to vote for movies about themselves—they'd written the Canadians out of the film and made it almost *all* CIA's triumph. That movie had been screened even more at CIA parties than in Hollywood.

"We need this in hours. We don't have time to create a fake movie." At least Drake knew his history, even if he had been born in the Stone Age.

"Television. Cable. Streaming. It's for a...brand-new

channel. Not announced yet. The Space Channel. Is there a Space Channel?" She tapped her intercom. "Is there a Space Channel?"

Her assistant answered in under fifteen seconds, "There's Sci Fi spelled like you'd expect. SyFy. S-Y-F-Y. NASA's is named NASA TV."

She hung up the line. "Perfect. Keep it simple. You can hide things in the cameras or their cases. Weapons, knock-out drugs, fake passports. Whatever."

"So, what are they doing there?"

"Filming new material for the grand launch of the brand-new channel. You'll pick up an escort, but they *love* showing TV people around—as long as you don't go near that satellite. When you...*shed* the pilots and loadmasters, you can shed the escort as well."

Clarissa waited while they looked at each other.

Miranda looked very unhappy, but that seemed to be her mode in life. Mike was worried, which seemed to be his main role on the team. Holly was the one to watch, and she was looking thoughtful.

Clarissa knew nothing about Major Swift, so there was no way to read what he was thinking, except he'd sat very close to Miranda. That was interesting in itself.

As if on cue, Holly sat up.

"Could you arrange for four passports and the appropriate equipment to be awaiting us in Ramstein?"

"Personally, I'd go with Warsaw. Fly in under your own names, fly out of Poland under Polish passports."

"Do you speak Polish?" Holly turned to Major Swift. Ah. He was part of the action team for some unknown reason.

He shook his head.

"Well, we can't make you Ukrainian. How about German?"

Major Swift rocked his hand, but Holly nodded.

"Let's go with being Germans then." Clarissa tapped her fingernails on the cherrywood of her desk, right where she'd had sex with Clark the very first time, to help her think. "You were...just in Poland interviewing their space agency. Do they have one?"

"POLSA. It's new and they're trying hard to get up to speed, at least on the industrial services side," Miranda stated in the lackluster encyclopedic voice she always seemed to use.

"You aren't one of the four, are you?" Clarissa didn't know why she cared. Let the woman get herself killed if she wanted to. Walk into the Progress Rocket Space Centre and steal a multi-billion-dollar asset?

Crazy.

Even by her CIA standards. That's why she hadn't offered one of her own teams. Her hold on this seat was still too tenuous and she couldn't risk a massive failure on her first day in the chair.

Miranda shook her head.

Clarissa didn't know why she felt relief, but she did.

She noticed that Miranda was doing something strange with her hand. Tucking her fingertips under her thumb joint and moving it back and forth over her lap.

Strange woman.

Then she noticed Holly wasn't watching the others. Or even watching Miranda as she often seemed to do, at least out of the corner of her eye. She was staring right at Clarissa.

Fine.

Let her.

What did she care what the woman thought?

46

HOLLY HAD PARTS OF AN IDEA.

The question was could she trust Clarissa Reese?

Drake had lectured all of them that Reese would have a game within a game within a game for every single thing she said, implied, or flat-out lied about.

Holly was plenty familiar with move and countermove tactics. They didn't serve a field team well. That called for hundred-percent reliability and trustworthiness.

But she didn't need trustworthy at the moment.

When everyone shifted to their feet, she was caught off guard.

What had she missed?

The film idea should work fine, as well as any other approach to this psychotic mission.

She recalled a few keywords: camera equipment, fake passports, transports. All arranged by the CIA. No one said a word about what would happen after they reached the plane. Jeremy wasn't mentioned again.

But she'd have to get any real details from Mike or Jon Swift.

As the others headed for the door, Director Clarissa Reese remained in her seat. A statement of power. *I don't need to rise to escort such people out.*

Holly stayed in her seat as well.

She could feel Mike hesitate by her chair, but she waved him out. Instead, she just stared at Clarissa and Clarissa stared back at her.

The door swung silently and closed with a soft click.

Holly didn't have time for waiting games, but she wasn't ready to speak first.

There was something...

So close...

"You're thinking very hard there, Ms. Harper."

"I'm wondering if I can trust you, Ms. Reese."

"In what way?"

"I know what you've done on your way to this new position. The drones, the extreme rendition sites in Iraq and Afghanistan, and I won't mention the mess in Oman or why a certain Saudi prince fell from high favor and is probably executed by now. Or the sudden exposure of your ex-Vice President's predilection for juvenile whores—though I'll personally offer a 'Well done' on that."

Clarissa did no more than arch her eyebrows.

Jeremy had found that Reese's history at the CIA was cloaked in some very nasty, aggressive code. He'd teamed up with a pair of CIA cyber-specialists that he'd met she-didn't-want-to-know-where. The three of them had very quietly cracked the shell, pulled a copy, and sealed it back up with no one the wiser.

"I take it this isn't blackmail or a threat. You aren't that foolish."

"No, Ms. Reese. I just like to know who I'm dealing with."

"As do I. Blow up any bridges lately, Ms. Harper?"

It took all of her training to reveal nothing of that gut punch. Holly allowed herself a ghost of a smile in response.

Of course, Clarissa would have long since had their whole team investigated.

She didn't trust herself to speak yet.

"We have a problem," a voice spoke up behind her.

Holly spun around to see Mike leaning with his back against the closed door. She wanted to chew him out, slap him down, or…something.

He moseyed forward until he was once again sitting in the chair beside Holly.

And she was *so* glad to see him.

Clarissa was infinitely slippery, but Mike was off-tap good with people, maybe he would know how to finish this clusterfuck she'd started. Holly had been dumber than a dipstick for trying this on her own—in so far over her head that all she was drawing up was mud deep enough to drown in. And the crushing blow of that image she couldn't hide.

She didn't give a damn what Clarissa saw, but Mike? She'd rather he didn't—

He was looking right at her. With sympathy.

"Worse than the 'Team' ghost?" His whisper so soft it barely reached her. Clarissa strained forward but her frown said she'd missed it.

Holly could only nod.

Mike didn't react. Instead he turned back to Clarissa. "Our problem is that we need a person…squelched." Of course, Mike had understood perfectly why Holly had stayed behind.

There had to be a way to take out Elayne / Elizaveta. But Zaslon operators were invisible, disappearing into the endless anonymity of the trackless wasteland between one black op and the next. This mission to grab the Persona satellite might be their one chance to get ahead of her.

"And you want to borrow an SOG asset?" Clarissa sneered.

"No. That's not the kind of mission that Miranda can ever be a part of. No wetwork. No assassins."

Again Holly stared at him in surprise.

"That's the old you, Holly. Not the new you," Mike said it with far more surety than she felt.

She wasn't so sure herself, but she liked the way it sounded when Mike said it.

"However, as I mentioned, we have a problem."

"This person?" Clarissa asked, all sweetness.

"No," Holly finally found her voice. "*You.* I expect that this total bitch is someone you'd very much like to meet." Two pit vipers of a kind. Dead-set real they'd be hell together if they teamed up.

She had to trust Clarissa to handle Elayne. But did she dare take the risk of even introducing them?

Mike folded his hands neatly in his lap. "We want a very simple arrangement. You can deal with her, but you cannot *make* a deal with her. Because if you do..." His shrug conveyed far more threat about ruining Clarissa's future than anything Holly could ever say.

Mike wasn't good. *He was amazing.*

47

"What was that about?" Jon asked Holly as they walked to the helipad in front of the CIA headquarters.

Miranda stayed close enough to listen. She knew that Holly didn't like Director Reese, therefore, remaining behind was an unusual action.

Holly merely shook her head and climbed aboard.

As they lifted off the well-groomed green square just above the Potomac, Drake placed a call.

"Have the jets ready to launch in five minutes and have a car waiting for me. Four passengers." He hung up and turned to speak to Lizzy.

Miranda turned to Holly and Jon.

She reached out to take both of their hands. It wasn't like her to do that, but this time she *wanted* the connection.

"I want you two to be careful."

"Yes, Mom," Holly smiled.

But Jon took it seriously. "Yes ma'am. I have no intention of not coming back."

"Good. Remember, you'll be flying an Antonov AN-124 below two hundred feet. With a wingspan eighteen feet longer than the C-5 Galaxy. Normally that wouldn't matter, but with a total wingspan of two-hundred-and-forty feet—one-twenty per side—that places your wingtip at only eighty feet above the ground in a hard bank. And it places your other wing above three hundred. Fly as level as you can. Slow turns."

She held up her hand with the thumb out and rested her other forefinger across it like a wing. Tilting her little mock plane side-to-side had her forefinger tipping low, then high.

"That's good, Miranda. That's really good. Thanks for the reminder."

Miranda saw a small shudder run along Jon's arm.

"Are you sure about this, Jon?"

"Yes. It's just...big."

Holly nodded. "The trick to any special operation is to remain both focused and loose. Focus on the next step, but stay loose enough to be flexible and appear natural. You can plan a whole mission ahead of time, but you can't let yourself picture it. If it becomes this large, any preconceptions fixed in your mind limit your ability to react. There's never been a spec-op that went a hundred percent, mate."

"Yes," Miranda had always liked Holly's ability to explain things. "It's like a crash."

They both eyed her strangely.

"You can't just *see* the cause of a plane crash. You have to build it in layers, approach it a piece at a time."

"Oh, okay. Sorry," Jon made a show of wiping sweat from his unsweaty brow. "I was just channeling my ancestor."

"Your ancestor's story," Miranda saw it now. "Picturing it like a crash is opening the door to the land of the Lilliputians. Picturing a crash *investigation* is perhaps a more proper analogy."

The helicopter was already descending toward the airfield.

Drake turned to them. "You abort at the least problem. I'm not happy sending in a civilian and a crash investigator, whether or not you're in the Air Force."

"Any better ideas, General?"

"Go to hell, Major Swift."

"Part of the mission plan. Yes sir, Uncle!" Jon saluted him sharply.

Instead of Drake getting angry as Miranda expected, he smiled. "Just bring both of you back in one piece and we'll declare this to be a success. Anything else you get is a bonus."

48

"REESE." CLARISSA ANSWERED THE PHONE WITHOUT EVEN thinking to look at it.

"Hey, honey." Clark was the only one she let get away with that endearment—or any endearment. "Something's come up at the White House. Roy wants me to join him."

"Social?" She really didn't have time for that right now.

"No. He's inviting me into a briefing. Wants to keep his Vice President in the loop rather than out of it."

"Good." That was very good. Also, she needed the evening free, and only now realized how disappointed he'd be if she canceled on him. It was better this way.

"You're not upset about us missing tonight?" He actually worried about such things.

"Are you moving out before tomorrow night?"

"No."

"Then we'll make up for it tomorrow night. Twice over."

"Sounds perfect."

"We could even make a habit of it." Clarissa winced. She usually played Clark better than that.

"Absolutely." Did he understand that meant marriage?

"I'll have to decide whether to put Second Lady or D/CIA on my business card," she kept her tone light.

"Do both!"

That had her glancing toward DC in surprise. Vice President Clark Winston was out there somewhere being... supportive. Not telling her to choose the wife-life because *he* and *his* position were what was important. But to be wife, Second Lady, *and* D/CIA.

"You're the best, Clark. Have I told you how proud I am of you?"

"Um..."

And for one second, a chasm was ripped into her world. Clark had just said such a wonderful thing—and now there was a *catch?* She'd fucking kill the man with her own bare hands.

"I, ah, didn't mean to propose over the phone. I meant to do that in person."

"Oh." Clarissa caught her breath, momentarily unsure how to proceed. She'd sworn to never, *ever* let a man control her emotions again. She'd almost let herself really care about Clark, and would have to be much more vigilant in the future.

Yet the image of Clark proposing formally... It was a nice image. One that should happen publicly with a newsie tipped-off to be there.

"You still there, Clarrie? Sorry if I upset you."

"I'm still here. And you can make it up to me by doing it properly next time we're together, maybe over a dinner at

Komi tomorrow *before* we go to your new house. A girl likes to have her moment." And where had *that* come from? She was sounding like a bad movie.

"Deal! Sure you're okay?"

"I'm fine. Go help President Cole; go learn from him. It's still my first day, so I have some things here I really should see to. I'm not *too* disappointed." She gave his ego the win.

"Perfect. Come home whenever you're done."

'Home' was another word that had lost all meaning years ago. Mom had made one, Dad had destroyed it. And she hadn't had one at all since she was sixteen and had helped dear old dad depart this life. She had a nice condo, but 'home' was just another lie.

"Now that you're Vice President, perhaps we shouldn't shack up until we're engaged."

"Ring's in my pocket." Again the good man. She wasn't used to that. Maybe never would be.

"I'll keep that in mind. Now go."

And he went.

Which left Clarissa in her office staring out into the darkness.

Clark, and whatever these stray feelings were, constituted the least of her concerns tonight. Time to shake all that off.

A Persona satellite.

She couldn't believe that they were actually going for it. It was mad, audacious, and potentially a massive intelligence coup with zero risk for the CIA—all on her first day.

Every arrangement that could be made, was made.

A Turkish charter company—a very discreet one that she'd had occasion to use before—would fly the team directly from Warsaw to Samara. The team would land at the international airport and get a cheap taxi to Bezymyanka Airport. The Turkish jet would be out of Russian airspace before the team even reached the Progress Rocket Space Centre to begin their fake interviews.

If they didn't get the flight—and weren't apprehended—the Turks could double back to fetch them.

She reviewed the plan they'd hashed out several times to be sure, but she'd missed nothing.

Everything that had been discussed was in place.

At least everything discussed in the group session.

There was still the proposal from Holly and Mike.

They'd left it to her as an option but Mike had made one thing very clear. If Clarissa did decide to do it, she'd have to play it one hundred percent the way they had mandated.

His threat if Clarissa didn't had been as clear as it was unspoken.

Had the threat come from Holly, Clarissa might have dismissed it. But from Mike it was a far more calculated threat. And they were each other's surety: one on the mission, the other under Drake's wing on the way to the White House.

Screw up in any way and Clarissa's past would be tomorrow's headlines. She'd lose the D/CIA, Second Lady, and eventual First Lady titles. It might even bring down Clark. Which, this close to the election and having just lost his first VP, would put Cole out of office as well.

It didn't matter where or how Holly had gotten her information; it was wholly accurate. If it all came out, the Saudis, Iraqis, and Afghanis would put out a hit on her—at the very least. Perhaps even the CIA, despite her being the director.

But, if she was instrumental in such an intelligence coup on her first day in the chair, she could ram it down every CIA department director's throat and several Senators who'd voted against her until they choked on it.

Holly's threat was real, so if she played Holly's game, she'd have to play that part of it straight.

Yet, it would be a hell of a game.

49

Gregor Federov woke up in his favorite place, tangled up with Vesna.

Only occasionally did she spend nights with him outside the club. But they were becoming more frequent, twice this month, and the month wasn't over yet.

But what had woken him wasn't the lovely Vesna. She slumbered soundly beside him.

His cell phone vibrated loudly on the nightstand.

He snatched it up before it could rouse her.

"*Ty ne znayesh', kotoryy chas?*" He asked, because he had *no* idea what time it was. Just dark.

"Hey, Monster."

"Hey, Beastmaster. I was just having a dream about..." Two dogs and a horse dying in the mud of the Siberian village he'd never expected to escape? Thankfully the dream faded fast. "...never mind."

Hearing from Clarissa Reese twice in a single night was...

He was going to say unusual, but he often didn't hear from her twice in six months. That meant—

He switched to English as Vesna shifted in her sleep and snuggled up against his back. "Oh, did that tidbit turn out to be something interesting?"

"Yes," Clarissa's tone was pleasant, but businesslike. Definitely not a late-night sex call. He pulled back the phone enough to glance at it. Four a.m. Evening in DC.

By her continued silence, he wondered if he'd missed something.

"*Very* interesting," Clarissa finally continued.

"You know I don't—"

"Get involved, Monster? Yes, I know that."

"Okay." He'd been worried there for a moment. He didn't mind passing on the smallest bits and pieces for amusement, but he wasn't going to be some deep mole who had his skin flayed from his body in some secret prison either. The old specters of Stalin and the KGB still loomed large in the modern Russian psyche.

"But I was wondering if you could do a small favor for me."

"What kind of a favor?"

"I need you to whisper something into someone's ear."

"Yours?" He considered whispering a few very suggestive somethings right now. But with Vesna sleeping against his back, he reluctantly decided against it.

"No. Where is that lovely creature you showed me earlier?"

Gregor shifted, but didn't answer.

"Ah, she's there with you. Well done, Monster."

"Why do you want to know?"

"I want to have something whispered into *her* ear. In fact, why don't you hand her the phone?"

"She's asleep."

"Oh, I doubt that, Monster."

"Vesna?" he asked softly over his shoulder.

She offered back a sleepy, "Hmmm."

He switched to Russian. "Someone, a friend, she would like to speak with you."

Vesna slid a hand over his ribs as if the phone was the last thing she was interested in, then up his belly and ribs, before finally reaching his phone. She kissed his back as she took it. She snaked the phone back over the same path.

"*Da.*" She shifted away from him a little.

He tried to overhear what Clarissa was saying, but couldn't make out a thing.

It was over a minute, perhaps two, before Vesna handed the phone back to him. She hadn't said another word.

It was still connected. "Yes?"

"I asked her to give you something."

Even as Clarissa spoke, Vesna's long, slim fingers began to wander over his hip.

"A special present from me."

Vesna ran a single fingernail along the inside of his thigh, which sent chills of anticipation running along his skin.

"And, Monster?"

"*Da?*" He managed as the fingernail began tracing other patterns on his skin.

"This is just from me to you as a way of saying thanks. Do *not* give any interviews today."

"Okay... Wait. *What?*"

But Clarissa was gone.

And Vesna was very, very present.

She began doing things she'd never done before...but Clarissa had.

And he'd loved it.

50

"Holy crap!"

Miranda looked at Mike with some surprise; he wasn't much given to even mild cursing.

"It's a common enough reaction," Drake simply smiled.

"It's called the White House, Mike," Lizzy appeared to be almost laughing as their car pulled up to the West Entrance.

Drake did laugh and Mike groaned.

A tease, Miranda decided. A tease? She decided to try one herself.

"Really, Mike. It's just a big house with a hundred and thirty-two rooms, thirty-five bathrooms. The Pentagon has two hundred and eighty-four, you know."

Mike just sighed.

Drake turned to her. "Two hundred and eighty-four rooms?"

"Bathrooms."

"Really?"

Maybe Miranda wouldn't try again with the teasing.

After they passed through security, Drake led them into the Situation Room.

Mike stumbled again.

"It's called the Situation Room, Mike," Lizzy teased him again.

Again Drake laughed and Mike joined in this time.

"How does that work?" Miranda asked Lizzy as they surrendered their coats and all of their phones.

"How does what work?" Lizzy leaned closer as a Marine held open the door for them.

"You were teasing him, right?"

"Uh-huh."

"I tried, but no one thought it was funny. Everyone, even your intended target of Mike, thought it was funny when you did it. I don't understand."

They crossed past the six reference specialists from the National Security Council working at their tiered desks and headed to the small conference room.

They were first through the door and the moment they entered, Lizzy snapped to attention and saluted.

President Roy Cole remained in his chair, but returned the salute.

"At ease, General. I can't begin to tell you how odd that is to say, even after three years. I stood down as a lowly captain."

"You're the Commander-in-Chief now, sir. Own it."

"Yes ma'am, General ma'am!" He saluted her again, far more sharply.

"There it is again," Miranda sat down at the President's right. "Can you explain teasing humor to me, Roy?"

Mike squawked. “You call the President of the United States by his first name?”

“He asked me to.”

“This must be your Mike Munroe. Welcome to the White House. I’m guessing you won’t be calling me Roy?”

“Not a chance in Christendom, sir. Or out of it. Uh... shutting up now.”

“I assume you didn’t arrive by attacking the White House with your jet again, Ms. Chase?”

“*That!* Right there. Humor, Roy. Specifically humor used in teasing.” Miranda didn’t want to lose track of the main topic by answering him.

But then the unanswered question itself was a problem.

“No. I didn’t. We arrived from Andrews Air Force Base by car.” she said it quickly, hoping they could stay with the first topic.

The man sitting across from her was smiling at her. It took her a moment to recognize him.

“Hello, Clark. Can you explain teasing humor to me?”

“Don’t you think that we should table that question for the moment? I’d like to—”

“No!” Miranda cut off Clark. She placed her hands flat on the table to show that she wouldn’t be discussing airplanes or hand models of airplanes until she had an answer. “I need to understand *one* thing, at least *one* thing that’s happening today. I have an unfinished game of Charades in which I don’t know the person I’m supposed to get Mike to say. I don’t understand why an Air Force C-130 pilot would think teasing about being able to land one-handed is funny. I don’t understand why someone sabotaged a hundred-million-dollar plane so that it blew up on an American runway and killed all six aboard, including a man reading pornography as his final act. Though I suppose it can't actually be called reading even though it was a magazine. And Drake's nephew—"

"Drake's nephew? Who's that? Dammit, Drake. You never told me, your Commander-in-Chief, that you have a nephew?"

"Never came up, sir. Nor his two siblings. Nor their dog. At least I think they have a dog."

"How can you not know if your brother's—"

"Sister's."

"—sister's family—"

"Big sister's," Drake grimaced.

"—has a dog?"

Miranda looked at the time on the wall clocks.

Washington DC and President's time zone both reported six p.m. Jeremy would be nearing Seattle right now at three p.m. local time.

Jon Swift.

Jon was just adding to the confusion of unknowns.

She wanted to ask Holly about him.

How to even *start* thinking about him.

But the Moscow clock, where Holly and Jon were heading, reported two a.m.

Her team was suddenly spread across eleven time zones.

Actually, Holly was headed to Samara with Jon, which was another hour east, so her team would soon spread over twelve.

Holly would say to focus on what was important.

There were a thousand spheres spinning. All different diameters. From the tiny sphere of the explosion that had ultimately destroyed the Antonov Condor to the massive sphere that could be a new Persona satellite in orbit high above the Earth.

How was she supposed to determine what was important?

"I wish—" She clenched her hands in her lap and stared down at the table when she realized she'd just interrupted Drake and the President. "I just wish I understood at least one thing."

The silence stretched out in the room.

"Ms. Chase," the President was the first to break the silence.

She studied the scuff pattern on the table. Whoever typically used this seat was left-handed. Tiny indentations in the surface finish indicated they would often tap their pen there. Two sets of indentations. Rocking it back and forth between their fingers rapidly. Tap-tap-tap-tap.

Probably when alone.

She'd learned that such habits could irritate others and did her best to only indulge them when she was alone.

"Miranda?" Roy asked. Miranda had no idea what the question was.

"Who usually sits in this chair?"

"My chief-of-staff. Currently running a budget meeting upstairs in the Roosevelt room."

"She likes bouncing her pen back and forth." Miranda ran her hand over the surface. The tiny marks were too shallow to feel.

"She does."

Too shallow to feel, but nonetheless real.

She looked up at Roy, not quite able to meet his eyes.

"I don't like not understanding."

"None of us do, Miranda."

"But that doesn't make the questions any less real, does it?"

"No," his nod was slow enough to be easily classified as friendly rather than dismissive. "But you're right, they're no less real for all that."

"Well, that's something, I suppose." Miranda set that aside and turned to the display screen at the end of the table.

She woke her tablet, synced it to the Situation Room's display system, and pulled up the first image she'd taken through the cockpit window of the C-130 as they'd approached the Condor's crash site at sunrise this morning.

"At 6:17 a.m. local time, that would be Central Standard—we really must talk about Daylight Savings Time someday, Roy, as you're no longer at the creative whim of the nineteenth-century New Zealand insect collector or the early twentieth-century British golfer who disliked dusk interrupting their hobbies—"

She could feel the others looking at her strangely. At least that was familiar.

"—we observed this aircraft disabled on Runway 23 at Fort Campbell, Kentucky."

"Disabled?" Roy exclaimed, then laughed. Short and sharp.

Miranda almost started thinking about why that might have been funny, but managed to stop herself. Perhaps she'd ask Holly about teasing humor versus other categories next time they were together.

Assuming she saw Holly again.

That thought was very upsetting, so she set that aside as well.

She selected the next image, "We traced the damage through the following steps."

And she also wouldn't think about the other items spread across the potential debris field of the upcoming operation.

51

Crossing the four thousand miles from DC to Ramstein, Germany, in just over three hours—a flight that normally took eight—with a midair refueling south of Iceland, was a brand-new experience for Holly.

She needed sleep, but there wasn't a chance of it. and it wasn't the new experience that kept her awake.

The back seat of an F/A-18F Super Hornet multirole fighter jet running hot wasn't a place conducive to sleep. The pilot had assured her that all of the weapon systems controls had been disabled at her position, not that there were any weapons aboard. Instead of missiles under the wings, the jet carried four auxiliary fuel tanks, doubling its range.

The weapons officer seat didn't offer much spare space, even for a woman, but that was fine.

Thankfully, the pilot seemed more than content to enjoy his unexpected night flight than chatting with his passenger. Of course, Drake might have said something about cutting off his balls if he bothered his priority passenger.

She wondered for a while if it was the mission keeping her awake.

Typically a deep-insertion mission took months of planning. After that, it often took weeks of preparation, training, testing different scenarios until every variation was reflex.

The SEALs who'd gone into bin Laden's compound had trained for months running literally hundreds of scenarios many times over. On site, when the main entry door had been bolted, the breacher already had his hand on the proper charges. Furthermore, he knew to warn the team working on entering from the other direction to stand clear of the blast.

But that wasn't every mission.

America's Delta Force in Iraq had perfected the on-the-fly mission profile. Hit the first site, gather intel, and based on what they found, immediately launch on the new site. They often did roll-ups of four, five, six sites in a single night.

All on the fly.

She was okay with that.

This was a little extreme perhaps. But once they'd picked up the two combat controllers in Germany, they'd have three Spec Ops plus Major Swift.

It wasn't *completely* off the track.

No, the mission, she'd be apples. Hopefully.

Holly glanced across the midnight sky. Or whatever time zone they were in at the moment.

Fifty meters away, a second F/A-18F appeared to be bolted to the sky. Visible only by the steady red left-wingtip light and, if she looked far enough aft, the flashing white of the tailfin anti-collision strobe.

Major Jon Swift was invisible in the darkness of his clear canopy.

She might as well be alone beyond the Black Stump. No one and nothing near her.

But she wasn't. Jon was off her wingtip. Mike and Miranda back in DC, lost in the wake of her exhaust but impossibly connected. Even Jeremy playing with spray painting a giant plane in Seattle. They were all connected. And soon they'd be picking up a pair of combat controllers?

The thought of 'team' still made her nauseous.

She wanted to talk to Mike about that. For the first time since that awful night, she *wanted* to try and hash out her feelings about being the lone survivor.

No one lost a whole team unscathed. Except that's exactly what had happened.

Then she remembered that scout of the Granite Mountain Hotshots. Nineteen wildland firefighters trapped in their fire shelters and dead from burnover. One lone Hotshot had survived by being out doing his job, scouting ahead.

How had he lived with that?

If she was the only one coming back this time, she just... *wouldn't.*

Holly didn't know how she felt about Major Jon Swift's obvious interest in Miranda, but she knew that it was reciprocated and she'd never be able to face Miranda without bringing Jon back.

Something she'd have to survive to achieve.

But that wasn't the worry either. Not really.

Her best estimate was that the mission was survivable. Possibly ugly, but almost dead set to be survivable.

Finally, Holly looked up.

Cruising at fifty thousand feet placed ninety percent of the atmosphere below them. Over the mid-Atlantic, in the middle of the night with the dashboard dimmed down for night vision, the stars seemed to burn in the sky above.

How many nights had she lain out and watched those stars?

Except they were wrong.

The stars of home were dominated by the Southern Cross, not the Big Dipper. And Orion didn't command the sky girded by his mighty belt and dangling scabbard. In the Southern hemisphere, Orion stood on his head and was drawn differently. Instead the belt was three brothers, and the downward-pointing scabbard was now the upward-leaping sawfish they had eaten against their laws. This had angered the Sun-woman Walu who created a waterspout and cast their canoe into the sky.

Getting away from the town lights of Tennant Creek wasn't hard. Three thousand people in the middle of the Northern Territory desert, with the nearest roadhouses thirty klicks north or a hundred and thirty south, didn't cast much of a glow.

As teenagers, they'd take their dirt bikes out into the Barkly Tablelands.

The Warumunga and Yapa, who made up half the town, had learned from their parents how to survive in the Outback. On school holiday, a whole group of them might go for a night and end up staying for a week. She'd learned fieldcraft out there. Holly had also lost her virginity to a lovely Yapa boy with skin the same brown-hued richness as the landscape's crimson sand. She'd often envied him the lazy brown curls of his sun-lightened hair.

She'd also had her first puking drunk out in the Tablelands. Not one of her better moments.

Not many of the white kids went along on the jaunts.

But one other did.

Her brother had always gone out with them.

Until he hadn't.

Holly closed her eyes but it didn't help, she...could still see him as clear as day.

Though it was dark, she slid down her helmet's sun visor. It blocked even the brightest stars.

She kept it down until she felt the jolt of F/A-18F Super Hornet's wheels contacting the runway at Ramstein Air Force Base.

52

"SET YOUR PHONE TO ENCRYPT. USE THE *Kontrrazvedki* department's code." There was a sharp buzz as the woman on the other end set her security code.

Elayne Kasprak stepped out of the flow of disembarking passengers. Surrounded by the comfortable buzz of Muscovites glad to be home, she'd been feeling warm and happy—until this moment.

She set today's code and drifted over to the window looking out at the Aeroflot plane that had just delivered her from London.

She didn't know the caller's voice, and she was good at voices. But the call had come in with a simple identifier that knocked all the warm out of the day.

Nobody wanted a call from the FSB. The Federal Security Service itself didn't *particularly* worry her though; she was above their parochial purview.

However, specifying that she use the Counterintelligence Department's code for encryption...

Their job was locating and "removing" spies. Nobody, not even a Zaslon operative, was wholly immune from their fearsome clutch.

The FSB were based in the Lubyanka Building. Those who entered against their will never again left the yellow fired-brick eight-story edifice under their own power. When the KGB had been headquartered there, it had become known as the tallest building in Moscow—because the prisoners incarcerated in its notorious basement dungeons could see all the way to the gulags of Siberia.

Elayne took a deep breath. "I'm here."

"I have a message for you." The woman spoke in perfect English, though with a heavier Russian accent than Elayne's.

"Listening."

"It was given to me in English, so I am repeating it that way. To Ms. Elayne Egorova. There—"

"Say that again!"

"To Ms. Elayne Egorova."

No one! Absolutely no one was supposed to know those two names were associated. Per Zaslon requirements, she'd killed Elizaveta Egorova. Actually, Zaslon had done it for her when she'd joined. Elayne Kasprak, as well as her other aliases, had then each been generated through distinct and separate channels. A crossover between aliases was a clear sign of a major failure—like a leak of the master agents' list.

But that someone had tied one of her current identities to her past should be impossible. That implied that *her* file alone had been exposed, not all of Zaslon's. Which was even worse. Command might assume that was her doing and they'd task one of her own unit with taking out the threat.

"Ms. Egorova?"

"I'm sorry, proceed with message." She leaned her forehead against the cold glass and stared at the jet that had just delivered her to Sheremetyevo Airport. It was too late to get back on it and escape. To anywhere. A heavy March snow was already blurring the plane. No way out.

"There is a satellite going to the sky. It won't get there and only you know why." There was a long pause.

"Is that it?"

"*Da.* Do you know what it means?" The woman asked as if she didn't know either.

"No. You really don't?"

There was a silence over the phone as if the snow had settled over their conversation as well. Finally the woman spoke softly.

"I don't know who you are. The person who gave me the message said you were Zaslon. I've never talked to a Zaslon agent before."

That's when Elayne heard something wholly unexpected in the woman's voice—fear.

The same gut-wrenching fear she felt to be talking to a counterintelligence agent.

"Okay. Let us both breathe. Just breathe."

The woman actually did, her breath heavy over the phone. "Yes, that is better…a little." The last was accompanied by a lovely laugh; brief but welcoming, setting Elayne's own shoulders at ease. A little.

"Maybe we can figure this out between us."

"*Da.* Maybe."

"I don't suppose you're willing to tell me who you are?"

"Nooo," she said slowly. "I would not be happy doing

that. But since I know your first name, I suppose you should know mine. I'm Vesna."

"Okay, Vesna. Can you tell me about the person who left the message?"

"She is a...friend. Of a...friend."

Elayne tried to read into the pauses. "But you spoke to her yourself?"

"Yes. She called him and asked him to hand the phone to me. I don't know how she knew I was there."

From one woman to another. Skipping over the middleman. If this Vesna truly was FSB Counterintelligence, which she'd almost have to be to have today's encryption code, she'd been tasked with watching the man. The snow falling from the heavy sky was becoming thicker, yet the snowflakes were more visible.

Daybreak was happening behind the heavy storm.

Vesna had just spent the night with the man she was watching—watching as a lover—and had only now gotten free to place this call.

"Your friend knows nothing of what the other woman said."

"That is correct. And she gave me your number."

How the hell had she gotten that? "Did she say anything else that might be useful?"

Vesna hesitated. "She made...threats. She knew what I did and the men I do it for. She also knew that I report to the FSB and threatened to expose me and all of the other women I work with."

Counterintelligence. Vesna and her friends would be well-paid spies. Spies paid to use their bodies to watch over some segment of the Russian elite. And if they were exposed, the FSB would either drop them back into the desperate cesspool of common whores or, more likely, they'd quietly disappear and never be heard from again because of the things they knew.

Elayne stopped worrying about the woman and returned to the message. "'There is a satellite going to the sky.' Do you know which one?"

Again the hesitating silence.

"Vesna, I can't help you if you don't help me."

Another deep breath. "My friend. He tells me that an important satellite is just finished and ready to send for launch. A 'Person?' Something like that."

A Persona surveillance satellite! It had to be. That wasn't just important. That was a major national asset. A new Persona launch was only a once- or twice-per-decade event.

Then her thoughts ground to a halt.

The second part of the message.

There is a satellite going to the sky. It won't get there and only you know why.

"But I don't know why." Elayne thumped her forehead on the glass and all she got back was a dull bass note as the glass vibrated.

"Are you okay, miss?"

Elayne snarled at the gate attendant who'd come up to her. She made a few observations about his shriveled excuse for male anatomy which he certainly possessed before he could scurry off. Then she moved to the center of the void between two adjoining gates for some privacy.

"If you are still confused, I am supposed to ask you a question that makes no sense to me to ask."

"Go ahead, Vesna."

"The woman said I should say, '*Where am I?*'"

"How the hell should I know?"

Vesna started to speak, but Elayne cut her off.

"No, wait." A Persona satellite. The Progress Rocket Space Centre. Samara. She knew exactly where Vesna was. What was more, she knew who Vesna was sleeping with—a high-level worker of Progress—because the state counterintelligence wouldn't spend so much effort on a mere employee. Either a department head or an executive.

But that wasn't her concern.

It won't get there and only you know why.

"Okay, I know where you are and roughly who you're..." there were many unsavory jobs for the State that must be done. "Who you're watching. I'm still not sure of the last part. Why me?"

"When you ask that question, I'm to tell you the very last thing that was said to me. Arfist."

"Arfist?" Are fist? ArFist, like misspelled artist? Perhaps an acronym.

"Yes. Arfist. Do you know what it all means now?"

Arfist! Russian for someone who played a harp. Harpist. Harper.

And she knew.

Holly Harper.

Who'd gotten her cell number from the ever-so-friendly Mike Munroe. She'd given it to him originally because she'd needed to know what happened to the sixth flight crew member.

"Tell me, Vesna?" Elayne smiled out at the swirling snow that no longer obscured anything. "Is there a Condor waiting to deliver the satellite?"

"A condor? Like the big bird?"

"Yes, an Antonov AN-124 Ruslan transport jet. Is there one sitting at the Progress factory in Samara?"

"I don't know the name, but the waiting jet is the biggest I have ever seen."

"Thank you, Vesna." Elayne resisted the urge to crow with delight. "You take good care of your friend. Very good care."

"He is kind to me. And is hanging very much like a horse." It was the first piece of idiom she'd gotten wrong.

"Hung, Vesna. He is *hung* like a horse. For you I hope he is hung like Catherine the Great's horse."

Vesna giggled.

Men wishing to denigrate Russia's finest ruler, the Empress Catherine the Great, had spread rumors of her taste for bestiality. Her death was widely publicized to be caused by the breakage of the truss lowering a horse onto her for her pleasure. Rather than being crushed by an equine lover, she'd died at her desk after saving Russia from itself for thirty-five years—starting with staging a coup against her insane husband-emperor.

But the story lived on.

They both hung up.

Elayne would worry later about flaying Vesna's lover for any betrayal to the Motherland—whoever the man's 'friend' was on the phone, she was connected to Holly Harper. That probably meant American intelligence. If Elayne was in a good mood, she might protect Vesna. She seemed nice for what she was. But ...she also hadn't turned in the man she was watching either.

Elayne would deal with them both—after.

First, Holly Harper.

In Russia.

Stealing a Persona satellite.

It was too perfect.

And Holly had made it personal, throwing down the gauntlet at Elayne's feet.

She'd *take* that challenge.

And when she delivered the Australian's head to the world's media as an American spy, they would give her the Order of St. George medal. Perhaps even the gold star of Hero of the Russian Federation medal.

Elayne dialed her phone as she spun around and began striding through the airport's crowded passenger halls.

"I need the fastest jet you have in Moscow. And make sure they include a field kit. I've been traveling and have no weapons."

The idiot started to protest.

"Now! Or by end of day you'll think that Lubyanka Prison is a luxury hotel."

Despite the thick crowd, a path opened wide before her as she strode ahead.

"And have them pick me up at Terminal D at Sheremetyevo, the first gate. If there is another plane there, get rid of it. You have fifteen minutes."

She hung up the phone.

It was just long enough to hit Sheremetyevo's Bosco store and replace her damaged jeans and jacket.

53

"THAT'S THE CRAZIEST DAMN THING I EVER HEARD." President Roy was slumped back in his chair.

But for all his apparent ease, Miranda suspected that his mind was highly engaged. He'd asked detailed questions throughout her presentation.

Clark had only spoken once when he said, "Clarissa did *what?*"

Roy's brief response had completely squelched him, "Keep personal shit out of this room and out of your job, Clark. Clarissa has a job and it's no longer yours."

Drake had added, "One of her contacts was the initial source, and she's also orchestrating the team's transfer from Ramstein to Samara. She is not cleared for any other aspects of this operation."

Clark's nod had been tight—in the displeasure category—and he'd kept his silence since.

Now, at the finish of her presentation, Miranda kept her

eye on the screen. She'd ended on a world map on which she'd superimposed all of the moving pieces.

"There's a call for you, ma'am." One of the NSC clerks announced.

Jeremy's face appeared on a side screen. "Well, it's aloft and I'm not on the plane."

Mike chuckled for some reason.

Miranda was simply relieved.

Jeremy placed an image of the repainted C-5A Galaxy on the screen. The Boeing paint shop had transformed the dull Air Force-gray into a shining white aircraft with a long, blue pinstripe. The Russian flag perched proudly on the towering tail.

The top crosspiece of the C-5 Galaxy's high T-tail had been painted black.

"The tail has a simplistic stealth coating. Nothing much, but enough to disrupt fifty-seven percent of the radar signature."

Lizzy leaned in. "What are the two stubs low on the tail? They're not part of any C-5 I've ever seen."

"Those are actually horizontal stabilizer elements that we hijacked off the 767 assembly line. The way we attached them, they're aerodynamically neutral and will simply flap up and down with any passing airflow, causing no significant induced-drag. Don't look very big on the Galaxy's tail, do they? However, they have highly radar-reflective coatings. They won't fool a visual inspection, but between the two coatings on the two sections of tail, they should give any radar the impression that this plane has a standard empennage like an An-124 Condor rather than a T-tail. What do you think, Miranda?"

"I think that's a wonderful job, Jeremy."

Jeremy looked ready to explode with pride.

"And the remote piloting is all configured?"

"Absolutely. Those guys at Davis-Monthan did a great job putting the control system together. Flew us, remotely, to Seattle with it. We can even do a midair refuel, though we won't need it. Her range with this little load is amazing. Also, did you know that if you're really careful, you can fit a KC-135 "Stratotanker" fuselage inside a C-5's cargo bay? We had to cut off the last twenty feet of the tail, but we got it in. We filled all those internal fuel tanks with just twenty percent of their possible fuel load—fourteen thousand pounds, about two thousand gallons. So, the tanks are mostly filled with explosive vapors. I hope that it's okay? I got the idea from what happened to your parents' plane."

Her parents had been killed by an accidental spark igniting the vapors in a nearly empty fuel tank. The explosion had ripped flight TWA 800 from the sky. It would shatter the C-5 Galaxy if done to the whole plane rather than just a single tank.

A part of her wanted to go hide in the corner of the room, hug herself, and maybe fly the airplane that was her thumb.

But a part of her knew Jeremy was counting on her. And Holly was counting on him.

She looked at only the slice of the solution that was the mechanism of TWA 800's crash and no other implications.

"Jeremy, if you found a way to make some good come from...that. I'm..." she checked inside carefully. Even being cautious, she was never sure quite what she'd find when she thought about her parents. But... "Yes. Well done."

"We set sparkers in the tanks to make sure any attack will trigger them all at once. If we can entice the Russians to shoot it down, it should make an incredible show and leave nothing bigger than a pea. That'll make them piss their pants. Pea, p-e-e, piss. Get it?"

"Yes, Jeremy, we get it." Mike was smiling.

Add pee and poo jokes as an entire humor classification that Miranda had never understood. Lizzy didn't look to be smiling either. Perhaps that category was a boy thing?

54

ELAYNE RESISTED THE URGE TO BEAT THE SHIT OUT OF THE pilot when he showed up at Sheremetyevo.

Did command send one of the brand-new MiG-35UBs capable of over two thousand kilometers per hour?

No!

They sent a thirty-year-old Su-28 that couldn't even break the sound barrier.

A twenty-minute flight was now an hour to reach Samara.

Then they were tenth in line for takeoff.

"Tell the tower that we are now first in line for takeoff."

"The snow is slowing everything. They're thinking of closing the airport and all of the flights are desperate to depart before they do," the pilot reported from the front seat of the aging jet.

"Tell those assholes that if I'm not in the air in the next thirty seconds that I'm going to have you fire a missile into their tower."

"I'm not carrying any missiles."

"Do you have guns?"

"This is a flight training aircraft, ma'am. It has no weapons."

A *trainer?* They'd sent her a *training* aircraft when she was in such a hurry? If Holly Harper slipped away from Samara, Elayne would never find her.

No, she could. She'd find that odd Miranda Chase and Holly would come running. Maybe she'd start by sending Holly a few body parts first.

Wait.

She herself hadn't known this was a trainer.

"Pilot, tell the tower you'll fire a missile at them anyway. I'll bet they won't know that you can't."

"My pleasure, ma'am."

When he did, they were immediately instructed to turn onto a nearby taxiway and cross onto the active runway ahead of everyone else.

"Is this enough room?" They were leaving a third of the runway behind them before they even started.

"Oh, yes ma'am. He may be old, but this jet is very capable."

"Fine. Prove it."

The pilot's answer was to throw the throttles wide open. They slid a little on the snow before it straightened out, but then it punched ahead. Hard!

They were aloft before she remembered to breathe.

When they were less than a hundred meters up, and the runway was still visible beneath them through the thick snow, he rolled the plane hard to the right.

In as many seconds, he spun through three wing-over-wings like he was drilling a hole through the sky. Then he pointed the nose nearly straight up and they shot aloft through the clouds.

He leveled out in the sunshine above the clouds while her heart was still pounding.

"He is also one of the foremost aerobatic performers in all of our air force," the pilot announced proudly.

"Captain," Elayne's body rippled from the forces that had slammed through her. "You have my permission to do that to me any time you want."

"It would be my pleasure, ma'am. But with my current fuel, Samara is at my range limit. Perhaps you would like a demonstration once we're there?"

Perhaps she would. She did so love taming a Russian officer's easy arrogance. What Miranda saw in the simpering Major Swift was a mystery to her.

55

"Now it's a question of timing," Miranda had tracked the Turkish plane, temporarily flying with Polish registration, from Warsaw to Samara and it was now headed back to Warsaw.

"We know Holly's team safely cleared customs at Kurumoch International Airport forty minutes ago. As they are only thirty kilometers from Bezymyanka Airport at the Progress factory, they should be there in the next few minutes."

Lizzy brought up some images from the NRO's satellites on one of the four large screens at the end of the table.

"There's the very edge of a storm over Samara, so we're peering through clouds, but you can see here that the Condor is still in place. Here's the image series we were able to capture in successive passes over the last two hours."

The images flickered by, one every few seconds. Sometimes the angle or lighting shifted, but Miranda could make out the ground action for herself as Lizzy explained it for the others.

"Here we can see them loading several large containers. This one," she circled it on the screen, "has the dimensions we'd expect for the Persona itself. Everything else we believe is auxiliary launch equipment, final fairings and such. The rockets would have traveled ahead weeks ago."

Smaller containers were loaded.

Many people were crowded along the path between the building and the plane as the loaders moved objects between the two.

Suddenly, the crowd dispersed. There were occasional flickers of people moving, but only a few.

"What just happened?" Roy didn't understand.

"It's all loaded." Miranda checked the image's time stamp and sighed with relief. "It was just a few minutes ago."

"Right." Lizzy pointed at the various people. "These will be the loadmasters doing their final checks. Look, there's a fueling truck. There's another already under the other wing. We still have some time. Each truck this size holds about fifty thousand pounds of fuel."

"Why pounds? Not gallons?" Clark looked puzzled.

"Military planes, we think in pounds of fuel."

"I forgot; you were a jet jockey. Carry on, General Gray. Pounds versus gallons?"

Lizzy cleared her throat. "Fifty thousand pounds is roughly seven thousand gallons of fuel per truck, sir."

"That's seven thousand, three hundred and fifty-three gallons, if their Jet A fuel mix is similar to ours, sir." Miranda looked around the room and decided that Holly was right and there were times she really shouldn't speak. "That's twenty-four-point-three percent of a train's railcar—another common unit for measuring fuel." *Really* shouldn't.

"If she's dry—" Lizzy continued, "actually he, the Russian's call their planes and ships by the male gender—the Condor will load up six fuel truck's worth."

One point four six railcars, Miranda whispered to herself.

"They'll keep the fuel loading as light as possible."

Miranda twisted to face Lizzy.

Mike spun as well.

No one else reacted.

None of them were pilots and they wouldn't understand the implications of that statement.

Holly and her team couldn't exactly drop into some quiet Siberian airport and load up an extra ten thousand gallons on the sly.

"How close do the Russians load fuel to their precise planned flight destination?" Mike found his voice before she could.

Lizzy shrugged.

"Close."

56

"READY TO ROCK?" HOLLY ASKED THE OTHERS AS SHE TRIED TO stretch the kinks out of her back. The only cab at the airport had been a thirty-year-old Zhiguli compact gypsy cab. The ride across Samara had been painfully cramped even with just the four of them.

Jon looked equally bent out of shape. Tim and Tom, the two 24th STS Air Combat Controllers who'd joined them in Ramstein, looked a little better off.

Holly had forgotten the smell of Russia. There was a dry-cold that pervaded every other scent. Cabbage and dry-cold. Aging, untuned exhaust from the Zhiguli, and dry-cold. The sagging industrial zone that surrounded the gleaming gray-and-glass facade of the Progress Space Rocket Centre's entrance, squatting atop a flight of concrete steps like a sleeping bear ready to awaken and crush them, smelled of rust and hydraulic fluid...and the dry-cold scent.

A woman with shoulder-length bronze-brown hair and a

classically Russian just-too-tight dress was coming down the front steps of the Progress Rocket Space Centre toward them.

"Wow! Talk about made for the camera," Tom spoke up and shouldered the Red 8K camera he'd been practicing with since they picked him up at Ramstein. He made the move look as if he'd done it a thousand times, rather than never having touched a studio camera until a few hours ago.

The woman certainly was: bright smile, smooth walk, and had clearly just brushed her hair to a shine and redone her makeup. She was remarkably photogenic.

Holly had last slept on the steel deck of a C-130 Hercules from Spieden Island to Kentucky, though mostly not-at-all because of Miranda's damn question about whether she was sleeping with Mike.

Clarissa had arranged for a change of clothes to be waiting for Holly in Germany—casual up-scale Euro that didn't feel like her at all.

Holly supposed that the slender black slacks, a trim matching blazer over a white silk, open-collar blouse, and wrap-around shades to go with the quick dye job into jet black hair and a neat trim had made her match her new passport.

And left her feeling not at all like herself. Except for the dirty-dishrag-exhausted bit. That was all too familiar.

The disguise, as much as anything, had pushed her back into SASR days when such togs were often appropriate during a reconnoiter. She'd forgotten so quickly what it felt like to be playing a role rather than just being her lazy self.

Jon wore dark contacts and a brunette wig that turned his military crewcut into something like an early Beatle—which was so out it must be back in.

It was surprising how much it changed both their looks, and the passport photos were doctored so much they were only barely the same person. Clarissa's team was smart; their identities would be almost impossible to trace back to a real person if anyone ever tried.

Nobody would pay attention to Tim or Tom as the technicians. They were just two guys who looked surprisingly alike, with tousled hair and rough-trimmed beards.

"Knows she's about to be on film. Bet that dress is less than an hour old." Tim held up his shotgun boom mic, covered in a long thick windscreen like a black foam rifle barrel. Which was appropriate because, if combined properly with the mic boom and three specific parts from his light meter, it turned into a very accurate sniper rifle in about sixty seconds.

Back at Ramstein, They'd debated between having Jon or Holly be the "on-screen" talent. Which would be better for bamboozling whoever they met?

Jon had finally hit the right idea. "We're cohosts. You take care of the hot men; I'll corral the hot women."

"And if they're lesbian?"

"I'll charm them anyway because I'm a charming guy."

He wasn't, but he was a *nice* guy.

Maybe it was time Holly stopped worrying about him and Miranda, and let Miranda just figure it out for herself. Maybe she'd take her own advice, and realize she didn't know shit. Perhaps she'd take Mike, a rack of long necks, and go on a blinder just to see what happened. If she drank enough, she wouldn't remember the morning after anyway. Or maybe she'd be able to knock back enough to block out the past, however briefly.

"He's so 'charming' that maybe I'll just swoon right here," Tim had clapped his hands to his heart and fluttered his eyes like a silent film dame.

"No, he's mine. All mine." Tom had given his buddy a hip check that sent Tim sprawling into the hangar's wall where they'd been quickly sorting their gear.

The two combat controllers had turned it into a fun team within the first ten minutes.

Ragging on her and each other.

Surprised the hell out of her. She was used to having to fight her own battles, especially among Spec Ops.

She couldn't ask why, of course. But eventually Tim had offered a side comment. "Ozzie SASR? That's some serious kick-ass, girl."

"Yeah, we'll all have to watch over Air Force here," she'd nodded toward Jon.

Tom had given her a high five that they were in on that program. And they'd been good from that moment on.

Now, on the front steps of the Progress Space Rocket Centre's admin building, they were three Spec Ops soldiers…and one pilot out of his depth but game to try.

She'd missed that a lot without even realizing it.

No need to ever question if they had her back, and they'd know that she had theirs.

"Last report said they're loaded and fueling. Let's do this fast." Holly turned just as the brunette beauty arrived a little breathlessly.

"Hello, I'm Tatyana Tarasova, head of media relations here at the Progress Rocket Space Centre. I was told that

Russian is acceptable for all of your crew. Would you prefer to work in Polish, German, French, or English perhaps?" No coyness to the smile or heaving chest of helpful excitement. Maybe she actually *was* good enough to be the polyglot head of media relations; just a very photogenic one.

"Please, let us stay with Russian. We are all comfortable with that. Also, at the Space Channel, we hope to capture the mood and feel of each country. POLSA was hard as Tomas has no Polish and mine is poor." Actually nonexistent, but Holly felt it was better to keep that to herself.

"Wonderful. I'm so sorry that there was a mix-up and we lost your scheduling. It never reached my desk, but no matter. Your credentials all check out—"

One point for Clarissa and the CIA.

"—and I was able to rearrange my meetings so we have the whole morning."

"That's wonderful," Jon stepped right in; his Russian was even better than Holly's so she was glad for him to take the lead. "We can never thank you enough. We actually aren't planning on shooting any real footage today. Instead, our interest is in establishing shots and story. We will then approach you for a full script approval, of course. Ultimately, SC—sorry, the Space Channel—is hoping to film a full mini-series about the Progress Rocket Space Centre from its very origins as it is one of the three most important in the world—along with ESA and NASA. Do you still have anyone who worked on the original R-7 Semyorka? I know it was sixty years ago that State Aviation Plant No. 1 was tasked with building that first rocket, but we are hoping someone still remembers the stories of that era."

"You have done your homework, Herr Schnell," the woman smiled prettily.

Holly had been surprised to discover that Clarissa Reese had a sense of humor. When they'd opened their false IDs, Jon Swift had become Herr Schnell, Mr. Fast. She'd become Hulda Musiker, maker of music. She supposed she should be thankful Reese hadn't named her Ms. Steaming Turdpile.

"As it happens, Progress maintains a retirement center nearby. There are still several members who worked on that first R-7 rocket that launched the *Sputnik* even before the manufacturing was given to State Aviation Plant No. 1, which became Progress. I will make a call that they should expect you."

"No. Let's keep it simple for now," Jon stopped her as she was already reaching for her phone.

"Simply knowing that we can conduct those interviews will be enough," Holly agreed quickly.

No time for delays.

"Our plan is to make this film backwards. So many stories start with the very smallest pieces and bring them together to the triumphant end. Our studies show that many people do not care without the bigger picture first. We will eventually start with a launch at Baikonur and then work our way backwards."

"Baikonur?" Tatyana bristled exactly as Holly had hoped. "That is in Kazakhstan. Why not start with our new launch center in Vostochny?"

"Oh, we simply assumed the Russian government would never let us film there. That would be wonderful if you could help arrange it."

Tatyana waved a perfectly manicured hand with tasteful

dark red nail polish—Holly had never worn nail polish in her life—as if it was no trouble at all.

"So, perhaps," Holly decided to really roll the dice. "We can start at the finished point, where you deliver a rocket to transport, and then start working backwards."

"Your timing is perfect," Tatyana began leading them around the side of the administration building. "We have just loaded our newest satellite onto a transport jet that will be leaving momentarily. I can't discuss the payload, of course, but I think it is okay to mention that it is headed to Vostochny."

"That's wonderful. Boys," Holly turned to Tim and Tom, "Make sure you capture any footage that Tatyana Tarasova approves. We will want to use that if we can't time our live filming with another delivery."

Tom grumbled something like, "Yeah, yeah. We know our jobs, lady," in surly German.

Tim just rolled his eyes.

Tatyana offered her a look of sympathy as someone who had clearly worked with too many grumpy camera crews.

Perfect.

57

Drake knew he used to be better at controlling his emotions.

He was sure of it.

At the moment he wanted to pound the Sit Room table with both his fists.

"What the hell is going on over there?"

Lizzy sighed. "The timing is awkward. I won't have another satellite overhead for seventeen minutes. And when I do, it will be a low-angle pass, so we may not be able to see much even if the approaching weather doesn't cover the site."

"Goddamn it," he kept that to a mutter.

Roy and Clark had been called out of the room to some other matter.

Mike was staring fixedly at the mission clock, which simply showed Samara-local time because they didn't have anything else more relevant to reference. The moment they crossed into Russian airspace wasn't terribly relevant except that each additional minute was another chance for everything to go to hell.

And they didn't have a mission-end time until they actually got that damn plane out of Russia. Not even an estimated one until they got it aloft.

Miranda was the only one staying focused on anything.

"What are you working on?"

She looked at him in surprise. Miranda always seemed to be shocked when directly addressed.

"Jeremy and I are working on two simultaneous crash reports. I currently have his latest draft of the civilian 767 accident at Nashville. And he is layering in additional information from his photographic analysis of the sabotage and explosion of the AN-124 Condor at Fort Campbell in case it's of use to the Air Force's AIB team. We've also been in touch with them regarding any new developments."

"And *is* there anything new?"

"Only one item. I'm not sure if it would be classified as new but it is definitely curious. For the team handover, Holly had insisted that I not mention the presence of an Antonov representative at the crash site. Apparently, one has just now called from the Ukraine asking if they had seen a plane that was past due for reporting their arrival at Fort Campbell. When informed that they had lost a plane, the Antonov factory complained about lack of notification. Which makes no sense as their representative was already on site."

Drake felt an itch.

It reminded him of one of his last missions. Task Force Falcon had deployed to Kosovo, including the Ranger's elite Regimental Reconnaissance Detachment, to help stabilize the newly formed country. Kosovo had fought a bloody and brutal seventeen months for its freedom from Yugoslavia, which had left the country in tatters.

Among the official count of forces involved in the war, an "unknown number" of Russian "volunteers" had supported Milosěvić's attempts at exterminating the Kosovan Albanians.

One particular "volunteer" was caught heading a rape squad, after the declaration of peace. Even as they drilled down on his identity, it seemed to morph. Yugoslav raping Islamic Albanians... No, an Albanian wanted for killing civilians who had aided...someone.

Then the volunteer had made one mistake, and they were able to identify him as Russian.

Within hours he'd been murdered in his cell...and the only likely suspect was a Russian who'd slipped through the perimeter Drake's own team had set up around the holding cells. Whoever it was had also left four dead Albanian guards inside. To get by a Ranger RRD team—and make five kills—took a degree of skill he'd never seen outside of Delta Force.

It hadn't taken a genius to know that the only person likely to pull off such a mission had been a Zaslon operative.

That same itch was back.

Had one of Russia's secret elite warriors been at the Condor crash in the middle of the secure Fort Campbell military base?

"Tell me about the man who was there."

"What man?" Miranda had drifted most of the way back to her report.

"The one who said they were from Antonov."

"I never said there was a man from Antonov."

"Then who?"

"A woman."

Drake hadn't expected that. He could feel Lizzy's smile at his back telling him he was still making assumptions. He ignored her.

"Then tell me about the *woman* who said she was from Antonov."

"Ask Mike. He spent the most time with her." Miranda turned away and Drake might as well be on another planet.

He looked across the table toward Mike, who was no longer watching the seconds tick by in the Samara time zone.

Now he was looking directly across at Drake.

His stare was dead flat.

Drake opened his mouth to ask.

Mike offered an infinitesimal shake of his head, then glanced over at Miranda. The message was obvious: *Don't say a thing about the Antonov woman around Miranda.*

Drake was sick of not knowing.

He jabbed a finger toward the door.

Mike shrugged before rising, and they both headed for one of the other Situation Room conference spaces.

58

"Wow! Is that an Antonov Ruslan?" Jon asked for Tatyana's sake. He still wondered why he'd agreed to this crazy endeavor.

He'd spent the entire flight over the Atlantic and then on to Samara, studying the Antonov manual someone had scared up for him.

The damn thing *was* a monster. And staring at it now parked on the Russian tarmac, it seemed to glower at him. Like the C-5 Galaxy, its wings drooped heavily when it was on the ground. It wasn't the natural state for either airplane. They belonged aloft; wings lifted near to level rather than drooping like sad rabbit ears.

"It is," Tatyana's pleasure at his surprise reminded him of his role.

Barely.

He wanted to yell to Holly. "Abort! Abort! Abort!"

But they were so far in. So close.

Then he thought about the five thousand kilometers to

cross Russia. And the thirteen hundred more to their planned refueling point at Sapporo, Japan on Hokkaido Island. Dependent on an unlikely twenty-four percent fuel reserve.

Maybe they weren't so close.

"Would you like to meet the crew?" Tatyana was flagging down four men walking toward the plane carrying small suitcases.

Jon tried to shout no, but his throat wasn't working.

"That would be wonderful," Holly effused with appropriate enthusiasm.

Tom, with his camera up, was already shifting toward a small windowless utility shed rusting beside the hangar. There were dozens of similar structures tucked in various corners and spaces around the edges of the main hangars. Whatever leading edge manufacturing happened inside the building, out here it was still the depths of the Soviet era.

"I think this would be the best angle. Really capture the plane in the background. Could you call them over, Tatyana Tarasova?" Tom appropriately used the polite form of her name whereas he and Holly were already on a first name basis with her.

As the crew arrived, smiling easily and happily flirting with Tatyana, Tim and his microphone circled around behind them.

Jon could only stand and watch as the other three slid into easy action.

He tried to reconstruct it many times in his mind's eye, but never quite succeeded.

Tim came up from behind and delivered knockout shots with a needleless jet injector about the size of a slim energy drink can. He just pressed it against the neck of each of the four members of the flight crew and Tatyana Tarasova, there was a click, and he moved to the next one.

Before their bodies totally failed them, Holly and the two STS operators had linked arms with the fading crew and hostess.

He himself should have been there to unlock the door.

To help.

Somehow.

But it didn't seem to matter. Holly shattered the lock and walked Tatyana into the shed even as she collapsed. Then she turned to help hustle the four other crew members into the tiny space.

And all Jon could do was watch.

Suddenly Holly/Hulda had him by the arm and was dragging him into the shed as if he too was one of the drugged.

It was run-down and stank of old oil and rust. Broken tools and odd bits of machinery were lying about. Hopefully no one would be checking it in the next six hours.

Tim and Tom already had two of them stripped of their uniforms and had pulled them on.

Holly shook him. "Now, Jon. We're committed. Without Tatyana, we can no longer safely traverse security back out of here. Let's go!" She shook him again.

Jon nodded twice. Once to Holly and once to himself.

He'd flown C-5's right through the heart of the Iraq and Afghan wars. Starting in the early years when field conditions were unknown, right through the peak era in the early 2010s where combat-landing a C-5 was as natural as breathing.

"Okay. Got it." He reached down to peel the suit off the next crew member.

"No," Holly stopped him. "You're the captain now. Take the captain's uniform."

Okay, maybe he didn't have it.

The small shed was crowded and there was a lot of elbow bumping. Hard not to notice a few things about Holly as they all changed in the cramped space. That was one crazy-fit woman.

Also fast. She was in her flightsuit in half the time it took any of the men.

"Let's go after the two loadmasters. We can't have them aboard either."

"Tom and Tim. You stay here. Find something to make sure they won't freeze to death before they wake up. Keep an eye out, we'll try to get the loadmasters over here."

"Twelve hours, they won't freeze," Tim poked one guy in the gut now bulging prominently above the waistband of his underwear.

"Living on too much beer," Tom agreed.

"A little fried brown bread."

"With that cheesy mayo-ketchup dip."

"Syrniki fried curd fritters."

"With honeyed sour cream?"

"Ah, Russia," they sighed happily in unison.

Holly just shook her head.

Then she thumped Jon hard enough in the gut that he lost most of his breath.

"Do I have your attention now?"

He nodded as he rubbed his gut.

"Just remember. You're the captain now, Major Karlov,"

she tapped the name on his uniform hard enough to hurt. "Act like it."

"Yes ma'am."

And she was out the door.

"Not a man around who could keep up with that," Tim stated flatly.

"Be fun to try though. You going for it, Major Karlov?"

Jon rubbed at his gut again. "Do I *look* like I'm insane? Get to work, you two." He snapped out the last with an outrageous Russian accent that earned him a laugh, then he followed Holly.

He had almost caught up to her when he spotted the refueling trucks.

One was just disconnecting from the left-wing refueling port. And there was no truck waiting behind him.

Under the right wing, the refueler was still connected to the two big fill-pipes in the side of the airplane. But even as Jon spotted him, he cycled down his truck's fuel pumps.

He strode over as the man was reaching for the disconnect.

"Let me see the fuel manifest."

The man waved a hand at a clipboard resting on the fuel truck's rear bumper and again reached up to disconnect the first of the six-inch semi-rigid hoses.

No, they were in Russia, it was—he didn't know what their standard hose sizes were here.

Twenty-five centimeter?

Thirty?

What the hell else didn't he know that was going to kill them?

He forced himself to focus on the manifest.

One hundred thousand pounds of fuel?

That was never going to work!

Kilos. It was in kilos.

Two hundred and twenty thousand pounds of fuel.

That was…it took him a moment to realize that probably wasn't going to work either.

"Hey! I need at least another twenty thousand kilos."

The fueler froze with his hands clenched around the coupling still attached to the fuselage. "You need *what?* We gave you exactly what you asked for."

It would get him to Vostochny, but not to Japan. "I changed my mind."

The fueler shrugged, then went back to his disconnection.

"Look, asshole—"

The fueler stopped what he was doing, hooked this thumb behind his front teeth, then flicked it at him.

Jon stuck his thumb between his clenched fore and middle finger, then flicked that at the fueler. He gave it the sideways twist and upswing that meant, roughly, *Forget about it, you asshole.* Rather than *Go to hell!*

Then, in unison, they gave each other the finger, just as if they were in the West.

They both laughed.

"I don't have another twenty thousand kilos. And if you call for another truck, the paperwork…*whoosh!*" He grunted, but he didn't go back to the decoupling.

"There's this storm coming in," Jon waved at the slowly thickening clouds that were barely an excuse. "I want more maneuvering room."

"It is seriously shitting snow and ice on Moscow, as it

should." He spat on the pavement. "That to all of the politicians. It will not come to Samara."

Jon sighed; he knew when he was beaten. "What have you got left?" Besides, his nerves wouldn't survive waiting for another truck to be called up.

The refueler shrugged.

"I want it."

He wiped his hands on his seedy coverall, pulled out a cigarette, looked up at the massive wing close above his head filled with kerosene-based jet fuel, grimaced, and stuck it back in his pocket.

"Who can tell with this old piece of shit. Hit the damn lever, let's see what you get."

Jon looked at the control panel, spotted the pump speed lever, and slapped it to high.

"I'm only filling the center tank, so your load should stay in balance."

That was good, because Jon wasn't so sure he could figure out how to rebalance the wing tanks without a little time to study it—like a month-long training course.

Then, from his perspective, he could see that Holly had done something so that two men were trotting toward the disused shed.

And there go the loadmasters. Sleep well, boys.

Two more bodies in there, it was going to be damn crowded. That should keep them warm.

59

Once Elayne Kasprak was out of the plane at Samara and standing on the ground, she dumped any thought of an aerobatics lesson.

All that mattered now was that bitch Holly Harper.

The tower parked them well away from the Progress building and there were no ground vehicles nearby.

She broke into a run. If someone came to arrest her, she'd commandeer their vehicle. But the Antonov was still on the ground and her Fendi calf-high boots were surprisingly good for running. They might have cost nine hundred euro, but she'd had to have them from the moment she'd spotted them at the Berlin airport last month.

She could sprint the American mile in under five minutes wearing track shoes.

She made it the kilometer to the plane in four, looking awesome.

The last fuel truck was pulling away. Close, but she was in time.

If they'd already taken off, Elayne could have ordered them back, or given them a fighter escort if Holly had already taken control.

But she wanted this one for herself.

The big clamshell rear doors were closed; the nose was swung down into place. But one of the crew was still fussing with something near the fold-out stairs to the passenger door.

She slowed her pace enough to even out her breath.

As she came up behind him, she made sure that her hair wasn't caught in her coat collar and it could flutter in the chill breeze—warm for late March at almost five degrees above freezing. An early spring.

"You, what's your name?"

The man glanced at her over his shoulder, then a predictable smile lit his face as he turned fully to face her.

He made a point of looking her up and down.

"What do you want it to be?"

"Name and rank?" She managed to keep her tone friendly. Holly Harper must be here, somewhere.

"Flight engineer Senior Sergeant Tomas."

"Is there a Holly Harper here, Senior Sergeant Tomas?"

He made a show of looking around them.

The refueler had driven off and the only people anywhere around were the two ground traffic controllers with their batons.

He even looked at the bottom of his boot.

"Just you and me, pretty one." There were only slight variations to the Russian language, but she heard the strangeness in him. Kamchatka or perhaps Yakutia. Definitely somewhere east past Siberia. They bred hardy souls out in the taiga forest, as she knew well from where the zone wrapped around her own native home in the far northwest. She liked him for that.

"I need to inspect this flight."

"Specialized cargo. It hurts me to say no, but I must."

She pulled out her normal high-level false identification card. "I *need* to inspect this flight, airman. In fact, I'm going to be with you every step of the way from here to Vostochny. Major Elayne Kasprak, Spetsnaz."

No one ever admitted to being Zaslon.

Thankfully, no one dared mess with Spetsnaz either.

Tomas did make a careful study of her identification. He earned points for that. But he didn't call in to verify it, which lost him those same points even if she didn't have the time to waste on such things.

He handed her card back.

"Fine. You've got the clearance to do what you want, *Solnishko.*"

Little sun. A nickname her first real lover had used when he toyed with her bright blonde hair. It was sweet.

"Personally, I'd be glad to have you along for the flight. Even if all I get to do is admire the view." Again he looked her up and down, but his smile was a little more tentative, appropriate considering he now knew her rank and association with special operations forces.

She patted his cheek as the first engine began winding to life. His thick beard coarse against her hand. "Keep dreaming, *Sakhorak.*"

"Be your piece of sugar anytime. Better hurry aboard if you're coming. We're twenty minutes past due for takeoff already. Some screw-up with the fuel," he shouted the last of it as the first engine stabilized at somewhere incredibly loud.

She sprinted up the stairs as the second engine started.

Inside the massive cargo bay, only a few lights were on. Cases of equipment were chained down to the deck in neat order. Near the center was a large container, which must be the Persona satellite itself.

It was like bad déjà vu.

Yesterday at this time, she'd been standing in the warm Kentucky sunlight on the remains of an Antonov AN-124 Condor that she'd blown up herself. She'd also been busy worrying that one of the pilots had survived.

Now, she saw that Holly and Mike had been manipulating her throughout most of that morning. Things she'd taken for incompetence and gladly brushed aside as a failing, hadn't been.

They hadn't been fooled either, or she'd never have received the phone call that had led her here.

No.

Driven her here.

Well, two could play that game.

The crew would all be up in the forward cabin, directly over her head, starting the plane and preparing for takeoff.

She pulled out the Grach MP-443 handgun from the kit they'd put on the old SU-28 jet for her. No aerobatics lesson today, not hot sex afterward. Pity.

Starting at the cargo deck's bow, she worked her way down the row of cases. Inspection time.

Every box. Every container.

No unsealed sides where a person could slip in.

No unexplained voids or shadows.

She checked the lids of everything except the satellite itself. If she needed to, she'd crawl up there and check it too.

As she climbed the stairs up to the rear passenger area, she saw that the engineer had pulled up the folding stairs.

It was a long flight to Vostochny. That would give her some time to interrogate Holly Harper on the way.

Elayne could only pray that she'd be uncooperative.

60

"So, Mike, who was that Antonov inspector?" Drake's nerves were definitely bugging him.

It was just he and Mike in a small, auxiliary conference room, little more than a box with four chairs and a round table. Not a bad spot to hold a poker night.

"Holly said that Elayne Kasprak was something dangerous—like the most dangerous Russian alive or something. Xerox, Zippo, Zabar's...? I never heard the word before."

"Zaslon?" Drake whispered it because he now knew that was who must have murdered his Russian prisoner in Kosovo. Though he didn't know that they had any women. Maybe that's how the assassin had gotten by him twenty years ago.

"Sure, that sounds right." Mike was leaning back in one of the big chairs as if he really was there for a friendly poker game.

"*Zaslon?*" It finally registered just what danger he'd sent this team into. Drake must be losing his mind. "*Zaslon!*"

Mike nodded calmly. "Holly was afraid of this Elayne somehow coming back after Miranda. Said she was going to take care of it. Never quite said how."

"Is she nuts?"

Mike nodded. "Not in the way you would use the word. But the way I as a civilian would have used the word, at least before I met her, yes. Brilliantly nuts, but definitely way out there."

Drake didn't know quite what to make of Mike Munroe. What little he'd noticed of him had always seemed to be... trivial in some way. Mike always had a smile and an easy handshake. People always liked him. He wasn't ex-military or very technical like the others on the team.

But at the moment, Mike was completely the cool professional.

"You think Holly is taking on a Zaslon operative one-on-one?"

Mike nodded. "Based on the extended meeting she and I had with Clarissa, I'd say that's a near certainty. If her plan worked."

Drake hadn't connected that, or even noticed that Mike and Holly had lagged behind. He'd been too busy discussing logistics with Lizzy, Miranda, and Jon.

"And you're calm?"

"No, General Nason. I'm not calm. Not even a little. Holly's got shit to deal with, past shit, just like the rest of us. She left the SASR for good reason. And now she's chosen to jump right back into the middle of an operation that I don't even begin to understand."

"You don't understand that we're stealing a Russian satellite?"

"No, I don't understand why we aren't sending in specialists in undercover aviation theft. The CIA *must* have the assets for that, but chose not to release them. I'd very much like to know why. Personally, I don't get why we're risking four people's lives by sending them into Russia—with no preparation—to steal a three-billion-dollar asset from a secure military base. And finally, I don't know if Holly is angry, vengeful, has a death wish, or just thinks she's that good. Or even worse."

"What would be worse than that?"

Mike was glaring at the wall over Drake's shoulder hard enough that he was surprised the wood molding didn't start to burn.

"Mike?"

He just shook his head.

"*Mike?*"

This time he whispered. "Or what if she really is that good?"

After that, he refused to say why that was a problem.

Drake didn't have any guesses.

61

ELAYNE FINISHED CHECKING THE REAR CABIN WHILE THEY WERE still taxiing. There were almost a hundred seats in the area formed by the very top of the hull.

There were no windows, and several of the lights were broken; it was a dull, dreary place for a flight. About a third of the seats had slipcovers that said the seat was broken.

Row by row.

It was like stalking in a shooting gallery during training—each corner could hold death. She'd always loved the high adrenaline charge.

And when she did stalk a target, they were never Special Operations. Political and rebel leaders were her normal fare.

Stalking a former SASR was such an adrenaline high that she could taste the bitter-metal of it at the back of her throat as she moved silently on her toes.

This was the most likely hiding spot, the vast passenger seating area.

But no Holly.

No one at all.

Which meant there was only one place left if she was aboard. *Please* let her be aboard.

Elayne slipped through the small tunnel between the rear passenger cabin and the front crew cabin. The sign on the door said that the passage through the wings' structural area was unpressurized in flight, so she was careful about sealing the doors behind her.

Entering the forward cabin from the stern passage rather than the stairs placed her in the sleeping area.

She glanced down and to the left.

Right…there! There was where she'd placed the Krakatoa charge that had shattered the Antonov plane that had stolen Russia's helicopters.

Now the Ukrainians had one less Condor plane. When Ukraine had split from Russia in 1991, the Antonov factory and most of their incredibly useful aircraft had gone to the West.

When the Russian Federation had taken back Crimea in 2014, it was still a long way from Kiev where the Antonov factory lay.

What the troops *should* have done was drive straight through after they'd taken Donetsk and the Crimea. She'd helped instigate pro-Russian riots all the way to Odessa. If they'd taken it while they could, the rest of Ukraine would have become landlocked from the Black Sea and been forced to return to the fold.

But that limp-dick Putin had no follow-through. He was all flash for the people and his fat-cat friends. All cautious about upsetting the West just so much and no more.

Mother Russia could have—should have—*owned* the whole of Ukraine in 2014!

Well, if blowing up one of their Antonovs brought the reunification of the great Russian Empire even one day closer, that was worth the price.

The jet turned, paused, and then all of the engines awoke with a roar.

The crew was behaving normally, all up front behind the cockpit's closed door. Perhaps she'd have to just wait for Holly to emerge and show herself.

After checking that there was no Krakatoa charge slipped under it, she sat on the last bunk.

Leaning against the rear bulkhead, she waited as the lumbering jet gathered speed and began jouncing down the rugged runway. It was amazing that the satellite could survive the punishment. Though, she supposed, the ride to orbit atop a mighty Soyuz-2 rocket was probably far worse.

Elayne found a girlie magazine tucked in beside the mattress and flipped through it while she waited for the climb to altitude. Russian porn was as lame as Western porn—the West too demure and the Russian too slutty. The Scandinavians had the best magazines. Just that thoughtful balance between fun and raunch.

When the flight leveled out, she tossed the magazine aside and continued her search.

Holly had to be aboard already and she was sick of waiting.

Unless she wasn't here at all, in which case Elayne was in for a tedious flight.

If that was the case, she'd have to hunt them down

herself, starting with that lame Miranda and saving Holly as the prize for the end.

It would be a long flight to Vostochny for nothing if Holly wasn't aboard. Maybe that flight engineer would be worth passing the time with. Or maybe she'd just go back to the porn—she'd never liked beards.

62

"Is that scrag here or not?" Holly couldn't keep her nerves at bay.

"She's here." Tom had reported that Major Elayne Kasprak was aboard when he'd closed the door. He'd been out there purposely waiting for her.

But now they'd climbed all the way to cruising altitude without a peep. What devilry was the woman up to?

Tim had taken the navigator's seat and was handling Russian air traffic control like an old hand.

She sat copilot to Jon's right, so her back was to the cockpit's door.

Jon talked her through the few things that he needed her to reach, and somehow they'd gotten aloft.

They still had to cross the entire width of Russia, pretend to crash, and sneak out of Russian airspace without anyone noticing.

And they still had to deal with Elayne.

Holly didn't dare to go hunting a Zaslon agent, but maybe she'd have to anyway. She really should have thought this through more carefully.

63

ELAYNE WORKED HER WAY FORWARD.

Nobody in the small lounge area. A few books. A gaming system and an impressive DVD collection. Only about thirty percent porn.

She kicked through the small personal luggage closet, but no Holly.

Where the hell was that bitch hiding?

There was nowhere else for her to be hiding. The only people aboard were she and the crew.

Shit! It was a dry hole.

Once she'd tracked down and exterminated Holly's whole team right in front of the chicken-coward bitch, she was going to rip the boobs off that goddamn Vesna whose phone call had sent her on this wild goose chase to begin with.

She glared about the tiny kitchen, so desperate for a target that her hands were shaking.

Except her hands *never* shook.

Blood sugar. Had to be.

Due to a tight connection, and all of the brainless-tourist delays at customs in London, the last time she'd eaten had been over the Atlantic.

She craved the bag of cucumber-dill Lays potato chips, but knew she needed energy for her system. A honey-sunflower seed *kozinaki* bar fit the bill.

She tucked her pistol in the back of her new jeans. Thankfully Bosco at Sheremetyevo had some lovely Etro jeans with a dark-grey paisley at the hips over black denim pants. The cropped top and the bell legs made it both sexy and allowed her to move easily. Thirty thousand rubles was still under five hundred dollars—she'd charged it to her Zaslon account. After today, they'd give her unlimited credit.

Except that Holly had chickened out.

Instead, Elayne had called up an emergency military flight from Moscow to Samara and flown to Vostochny. Command was going to be so livid they'd probably leave her there to rot for a while.

She peeled the plastic off the bar, and continued headed for the cockpit as she ate.

At the air-tight hatch to the ladder down into the cargo bay, she glanced through the small round window. A few work lights below, nothing moving. If Holly was down there, she'd be knocked out by now unless she had an oxygen kit. The Antonov flew with the hold at outside atmospheric pressure.

Please let her be trapped down there. With the pressure at thousands of meters higher than Everest, her brain cells would be dying by the truckload. Even a brain-dead Holly would be better to show Command than nothing at all.

The cockpit door swung open as she neared it.

Tomas looked at her in surprise, then offered that lazy smile of his.

"Was wondering where you got to, Sunshine." No mistaking his pleasure.

She glanced into the cockpit. There were four seats facing two-and-two to either side, only one was occupied. The pilot and copilot were facing forward. A man and a woman with neatly trimmed black hair.

Where the *fuck* was Holly?

If she wasn't onboard…

But Holly had wanted, had *arranged* for Elayne to be onboard…

That meant they were planning to shoot down the plane.

"You must land this plane immediately."

Tomas just blinked at her like some stupid horse.

"We're in grave danger. We must land now. No, wait." Then she remembered her own booby trap on the Ukrainian Condor. It had been set to destroy the plane *upon* landing.

Had Holly done the same?

Were they safe *until* they tried to land?

How to know?

"I must speak with the pilot."

Tomas shook his head. "Sorry. Not possible at the moment."

To emphasize his point, he stepped toward her and pulled the door shut behind him.

She could hear the security lock click into place.

That left three crew in the cockpit and one facing her.

One final memory came to her as she stood there with her mouth half full of the taste of honey and sunflower seeds. Elayne recalled lying through her teeth when she'd claimed she knew that "We, Antonov Cargo, fly with flight crew of four and two of loadmasters."

Two loadmasters.

She didn't know if the number was right, but she knew that no military cargo plane would ever fly without any loadmasters at all.

64

"SO, THERE'S NOTHING WE CAN DO FROM THE GROUND TO HELP them?" Drake already knew the answer, but had to ask it anyway.

Mike shook his head. "That's why I've been keeping my mouth shut. I can't beat someone up like Holly, or shoot them like you probably can. So basically I'm screwed. All that talking about it would do right now is freak out Miranda. Until this thing is done, I want her functioning at a hundred percent. It's the best way I know how to help Holly."

Drake nodded. So did he. He didn't know how Miranda did what she did, but this was one of those times when having her close by felt like a good thing. He'd long since learned to trust his gut on that.

"Okay. Thanks, Mike. Keep doing what you're doing."

"Worrying myself sick? Not a problem; I've got that one down."

They shared a laugh, though not a happy one, and returned to the main conference room.

Lizzy started speaking the moment they walked in.

"On the next satellite pass, I was able to just get a peek under the clouds. And their parking space was empty."

"They're underway."

Lizzy changed the view.

A large white plane with a blue side-stripe and red flag on the tail floated above the clouds.

"Thank ya, Jesus!" Mike raised his hand and Drake slapped it a high five.

"I like the sound of this," President Roy Cole and VP Clark Winston came back into the room.

"They're aloft," Lizzy announced.

A message pinged up in the corner of her screen.

Aloft.

"That's from Holly's satellite phone direct to my system at the NRO."

"Goddamn, that's amazing, Drake. Well done." Roy came over and shook his hand.

"Thank you, sir."

Miranda looked up at the screen for a moment, then turned back to her own with no obvious reaction.

Drake could barely hear her comment to Jeremy over the others' good cheer.

"They still have six hours to Vostochny and have to fool the entire Russian military."

Over her shoulder, he could see Jeremy's nod in a small chat window. He appeared to be in a small conference room with a Boeing logo behind him. Then they both went back to work on their reports.

Drake glanced across the table at Mike.

He hadn't heard.

Instead, he was back to staring at the clock displayed beside the plane.

65

Holly heard the click of the cockpit door latch just as she tucked her satellite phone in the cupholder beside the copilot's seat.

She knew she shouldn't look—the risk of revealing her face to Elayne too soon could be disastrous.

Unable to resist, she swung her hair forward and turned just enough to see through it—black hair was much harder to see through than blonde.

The door was closed.

Jon sat in the left-hand captain's seat.

Behind, only Tim sat at the technical consoles. Tom was nowhere to be seen.

"Shit!" She tore a nail bloody as she scrabbled at the unfamiliar harness release trapping her in the seat.

Even as she did so, there was a hard thump against the door.

Hopefully that wasn't Tom's dead body.

Tim launched out of his seat faster than she could.

"No!"

But he'd yanked the door open even as she screamed her warning.

Only luck saved him having his windpipe crushed.

While crawling out of the copilot's seat, Holly snagged her foot on the control yoke because she'd forgotten to slide the seat back first.

Jon cursed as the plane gave a twist to the side and up.

Instead of Tim's throat, Elayne's strike slammed into his shoulder hard enough to slam him aside. He grunted at the force of the blow.

Tom lay at Elayne's feet, groaning.

Free of the harness and seat, Holly grabbed onto the back of the seats and kicked her control yoke—hard.

Jon had remarked about how impressively easy the Condor was to fly and how light it was on the controls.

Her kick against the copilot's yoke was hard enough to jerk the linked control wheel right out of Jon's hands. The yoke slammed full forward and caused the massive plane to nose-down sharply.

Elayne and Tim were thrown to the ceiling. Not hard, but enough to take their feet out from under them.

Holly's grip on the seats kept her in place.

Tom, bleeding profusely from the nose and mouth, managed to wrap an arm around Elayne's legs.

Too bad. It stabilized Elayne just enough to land a blow to Tim's sternum.

He wheezed, but didn't drop to the deck. Instead, like the trained fighter he was, he managing to grab one of Elayne's arms in both of his and pin it.

Holly used the plane's momentum from Jon's recovery

from the dive to plant her feet firmly and lunge toward the rear of the cockpit. For this brief moment, she was sprinting downhill.

And she needed every bit of speed she could get.

Elayne, at the far end of the cockpit, was at least twenty feet away.

Already her arm was in motion to draw a weapon.

Twenty feet.

Tueller's Law.

Twenty-one feet was the outer limit of his testing.

Under twenty-one feet, a charging assailant could outrace their target's time to draw, aim, and fire accurately enough to hit the primary body mass.

Over twenty-one feet, the charging assailant might reach their target, but they'd probably do it with a bullet through their chest.

In SASR they'd practiced techniques to shave tenths, even hundredths of a second off the time to draw, aim, and fire.

Elayne would have done the same.

Plus or minus three feet could make all the difference in the world.

The full charge of adrenaline slowed down Holly's perception of time.

The increasing pressure on the bottoms of her feet as Jon continued pulling the nose up to recover from the unexpected dive gave her extra traction.

Tim and Tom must be unaware that their hard clenches on Elayne's arm and legs were serving to stabilize her.

The arc of Elayne's arm indicated that her primary weapon was in the waistband at the small of her back.

Holly shifted her planned trajectory to the right.

The narrow cockpit aisle didn't allow much flexibility, but every additional millimeter that Elayne had to bring her weapon around for a cross-body shot bought Holly another little slice of time.

Past the senior engineer and radio operator chairs.

Elayne's hand disappeared out of sight behind her.

Now Holly was even with the empty and little-used assistant engineer and navigator stations halfway between the pilots' seats and the cockpit door. Antonov AN-124s, like most Soviet-era aircraft, was a brute force solution—more bodies, less technology. It made for a painfully long cockpit.

The direction of Elayne's motion was shifting.

She had the weapon.

Holly wouldn't be too late this time. Not. This. Time.

Elayne would *not* take down this team.

Never again would Holly be one step short.

So few, grasping, desperate inches from saving her brother.

As the pistol—a Grach MP-443—came into view alongside Elayne's hip, Holly launched.

She didn't try to catch the gun arm—always a difficult target.

Nor did she go for the obvious pain points of sternum or eyes.

All she could see was Elayne beating Miranda.

Killing Mike.

No.

Against all of her training, Holly's outstretched hands were aimed to grab Elayne Kasprak by the throat.

66

Drake was considering going home for a couple hours' sleep.

Last night, he'd foolishly checked his phone at midnight and seen the message about the Condor exploding on the Fort Campbell runway. Now it was eleven at night, twenty-three sleepless hours later. The next expected event was the plane switch planned for three a.m.

But he didn't want to be the only one to leave. He expected that removing Mike would take some serious explosives, and Miranda never appeared to sleep.

The President and VP had left, but they didn't really count.

"Hey Lizzy," he fought off a yawn. "What do you think about—"

"What was that?" Mike jerked upright in his chair.

"What was what?" Drake hadn't noticed anything.

"Wind it back." Mike was up on the edge of his seat, practically shouting at Lizzy.

The Situation Room was dead silent as Lizzy backed up the satellite image and restarted it.

Their stolen plane was in straight-and-level flight. It was, he checked the screen clock, nine a.m. local time for the airplane. The sun shone brightly off the white paint. They were clear of the storm's edge that had obscured their Samara departure and the plane was now etched against the rugged green of the Ural Mountains.

He was just about to ask again when it happened.

The plane pitched up and left for a moment.

As it was recovering, it twisted hard right and down. The change was awfully abrupt for such a big plane.

Then it recovered and restabilized...mostly.

It continued to wander along its track as if the pilot wasn't paying attention.

"Run it again," Miranda's voice cut through the silence.

Lizzy did.

Drake learned nothing new by watching it again.

"Once more. Can you zoom in until all we see are the ailerons and elevator."

Lizzy did her one better and used all four screens at the end of the table.

Upper right was the satellite overview of the plane.

The mission clock was upper left.

The tail section's elevator, which, Drake had to remind himself, controlled the up-and-down pitch, was lower left and the wing's ailerons for turning were on the lower right screen.

The images were fuzzy and the angle sucked; due to the satellite descending again, he supposed.

"The moment arm of force isn't commensurate with air

turbulence. That descent was pilot-initiated." Miranda had tipped her head as she dispassionately narrated the image. "A small initial mistake. The control yoke was briefly pulled back and twisted to the left. It was rapidly recovered. Less than a second later, there was an extreme maneuver pitching the nose sharply down and right. A slight delay and then a more controlled recovery, though not as smooth as the first one. The continuing irregularities of motion are still being generated by the cockpit—as if the pilot was very distracted."

Drake didn't need to see Mike's face turn sheet white to know that they were having exactly the same thought.

67

"SHIT!" JON LET GO OF THE CONTROLS AS HIS ALTIMETER shattered.

Only after he saw the hole in the center, and the sparks spitting at him, did he register the sharp crack of the gunshot.

Gunshot.

Aboard a plane.

That was very, very, *very* bad.

Another round dead-centered the autopilot, which was no great loss as he hadn't yet had time to figure out how to use it.

The Antonov wasn't at all like the C-5M Super Galaxy he'd last flown. It wasn't even like the C-5B Galaxy he'd first certified on. The Russian AN-124 made a fifty-year-old, first-generation C-5A look like rocket science.

He got his hands back on the controls, then turned to see what was happening behind him.

Twice a waving gun swept the empty void of its barrel across his face.

He tried to flinch aside, but the seat harness kept him pinned in its sights.

Then someone struck the wrist holding it and the weapon skittered along the floor.

The first thing he did was check the windshield. No star cracks. No shattered glass.

Okay.

No autopilot.

He couldn't go and help in the fight even if he'd known how to engage the autopilot when it was intact. First he checked the duplicate altimeter in front of Holly's copilot position. It was mounted to the right of her control yoke, so it was a pain to see, but he could make it out.

He pulled on the oxygen mask as a precautionary gesture, just in case someone with a death wish shot out his windshield, then looked behind him again.

There was blood.

Lots of it.

Not arterial, but a lot of it. It was smeared on the steel door, along the frame. A pool of it was being trampled into the carpet. But most of it was on the people, especially their hands.

It wasn't something he was used to seeing in flight. Even as a crash investigator, it was typically rust brown by the time he arrived on site. This was alarmingly bright and very red in the sun-filled cockpit.

Tom, on the floor, took a brutal kick to the head and rolled backward out of sight.

Tim had both of his arms wrapped around one of the

attacker's and had one of his legs hooked around one of...hers.

In the center of the melee was a fierce blonde. It took him a moment to remember that Holly had died her hair black.

That meant...

Elayne?

He'd overheard Holly briefing Tim and Tom about her on the flight to Samara, but he'd been too busy studying the flight manual to pay any real attention. Secret agent or something.

The fight seemed interminable as each person struggled for any advantage.

A knife appeared—was knocked aside.

Punches blocked.

Grunts when they connected brutally.

Then a knee got through Elayne's defenses.

He'd heard that being kneed in the crotch was as painful for women as it was for men. Not that he'd ever believed it because—*Damn.*

Until now.

Holly's knee lifted Elayne a foot in the air.

Her scream sliced through the cockpit.

Then Holly and Tim literally fell on her until she collapsed beneath their shared weight.

He glanced forward and corrected back to level flight. A quick glance at altimeter and artificial horizon. Corrections confirmed out the windshield. Shit, he was flying like a first solo in a Cessna.

This time when he turned, he saw a struggling Elayne clawing at Holly's arm pressed across her throat.

Even as he watched, her struggles faded.

Holly's face was bloody and he could see the claw marks on Holly's cheek and arm.

Tim had his own share of cuts and bruises, which included a bloody scalp wound.

But Tim didn't pay any attention to it.

Even though Elayne had stopped moving, Holly didn't ease up until Tim had layers of duct tape around Elayne's ankles and knees.

They hauled her limp body and dropped it into the assistant engineer's chair, then (after the removal of another knife from her sleeve) they taped her to the chair.

Holly picked up the gun, then moved to sit in the radio operator's seat across the aisle yet up one row position.

"Go check on Tom, then get some strapping. Salvage some seatbelts or something."

"She's not going anywhere," Tim growled, then spat blood out of his mouth onto Elayne's pants. "But if she does, shoot the bitch."

"I promise."

The sudden silence in the cockpit was almost alarming.

Jon looked forward and fixed a five-degree bank, checked his heading, then climbed back to his assigned flight level.

"You okay, Holly?"

"Think so. You?"

"I got shot in the altimeter and autopilot, but otherwise I'm good." Jon had flown through mortars and machine guns at Bagram. Small-arms fire and RPGs at Kandahar. And he'd never understood the dry humor of aftermath among warriors as well as he did at this moment. For this instant in time, it kept all the horror and fear at least one step removed so that everyone could keep functioning.

When Holly didn't respond, he twisted back to look at her. She was wiping at a bloody nose, not realizing that was probably the least of her injuries.

"How did she even find us?"

Holly offered him a bloody smile through cut lips. He'd seen entire bar brawls with fewer injuries. She'd taken a hit right in the mouth, but appeared to still have all her teeth.

"I invited her to fly with us."

Jon watched for a moment to see if she was joking. When he decided that she wasn't, he turned back to flying his plane.

At least that he understood.

68

All secure. On plan.

The flight had straightened out twenty minutes ago.

"She wasn't scheduled for a check in," Lizzy was checking her log.

Drake nodded to acknowledge what they all knew. Whatever had happened, it had taken twenty minutes for them to recover enough to send reassurance.

Lizzy cleared the message.

There was nothing else on-screen because of the recon satellites' positioning. They weren't heavily scheduled over central Russia, but Holly's satellite phone had reached up to a secure, low-orbit comm bird, which had forwarded the message.

Drake did his best to nod sagely.

Mike still hadn't moved from the edge of his chair.

"It's okay, Mike."

"Huh?" His eyes weren't exactly focused.

Drake wondered when the last time was he'd taken a breath.

"Right. Oh right." But Mike didn't relax very far.

Drake knew that Miranda didn't actually miss much, no matter what Mike thought. But if she'd made any conclusions, she kept them to herself.

69

By the time Holly returned to the copilot's seat, the fiery pain of the fight was burning through her system. As well as the fury. Tom was a mess. And Tim wasn't exactly going to heal overnight either.

"Sorry to leave you on your own for so long, Jon." Even lowering herself carefully into the seat caused different body parts to clench or spasm. "It was a hell of a Barney."

"Barney?"

"Brawl. Dust-up."

"Oh. You realize that you have more bandages than an entire Tour de France team after a high-speed crash."

"Feels worse than a slap with a wet fish, I can tell you that much." She buckled her seatbelt carefully, hissing at the fingernail she'd torn bloody getting out of the chair, but hadn't noticed during her cleanup.

"The others?"

"Elayne is still out. Thankfully, it's a military flight, so the med kit has morphine. We dosed up Tom and belted him to a bunk. Couple of broken ribs, broken arm, and his nose is going to have a very distinctive angle for the rest of his life. Tim's about in my condition, at least what he'll admit to."

"That's 'cause I'm made of hardier stuff that some Ozzie chick."

Holly turned in time to see just how gingerly he sat back in his own chair.

"You done good, Tim."

"You too, Hol. Remind me to never piss you off."

"Deal. Same to you." She hated that nickname, but was too sore and too grateful to Tim to complain.

They traded nods and Tim began checking over both the navigation and engineering instruments—wincing each time he had to reach out to one.

Jon didn't say a word for the next couple hundred miles, but Holly could still hear his question: *What was that about?*

"I invited Elayne Kasprak to join us for one reason. The instant I found out she was Zaslon—"

Jon cut her off. "That's when you started lying about what we found on the blown-up Condor."

"I only suspected at that point. But Miranda was seeing things that Elayne didn't want seen."

"Like the explosives detonator."

"And the trigger I found," Holly liked that Jon was sharp. "But it wasn't enough. It's very hard to make Miranda appear incompetent."

"But you *did.* At least enough to satisfy Elayne."

"Not enough." Holly leaned back and closed her eyes, but there were no comfortable positions. "Elayne is smart. She'd figure it out eventually. She'd come after us. After Miranda. I doubt if Miranda has ever looked over her shoulder in apprehension. And I couldn't risk looking over my shoulder for the rest of my life, not even for her. I've already done that for too long."

"So you took out the threat. Why didn't you just kill her?"

"That was my first idea. Mike had a different one."

Besides, Mike was right. Miranda wouldn't have liked that. Not at all. And Holly had been left with the decision of killing Elayne, as she should have, or of staying on Miranda's team. It had been a close thing in Clarissa's office, but Mike had won.

70

Jon let the solid drone of the engines wash more miles away.

They'd been flying east, later into the day. By his best estimation, it was well past midnight for his Kentucky body time, two hours earlier for Holly. He'd been rousted after five hours sleep. According to Miranda, that was an hour more than they'd slept on the C-130 Hercules from her home to Kentucky.

Here it was past late afternoon.

The low March sun streamed in behind Holly and made her hard to see.

She might have slept, but each time he thought she was out, she'd open one eye and scan about before closing it again. Her bad one wasn't quite swollen shut, but she'd have a pretty good shiner.

Tim's low grunts each time he shuttled across the aisle between the engineering and radio/navigation stations said that despite his injuries, he was still doing two people's jobs.

Holly offered to help, but Tim declined. "Rather do something to keep moving. Otherwise I'd start thinking. Hate it when I do that kinda shit."

They'd shared a laugh, then both groaned at the pain that induced.

"You just fly the plane if Jon has any problems."

That had bought Tim a laugh from Holly, but Jon wasn't so happy about it. Tom had been his backup pilot. He supposed he was damned lucky that Elayne had only shot the autopilot and not the live one—or they'd be in a whole different world of hurt right now.

For the moment, that wasn't a problem.

But they were fast approaching the changeover between planes and that was going to be a very different challenge. Things were going to get busy and he'd really planned on Tom's help from the copilot's seat.

He needed a distraction. And he expected that not all of the pain on Holly's face was from her injuries.

But he didn't dare come straight at it. Holly would just brush it off.

"You really think Miranda doesn't look over her shoulder?"

Holly again proved she wasn't sleeping when she one-eyed him carefully.

"It's not like I'm fishing for insider information on her."

"You *so* are." At least she was speaking. Getting her started seemed to be half the battle.

"Maybe a little, but that's not my point. I wish she did a little *less* looking over her shoulder."

"Different meanings," Holly twisted around to check on Tim and the tied-up Elayne.

Jon looked as well.

"Still out?"

Tim stuck out a foot and tapped Elayne's knee as if it might be toxic or electrically charged. "Still out. Does a damn good job of looking harmless, doesn't she?"

"So not," Holly eased back around until she was facing out the windscreen again.

Jon figured he'd lost the battle to get Holly talking. He was about to try engaging Tim when she finally spoke.

"Miranda looks back at her past with loss and wonders how to move forward. I hate looking back because every time I do all I see is death. But I have to keep looking, because death hunts me. Sometimes in the form of pretty-bitch Zaslon operatives, sometimes the ghosts of my old team."

"Or of your brother?" Oo! *Not* smooth.

71

If Jon expected Holly to flinch, he'd be disappointed.

She'd long since learned how to cover every time the past tried to drive a knife into her gut. It was easy; all she had to do was die a little more each time.

"How?" How the *hell* had Jon known to ask that question?

"Miranda."

"You shittin' me, mate?" The chance of Miranda noticing someone else's feelings were...apparently not as low as Holly thought.

"She told me what she knew, which wasn't much. Mostly she saw you change any time he or your family came up, but especially him."

Holly thumped her head back against the headrest. Her eye exploded with pain that yanked a gasp out of her. She needed to do it again—beat her head hard against *something*—but the pain was too much.

She was lucky to still *have* an eye. Elayne had aimed a

two-fingered gouge at her left eye and only missed because Holly had stumbled over Tom's prostrate form. Instead she'd gouged a long cut on Holly's cheek. The blackened right eye? She wasn't sure when that had happened.

"Such is life. That's Ozzie for 'The past sucks.'"

"Thank God the past is in the past. Thought you were going to tell me something I didn't know. Guess not."

Holly glanced over at him.

Jon was smiling.

Not sympathy she'd brush aside or a prod and a poke for more details.

Instead he was telling her that the past was just some... thing. Like hers and Miranda's pasts actually didn't matter.

Hadn't she told Jeremy the same thing during the A-10 Thunderbolt crisis?

Hadn't learned that lesson for herself, had she?

She started smiling, which hurt her cut lips, but she didn't care.

It was too crazy. She was on a stolen plane in the middle of Russia and had just defeated a Zaslon operative.

Their chances of survival still weren't impressive.

And she was worried about the *past?*

Jon was right—totally trivial.

It was the present that was going to kill them.

Then she made the mistake of glancing at him at the same moment he looked over at her.

They both started to laugh.

"Oh God," she gasped against the pain in her ribs.

But it was a good laugh and she couldn't stop it.

72

Elayne climbed back up along the sound of laughter in a whole world of hurt. Every single part of her body throbbed or ached.

Elayne felt like she'd fucked an entire hockey team—only worse.

Only one of her eyes would open and she didn't like what she saw when it did.

Her arms were duct taped and strapped to the chair arms. Her calves and knees were likewise bound together. When she tried to swing her legs forward, her right knee screamed with complaint.

But her feet didn't move.

A little testing. Also bound to the chair.

Straps across her chest and stomach were all that were keeping her upright.

Loud.

The sound was loud and humming.

The Antonov AN-124. She was still aboard.

"Hey, we've got some life here." The flight engineer called out.

He looked as battered as she felt.

Good.

Pilot and copilot, but the other man wasn't here.

"Where's your buddy?" She croaked out.

His scowl went dark.

Even better.

She thought she'd gotten one of them.

Then she remembered.

Elayne cursed as she twisted too quickly to look at the dark-haired copilot climbing out of her chair.

Black hair. Neatly cut.

But when she turned and leaned back against the console beside the engineer, she had Holly Harper's face—just as battered as the engineer's.

She'd *wanted* to rip it off, but three against one? She hadn't succeeded.

"Where are we going?" Her throat was dry...and incredibly sore.

Right.

The bitch had gotten her in a chokehold. Even swallowing hurt like hell.

"Water."

Tim reached for a bottle.

"Aspirin too if you've got it."

"Go to hell!" He held the bottle for her, yanking it away before she'd had half-enough.

He wasn't the problem.

Holly was.

"Where are we going?"

"Somewhere you won't like at all." Holly spoke for the first time. One eye a clear blue, the other like a fake watercolor in contrast to the field of purple that surrounded it.

"I gotta pee." Maybe if she could get out of this chair, she'd have a chance. Holly and the one remaining man looked much the worse for wear.

The pilot hadn't left his seat for the fight, but neither had he come to her rescue. Noncombatant. Good to have around as she couldn't fly the Antonov if she overpowered the other two.

But she could certainly hold a gun on the pilot and make him go where she wanted.

"Not a chance," Holly said it softly.

"Piss your pants. I couldn't care," the guy folded his arms over his chest.

They'd both been very good.

Only surprise had gotten her past the first fighter's guard. Even down, he'd pinned her legs. Special Ops. American Special Operations.

And Holly?

What woman fought like that?

"What are you?"

"Australian SASR."

Elayne could only gape at her. What was an Aussie SASR doing on an American accident investigation team?

That meant that Holly knew far more than she'd said. Worse, Holly had played her all along.

If Holly knew enough to entice her aboard... That meant that Miranda's cute little "I'm so odd and quirky" game had been a complete and total sham.

Goddamn it! And she'd fallen for it.

Now the pieces were falling into place.

Persona satellite.

Holly and her team aboard the transport craft.

Holly hadn't missed the flight or sent Elayne on some wild goose chase. They'd hijacked it right out of Samara and then egged her on until she'd just walked aboard.

The Americans had a plan to steal it and Elayne was the only one who even knew about it. She was also the only one in a position to stop them, except she'd lost.

She didn't look down, but she did flex different combinations of muscles. They all hurt, but there was little give. Not even enough to get free.

Something was missing.

Her back pocket was empty. Her phone—

She spotted it on the console beside the engineer. Disassembled. Battery and SIM card extracted.

No use to her now. Several other weapons lay alongside it—the knife she'd put in a leg sheath, and the leg sheath, plus her backup Markov pistol. Every single item from the kit that the Moscow pilot had supplied her was there. So close and yet completely out of reach.

Elayne had held it in.

Played it cool.

But this was too much. She was hurting. And she was about to lose a two-hundred-billion-ruble satellite to this...toad!

Elayne screamed. She unleashed everything she had, managing enough freedom to thrash a fist on the chair arm.

Who knew what else might loosen.

As much as it hurt physically, she threw a full-blown

tantrum—jerking and twisting for all she was worth—while she described Holly's asexual nature being the reason Mike had never touched her. She—

"Wow. She's chuckin' a proper wobbly. Dose her." She heard Holly say.

One of her ankles came partway loose just as the engineer pulled out a field injector.

"About fucking time," he jabbed it into her neck.

His mutter was the last thing she heard as the drug took her under.

73

"MIRANDA?"

"Yes?" She turned to Lizzy.

"Holly wants to speak to you. An actual call, which is risky, but encrypted, so a short one should be okay."

Miranda looked at the main screen. The timer said they were still an hour from the airplane switchover point.

She'd done her best to distract herself with work, but each passing minute made it harder and harder.

"Put her on."

Lizzy tapped the conference phone.

"Are you okay, Holly?"

"Yes. Where's Jeremy?"

"He's still in Seattle, but I've kept him on conference call in case you need him."

"Hi, Holly," Jeremy spoke right up. "What's it like flying the Antonov? I wish I could fly it to compare it with the C-5 Galaxy we took to Seattle. Not that I flew the C-5, but I felt what it was like to fly in it and I was thinking...."

Holly's laugh was a little rough, like it hurt. Miranda had never laughed until it hurt, but she'd cried until it hurt. She'd cried for three days when she found out about her parents' deaths. They said you can't remember pain, but she remembered everything. Including that her voice had sounded like Holly's afterward.

"You sound...tired."

"It's been a long day," Holly admitted.

"It has." Twenty-six hours ago she'd been worried about the identity of Ewan MacGregor. She'd taken a moment when no one was watching to look him up online. She now knew who he was, but it didn't help her figure out how to describe him in Charades. So, he was still in a corner of her mind, worrying at her.

"I want to try something," Holly continued. "I've got a Russian cell phone here. My question is how do we cheat its signal onto the other plane, the decoy. After the switchover. Can we do that?"

"It's Elayne's phone?" Miranda didn't know why she made it a question. It was the only logical conclusion.

Everyone twisted to look at her in surprise.

Jeremy's exclamation of "What?" was the only sound.

Holly sighed. "Was trying to keep you from knowing about her."

"It's a logical conclusion based on your actions at the crash site and the difficulties you had in flight a few hours ago. Is she...alive?" Miranda hated to ask but she needed to know.

"Yes." Holly's answer was short and flat.

"Okay. That's good." Miranda could only feel

overwhelming relief. She couldn't have faced Holly again otherwise.

"So much for keeping you safely in the dark. Sorry, Miranda. I won't try that again. Anyway, Elayne Kasprak is insanely dangerous, Russian terrorism squad—they'd call it counterterrorism. She took out the first Antonov and she almost got this one before we stopped her. I want to spoof her phone signal onto the decoy plane so that when the Russians shoot it down, they'll think she's as dead as the Persona satellite. Maybe even think she's the one who tried to steal it, casting doubt on her past and maybe her entire cadre."

"I like it," Drake muttered. "It's nasty, underhanded, and I like it. What are you going to do with her?"

"Well, if she behaves, I won't shove her out a hatch. Though she's definitely tempting me. Don't worry. I've put her on a road train to nowhere. About the phone?"

"I'm working on it," Jeremy announced.

In the small video link they'd been sharing, Miranda could see him working fast on a keyboard.

"Um, neither plane is equipped for it."

Holly sighed. "Oh well, it was worth asking. Everything in place for the switchover?"

"But I have an idea. What if we do the switchover near some remote cell tower? Have her place a phone call, then unplug the SIM card?"

"What would that achieve? Who would she call?"

There was a brief silence.

Then Drake began to laugh softly.

Miranda studied the sound. She was fairly sure that it was a joke meant for one single person, Drake himself, rather than a group. Indeed, no one else joined in his laughter, but she couldn't identify any unique distinguishing characteristics that would assist her in the future.

She slipped out her personal notebook and marked it as yet another category of humor.

Drake read off a phone number with a country code that Miranda didn't recognize.

"Who's that?"

Drake smiled. "Trust me."

Miranda did.

But did Holly?

Holly answered the question for herself.

"Thanks, Drake." And Holly was gone.

They were a good team. Miranda could definitely get used to the idea of having a team of people close to her.

Who else would she keep close to her?

Now *that* was an interesting question.

74

"You ready for this, Jon?"

"No! Not as if I have any choice. Why did you even bother asking?"

Elayne registered the words as she woke up. But it took her a few moments to make sense of them.

She was still on the plane.

Careful testing proved that she was still tied down.

"Oh, man. I fell for that, didn't I?" Major Jon Swift. She hadn't noticed him earlier, but she recognized his voice from Fort Campbell, Kentucky. He must be the fourth crew member, the pilot. The noncombatant.

"You bought it hook, line, and sinker, mate," Holly crowed.

Then her voice came closer.

Elayne still didn't move, just letting her head hang forward. Her hair masking her face to either side.

"Okay, let's wake her up."

"Uh," the engineer's deep voice. "I brought knock-outs, not amphetamines."

"How deep did you dose her?" Holly poked at Elayne, but she managed to repress any reaction.

"Not as much as the flight crew or Tatyana Tarasova. Hated to do that. Seemed like a nice lady just doing her job. Actually, I'm surprised this bitch is still out."

Holly grabbed Elayne's hair and used it to yank her head back.

Elayne screamed as loudly as she could. Not because it hurt like a bitch—though it did—but because she was hoping to break Holly's eardrums.

"What the hell do you want?"

"Hello," Holly said complacently, giving her hair another painful yank before letting go.

"Hello yourself, you bitch."

"Let's just have a jabber."

"About what?"

"Let's start with what your real name is, Elayne Kasprak or Elizaveta Egorova?"

Elizaveta was dead. "The first one."

The irritating bitch just raised an eyebrow at her.

"Elayne Kasprak. This is something that you'll never live to report to anyone."

"Zaslon, right?"

"Yes, I'm Zaslon. And we are going to eat your country alive for this."

Holly leaned back comfortably against the opposite flight console. "How much would it be worth to you for me to be dead?"

"Ten million in hard currency! US dollars. In a heartbeat. I promise that I'll give that to anyone who kills you. Twenty if they bring you to me alive so that I can off you myself. I have slow and painful plans for you." She looked at Tim, who didn't react. Twenty million could buy any American—any *ten* Americans before the politicians drove the price up so much.

"Real deal?"

"Real deal," Elayne confirmed.

"Huh. Thought I'd be worth more than that." Holly shook her head and made a tsk-tsking sound.

Elayne focused on Holly's black-and-blue eye and imagined whipping her with a truncheon until every square centimeter of her body was that same color.

"What can you tell me about the payload on this flight?"

"You already know."

"I do. Tell me anyway."

"I will ram this two-hundred-billion-rubles' worth of Persona surveillance satellite up your ass. You'll never get to keep it. We will destroy you for taking it."

"So you mentioned. But who said we were taking it?" Holly made it sound as if she was innocence itself.

"What are you talking about?" Elayne tried to imagine what she was up to. It didn't make any sense.

"What crew would you hire to transport it?"

"If I hired a crew, it sure as hell wouldn't be you."

"Aww. I'm so hurt. Where do you think we're going?"

"Not America?"

"Not America," Holly agreed complacently.

"Japan."

Holly shook her head.

"China?" But that was impossible. America and China

hated each other. But if their goal was to damage Russia, giving a Persona satellite to the Chinese would be an exceptional way to do it. "China. Better them than you."

"Think that's enough?" Holly turned to Tim.

"That's plenty." Tim turned away and pulled on a set of headphones.

"Good," and Holly turned away as if they hadn't just been speaking.

Elayne looked back and forth across the three crew members, but they were ignoring her.

About two minutes later, Tim called out, "Got it. A little rough, but I like it."

Elayne heard her own voice speak into the cockpit.

"Hello...China. This is...Elayne Kasprak...I'm Zaslon. I have...two-hundred billion-rubles...Russia...Persona surveillance satellite...as ...I promise. For...twenty million in hard currency. US dollars." The spliced pauses were short enough to be ignored during a radio transmission.

Elayne started to struggle.

Holly didn't even turn around. "You want another knock-out dose?"

If she was knocked out, there wouldn't be opportunity.

She stopped, but she was far from having given up yet.

75

"Any bets?" Holly called out.

Jon certainly wasn't taking any. The fact that he was the pilot and still wouldn't bet probably wasn't the best vote for success, but it was all he had.

"Tim?"

"Twenty on the good guys."

"Cheapskate. I'll go fifty, Australian."

"Is that even real money?"

They both laughed.

"Any takers? Elayne? No?" Either Holly was cocky or simply irrepressible, and Jon hadn't decided which yet.

"They ready, Mike?" Holly had her satellite phone on speaker now.

Mike had become the liaison to the Groom Lake pilots flying the C-5A Galaxy from its paint job in Seattle to the pending switchover here in Russia.

Jon had followed their route as they'd arced the remote-controlled C-5 in along the Great Circle route, crossing toward Japan until well out on the Sea of Okhotsk. They had finally slipped down below radar before Sakhalin Island. The C-5 pilots were now circling the plane in a low holding pattern of an uninhabited stretch of forest, four hundred kilometers northwest of Vostochny Cosmodrome.

It was a route that he hoped to follow back out of Russia very soon.

He'd flown the Antonov Condor through a complete day-cycle into the future—six hours flying plus five time zones east. Evening's darkness would hopefully hide their next actions.

The thing about Vostochny that played to their advantage was its position. It was close by the Russia-China border. And to the west, the Chinese border curved five hundred kilometers to the north. To stay in Russian airspace, Jon had flown far north of the best Great Circle route and was only now turning almost due south toward Vostochny.

"They're ready," Mike reported. "Came in so low I'm surprised they didn't smack a fishing boat or something." For added security, the American pilots remotely flying the C-5 Galaxy only knew their route. They knew nothing about why or about Jon's Condor. Mike was the filter there.

"Why Mike and not Miranda? I thought she was the more experienced pilot," he'd asked Holly.

"She's so freaking good you can't imagine. But she's also our wildcard and isn't the best at thinking about multiple things. I don't want her thoughts focused on the flying."

Even in that simple statement, Holly's protectiveness of Miranda shone clear as day. Her entire team had made it obvious that protecting Miranda was one of their highest priorities. It just confirmed his own assessment; that Miranda was an amazing woman.

Even his uncle and his general-girlfriend seemed to agree.

However, Jon suspected that Miranda needed far less protecting than the people closest to her seemed to think.

"We've got a cell signal. Let's do this." Holly took Elayne's cell phone and dialed the number Drake had given her.

76

General Zhang Ru of the Chinese Central Military Commission answered his phone, raising his glass of Kentucky bourbon whiskey to General Zuocheng Li in apology as he did so.

Between them, they'd just managed to oust a recalcitrant committee member and replace him with a far more compliant one—one who had a past gambling problem that would ruin him if it was ever revealed. He'd straighten out now, assuming he valued his family's lives.

Tonight was a little private celebration. With Ru's help, Li now directly controlled fully two-thirds of the Commission's votes, making him the second most powerful person in China after the President.

Of course, Ru would have to wait until they parted before he found himself a whore. Li was curiously devoted to his wife and was even now pushing Ru to find himself a permanent spouse. Ru didn't like the idea, but they both knew that Li could have him ousted, disgraced, and executed on a whim. All he'd conceded, so far, was that he'd *consider* the suggestion, but he could feel the day coming soon where he'd better be taking a wife.

She'd have to be as skilled and elegant as Chen Mei-Li had been.

He still couldn't believe what his spies had reported—that her lover was Zuocheng Li's most-favored granddaughter. The two of them were proving to be incredibly valuable to him as assistants, so he wouldn't interfere. But it made him rock hard just thinking about those two perfect young women fornicating like rabbits.

Maybe he'd find a way to have two wives.

"Zhang here," he answered even though he didn't recognize the phone number.

"Hello, China. This is Elayne Kasprak. I'm Zaslon. I have two-hundred-billion-ruble Russia Persona surveillance satellite, as I promise. For twenty million in hard currency. US dollars."

Ru didn't even know what to say.

He was just about to speak when the woman continued, "What the hell..."

Then an inarticulate scream sounded over the phone so loudly that he had to jerk the phone away. The signal cut off before he could return it to his ear.

"What was that?" Li asked.

"I'm not sure." Was it a real offer to sell Russia's most advanced spy satellite? It couldn't compete with the Americans', but it was far better than anything China had been able to design.

Or had the offer died even as it was made?

The number hadn't been blocked.

He called his chief of security. "Find out anything you can about the number that just called my private phone and look for the name Elayne Kasprak...No, I don't know how to spell it. Check every damn spelling and call me the second you have anything. Anything at all."

When he hung up, General Zuocheng Li was watching him closely.

It would be such a coup if he managed to capture it. Perhaps even secure his place on the CMC enough that Li couldn't remove him with a flick of his finger.

An intact Persona spy satellite ready to launch?

Twenty million would be a trivial price. For an asset like that, he'd pay a hundred million in a heartbeat.

But to almost have it and lose it would be a black mark from which he might never recover.

"I...think that it is a prank. But it is so strange that I want to be sure. Please, I would like your opinion as well." And he did his best to repeat the call word for word.

Between them they puzzled over it and waited for a report.

77

THE INSTANT THE CALL WAS OVER, JON PULLED THE ENGINES TO idle and began to slalom the plane back and forth in a steep dive.

Holly had returned to the copilot's seat and was calling out the altimeter readings from her dial.

"Thirty-five thousand. Thirty thousand. Twenty-five thousand."

"Now," he and Holly called out in unison.

Tim got on the radio. "Vostochny Tower. Vostochny Tower. This is Antonov AN-one-two-four military flight eight-niner. We've lost power and control. We are in a steep dive. I'm declaring an emergency." His voice was rock steady because a military operator wouldn't panic.

The tower responded immediately. "Roger Eight-niner. We have you on radar. three-zero-five kilometers north-northwest. Confirm you are declaring an emergency."

"Confirming emergency. Engine restart failure. All

gauges show sufficient fuel. We are again attempting engine restart."

"Roger, Eight-niner. We report negative possible airfields within your glide capabilities. Keep us informed."

"Roger, Tower."

"Ten thousand. Now," Holly whispered.

Jon nodded. That should place them below radar due to the Earth's curvature at three hundred kilometers distance. But not out of radio contact yet.

"Possible restart Engine One," Tim reported.

"Roger, Eight-niner. We've lost you on radar."

Perfect.

At five thousand feet, Jon eased back on the control yoke and slowly fed power back to the engines. Causing a flame-out at this point wouldn't be good.

"Three thousand," Holly reported. "Two thousand...one."

"Turning off the transponder," Tim called from the radio operator's station.

Now their plane was no longer producing a broadcast of its position.

"Turning off all exterior navigation lights," Tim reported as he moved to the engineering console.

Jon fully leveled the plane and restored all the engines to cruise thrust. Then he turned east, but kept his altitude at a mere five hundred feet above the local terrain.

Then he began to pray.

78

Major William Straitsmouth pulled back on the control yoke inside his coffin at Groom Lake, Nevada. The air-conditioned white shipping container was where he usually remotely flew test planes and other drones for testing at Area 51.

He wasn't even sure what kind of plane they were flying tonight. Based on the minimum elevations, four engines, and response time, he surmised that it was one of the big cargo lifters. But whether it was a C-17 Globemaster or a Boeing 747, he had no way to tell. It could even be one of the Russian or Chinese transports for all he knew.

His control suite was very limited compared to the usual full linkage or full instrumentation. He'd never heard of any of the big jets being set up for remote flight, so that wasn't a clue either.

Major William Straitsmouth also didn't know that he and his copilot, Captain Sam Thatcher, were the plane's fifth flight crew in the last twelve hours. Other crews had departed Tucson, landed in Seattle, departed Seattle, and flown from the Aleutian Islands into Russia.

He and his copilot had taken over the flight already well into Russian airspace.

"Transponder on."

"Transponder on," Sam Thatcher replied from the copilot's seat as he turned it on and dialed in the code that was listed on the mission sheet.

"Climb for twenty thousand feet."

"Climbing."

"Heading southwest two-two-five."

"Two-two-five, Roger."

Nothing much happened as they climbed to altitude.

"Any thoughts?" Sam asked him.

They'd met five years ago flying Air Force and CIA drones into Iraq and Afghanistan from Creech Air Force Base. For two years now they'd been assigned to any number of tests and missions from Groom Lake.

But William had never flown a mission like this.

"Aren't we supposed to shoot each other if we ask any questions?"

"Yeah," Sam admitted. "I'll buy a bottle of Wild Turkey whiskey. You buy the pair of shot glasses. We'll have a Turkey shoot and call it even."

"Deal. And no, I've got no idea why the hell we're flying from Russia into China. That's gotta be bad, right?"

"Gotta be."

"I mean, if there's even a plane out there and this isn't another goddamn simulation."

"Doesn't feel like one."

Sam was right, it didn't. Not that anyone was ever going

to tell them what this was about. And their security clearance said they'd never be able to ask.

So, they stuck with their orders and continued straight-and-level flight at twenty-thousand feet, heading straight for China.

79

"Is that you, Eight-niner?" The question sounded over the Sit Room's speakers.

Miranda couldn't focus on anything since the Antonov had begun its "out of control" descent.

Lizzy had managed to position a satellite so that they could see the infrared heat blooms off the Antonov's engines as it flew southeast toward Japan. But it had gone silent, no lights or radios. If they lost track of it, they'd never find it again in the vast wilderness.

Mike had a phone to his ear, one connected to the decoy C-5 Galaxy's radio via an encrypted satellite link.

"This is Eight-niner," he spoke in passable Russian. "We have successful engine restart and are back at safe altitude."

"Excellent. Congratulations."

"That was close. Save vodka for me." Mike joked in Russian.

Miranda winced a little at the translation, but since he'd

supposedly just barely survived a crash, it would probably be ignored.

"Roger, Eight-niner. Correct heading to one-seven-five."

"Roger," was all Mike said.

The plane didn't turn, of course. It was under the command of two pilots out at Groom Lake who would never know that the Russians thought they were off course.

After sixty seconds, the tower called back.

"Antonov Eight-niner. We show your heading two-two-five. Please correct immediately to now one-seven-five."

"Roger." Mike replied and waited.

It bought them only thirty seconds this time.

"Military Eight-niner, are you experiencing control issues?"

Mike barely paused. "Negative."

"Correct your heading immediately south-south-east. You are eight-zero kilometers to the Chinese border. Six minutes out."

"Roger."

There was a long pause this time. Longer than Miranda had expected.

"Eight-niner. This is Vostochny Tower. Do you have an Elayne Kasprak aboard?"

"They intercepted her phone call to the Chinese," Drake sounded pleased, but sat forward with his hands clenched white on the light oaken table.

Miranda squeezed her own fingers together and noted how hard she had to do so to turn them white. Drake's tone belied his mood. She wished he wouldn't do that.

"Roger," Mike said calmly.

"Request immediate communication with Elayne

Kasprak," the tower operator was sounding even more stressed than Drake looked.

"Roger," Mike said, pausing briefly before he continued, "I'm afraid she busy screwing with Captain at moment." Mike grinned like he thought he was more fluent than he was.

Miranda tried a Holly expression and glared at him.

Mike straightened up in the chair and looked much more serious.

"Eight-niner. Be aware that you will be shot down if you do not immediately alter your course and connect us with Elayne Kasprak."

"Roger," Mike returned to his planned script.

Lizzy spoke softly as she marked circles on the screen. "By these heat plumes, they're scrambling fighters out of Vostochny. Too little too late. The C-5 Galaxy will be well into China by the time the Russians arrive. If they violate the border..."

"We can't have that," Drake was shaking his head. "Have them turn away from the border. We are not trying to start a war."

"No," Mike protested. "If they turn, then the Russians won't shoot them down. If we even slow they might give our decoy flight the benefit of the doubt."

"But—" Drake waved a hand helplessly at the screen.

"The Chinese are launching jets," Lizzy reported. "But they're over seven hundred kilometers away."

"That was my phone contact," Drake admitted. "They're probably scrambling to protect the asset if it can make it over the border."

"I don't know about this," Mike was shaking his head.

"I do," Drake jabbed a finger at the screen. "That's World War III. Right there. Turn it around."

Miranda had an idea…

Perhaps.

"Mike. Say goodbye."

"Goodbye?"

"Not to me. Over the radio."

"*Proshchay!*" Then he covered the phone and looked at her.

"Wait for it."

Drake sputtered in frustration, but the others waited.

For thirty seconds, nothing changed.

The C-5 Galaxy, beeping with the Antonov AN-124's transponder code, continued flying toward the Chinese border.

The flight of Russian fighter jets raced from Vostochny. But they'd still be hundreds of kilometers away by the time the C-5 crossed the border.

The Chinese continued to drive north, but from much farther away.

The silence was so loud that it hurt Miranda's ears.

"What the hell's going on here?" The President stormed into the Sit Room like a thunderclap. "Are the Chinese and Russians at war?"

"Not yet," Drake spoke through gritted teeth.

Roy's face paled as he scanned the information on the monitor.

"Did your damned operation just start a war?" He practically screamed into the room. Miranda wanted to cover her ears and hide even though his ire was directed at Drake.

Instead, she forced herself to speak.

"Give them a moment more, sir," Miranda kept her eyes on the screen.

For another twenty seconds, the room was dead silent.

Then it happened.

A pair of new missiles launched from the Russian fighter group. Except there were no jets flying quite at either track's point of origin; exactly as she'd suspected.

"They're too late," Drake declared. "And they don't have the range."

"For any conventional missile, yes. However," Miranda nodded toward the screen and thankfully everyone went silent again.

"Oh," Drake whispered softly, then Lizzy nodded in reply.

It was actually incredible to watch the relative speeds.

The C-5 Galaxy was approaching the Chinese border at Mach 0.75, three-quarters the speed of sound.

The Russian jets were close to Mach 2, as were the far more distant Chinese jets.

And like a drawn pencil line, two parallel tracks were tracing in an invariant line from the cluster of Russian jets toward the C-5 Galaxy.

The lines raced away from the jets, despite their Mach 2 speed.

Lizzy kept zooming in, but the missiles' implacable tracks were unmistakable.

When the two dots ultimately coincided with the third—the new missiles and the C-5 Galaxy—less than ten kilometers from the Chinese border, all three signals cut off immediately.

80

The Sukhoi Su-57 "Felon" fighter jets were the newest supersonic stealth jets in the entire Russian fleet. Two of the only twelve in existence had been stationed at the remote Vostochny Cosmodrome for testing.

Their testing mission was a brand-new capability to carry the Kh-47M2 Kinzhal "Dagger" missile.

In desperation to stop what the Russians thought was the defection of an Antonov AN-124 carrying a Persona satellite, the test aircraft had been ordered aloft along with the other conventional fighter jets.

The American satellite was unable to detect the Su-57s from orbit, though it could see the other five jets they were flying with.

But once it was launched from the Su-57, the Dagger missile didn't trust to stealth but rather to speed.

In the first two-point-seven seconds, the missiles accelerated from the jets' Mach 2 to Mach 10. The Dagger wasn't capable of the Mach 12 claimed by the

Russian media releases, but that was of little consequence.

At twelve thousand kilometers an hour, it could cross the continental US in under thirty minutes. As it was constantly maneuvering, even at hypersonic speeds, no missile defense system would be able to stop one.

It took the next eighty-three seconds to traverse the remaining three hundred kilometers.

At such speeds, a direct hit was nearly impossible, but that wasn't necessary.

The pair of two-hundred-kilo warheads both exploded less than twenty meters from the C-5 Galaxy.

The blast had sufficient force to shred one of the wings.

But that wasn't what destroyed the aircraft.

Even as shrapnel from the explosion penetrated the fuselage, Jeremy's accelerometer that he'd had installed at Davis-Monthan detected the extreme jarring of the explosion. It ignited the sparkers that had been placed in every partially filled fuel tank of the KC-135 Stratotanker's fuselage that had been placed in the cargo bay, as well as each of the C-5 Galaxy's own mostly empty fuel tanks.

The fuel vapors ignited.

In under three-tenths of a second, the explosion of the fuel vapors had ripped down the length of the plane and out the length of both wings.

The twenty-thousand-gallon capacity of the KC-135's fuel tanks and the fifty-thousand-gallon capacity of the C-5's own tanks were now mostly filled with a thick hydrocarbon haze.

What would be a relatively safe three hundred gallons of liquid Jet A fuel was now seventy thousand gallons of highly explosive vapor.

To any meaningful measurement, it all ignited simultaneously.

The equivalent of six tons of TNT shredded the aircraft past any chance of recognition.

Any team that was sent into the remote reaches of the Russian-Chinese border of the Amur River would find little to identify, even after the deep snows had melted.

Every screen in the Groom Lake control coffin blanked simultaneously. Major Straitsmouth and Captain Thatcher would never know why.

81

ON THE VISUAL TRACKING FROM THE SATELLITE CIRCLING IN low Earth orbit, a massive bloom of light appeared.

"One minute and forty-seven seconds," Miranda noted.

"What the hell was that?" President Cole dropped into his chair.

"Hypersonic Dagger missile. Probably fitted to an Su-57 Felon as we didn't see a jet at the exact firing position."

"You know," Jeremy spoke up over the intercom from Seattle, "Mach 10 is pretty amazing. I wish they'd had time to use their new Avangard hypersonic glider. It can travel at Mach 27, but first the ICBM has to launch it into space so that it can fall that fast. Not enough time for the launch and reentry before it reached China, but that would have been something to see."

"Goddamn," Roy rubbed at his face. "I never wanted to see either of those things launched. Are our people safe?"

"Um..."

Everyone turned to Lizzy.

Miranda waited while Lizzy searched her satellite feeds. While they'd been tracking the fate of the decoy plane, they'd lost track of the primary one.

At long last, Lizzy shrugged uncertainly.

82

"What just happened?"

"Turn the jets around," Zhang Ru told the base commander. "It was a false alarm. Well done, Colonel." The fewer who knew about this the better.

He hung up and turned to Zuocheng Li.

"It would seem that the defector who called me was unable to deliver. She was shot down five kilometers from our border."

"Pity," Zuocheng Li refilled both their glasses. "What about that girl in your office? Dandan? Dongmei?"

"Daiyu?"

"Yes, that one. What about her?"

Ru considered. She was hardly a girl—she was thirty-three. But she was *very* athletic. Perhaps. Perhaps she had a sister or a girlfriend as well.

It was an interesting thought.

Almost as interesting as what his aide had described about the Russian Dagger missile the Russians at Vostochny had been forced to unleash. To intercept the defector's plane, it had briefly crossed over a curve in the Chinese border. His people had acquired excellent infrared images and signals intelligence.

Perhaps he could trade that to the Americans for help in stealing the design. He'd very much like to deliver that to the Central Military Commission himself.

83

"I CAN'T BELIEVE IT WORKED! BONZER FLYING, MATE!" HOLLY reached out and grabbed Jon's arm, careful not to shake it as he was flying.

Tim was out of his chair and gave her a kiss on top of the head and a hard hug that hurt like blazes and felt wonderful.

"Never. Not in a thousand years. I can't believe you did it."

"Me? Took a mess of us to pull this off."

Tim laughed, let her go, and gave her a quick kiss on the lips. Then he turned and did the same to Jon.

Though it did get Holly thinking. She hadn't kissed anyone since...joining Miranda's team? Since...leaving SASR? Too damn long.

And it wasn't Tim she wanted to kiss.

Goddamn Miranda and her stupid question. This was not a moment Holly wanted to think about Mike Munroe.

But she was, wasn't she?

"Awesome flying, buddy," Tim was far less restrained

about thumping Jon's shoulder than she'd been. "Awesome. Definitely buying you a round at the next bar."

"That was nothing compared to what comes next," Jon said calmly.

"Yeah, right. We just cruise along and we're good."

Jon's glance at her said it wasn't nearly that simple.

"Spill it."

"Well," Jon kept staring down at the instruments. It was just seven p.m., local time, not much to see out the window. "We burn a lot more fuel flying at five hundred feet than we do at thirty-nine thousand."

"And how much do we have left?"

Tim went back to his seat. In moments she heard the bright tapping of his fingernail against various dials as if hoping they'd change.

"Uh…"

Elayne started to laugh. It wasn't loud, but it was mean.

Tim ignored her and looked at Holly.

"Not a whole lot."

84

"We're not going to make Sapporo, Japan." Tim announced.

Jon rather expected that.

"At least a hundred kilometers short."

"If I dared to climb to over twenty-five thousand feet, I could glide that far to Sapporo except, wait a minute, I don't have the fuel to climb. As a bonus, as soon as we popped up on their radar, the Russians really would shoot us down."

"Okay, I vote against that," Holly could always be counted on for a steady bit of humor.

"Okay, Holly. Any bright ideas? I'm way out of practice on ditching massive cargo planes at sea without killing everyone aboard."

"I'll vote against that one," Tim joined in the game. "The Sea of Japan in March? No way, man. Just no way. I'd freeze my balls off."

Holly left her seat and began prowling through the

cabin, opening drawers and cases behind him. Flying this low, he didn't dare turn to see what she was doing.

"Oi, this is worth a gander."

She and Tim were making a lot of hmm and ahh noises, clearly messing with him.

"Careful, or I'll crash the two of you and just save myself."

"He's Air Force. I don't know if we can trust him not to do that," Tim spoke up.

"So are you, jerkwad."

"Rishiri," Holly cut them both off.

"What?"

"Keep this heading. There's an island called Rishiri just off the northern tip of Japan. Almost two hundred klicks closer. Tim thinks we have the fuel for that."

"Awesome. Tell me about it."

"Winter population under a hundred and we'll be landing past ten p.m. local time. Elevation ninety-nine feet."

"Good." Jon wouldn't have to waste any fuel climbing.

"Runway 7/25."

He'd have to check the winds before he decided which way to land, if he had time to choose.

"Length is over a mile."

"How much over a mile?"

"Five thousand nine hundred feet long."

"Oh shit."

"What's wrong?" Tim and Holly crowded around him.

Jon sighed. "I can land there. But if we add enough fuel to get to Las Vegas, where we're supposed to deliver this mother, I can't take off again."

"What?...Oh." It didn't take Holly long to see the problem. "Let's get there. Then I'll call Miranda. She'll know."

85

THE SOLUTION WAS SIMPLE.

Miranda was a little surprised the others didn't see it. Perhaps they hadn't made as intense a study of the world's airports as she had.

Based on the loading of the Antonov, especially if it wasn't loaded to full fuel, taking off in a mile at sea level was easily achieved.

Also, it was March in the northern Pacific, so the colder-hence-denser air was better for lift.

At her direction, they took on just sufficient fuel at Rishiri to fly the eighteen hundred miles to Attu Island. The abandoned US Coast Guard station lay at the extreme end of the Aleutian Island chain.

Several KC-130J tankers flew out to Attu Island to meet them. They were told a Russian plane had gotten in trouble and they were to assist its safe return. Holly's crew had stayed aboard the Antonov.

It was convenient as well, as they had to wait out five

hours of daylight on Attu so that it was after dark before they crossed over American soil. It wouldn't do to have an overeager plane spotter posting pictures of a Russian military cargo plane arriving at a secret hangar in Nevada.

The six hours to Las Vegas had them arriving just after eight p.m. local time.

Hangar 33B lay at the far southern end of the Groom Lake runway, over a mile from the next nearest building.

Miranda shivered and waited as the blacked-out plane arrived.

She heard the distant screech of the tires before she saw the vague shadow of the massive Antonov.

Groom Lake was used to handling unscheduled and top-secret flights. No airport lights shone toward the runway where it might reveal the aircraft that operated here: ones so secret they often only flew at night.

The welcoming committee was very small.

She and Mike had been flown in on a C-21A Learjet from DC. Jeremy on another from Seattle. The Lockheed engineers would be arriving tomorrow to begin studying the Persona satellite.

An ambulance was waiting.

Other than the technicians in charge of the hangar, the only other person there was one that Miranda hadn't anticipated. Though in hindsight, she should have.

Clarissa Reese.

She had arrived in her own jet, with two very substantial bodyguards.

Only after the technicians had placed wheel chocks on the Antonov, hooked it up to ground power, and closed the hangar doors had the Antonov's passenger door opened and the ladder lowered to the ground.

The two medics hustled aboard.

The first person to disembark was Tom, strapped to a stretcher and complaining about it to anyone who would listen.

Tim was doing his best to make Tom laugh, even though it appeared to hurt both of them.

Humor to deny pain?

Humor to declare continued life sustainment against long odds?

She didn't have a chance to ask them before they were gone, and Holly and Jon came down the stairs.

"We didn't dare untie her. She's in the cockpit."

The two bodyguards stalked aboard, closely followed by Reese.

Now it was just the five of them.

Holly was limping, her face was battered, and her arm was wrapped in bandages.

"Oh, Holly." Miranda wasn't sure what else to do with everything that had built up inside her. All those hours of just sitting and waiting. Trying to imagine how she could have planned it differently. What might she have missed that would kill the team?

Unable to keep it all in but at a loss for words, she simply stepped up to Holly and wrapped her arms around her.

"Whoa!" Holly sounded shocked.

Miranda could feel the vibrations of Holly's exclamation as much as hear them.

Holly hugged her back.

"Never again, Holly. Never again. We investigate crashes. We make things safer. That's what *we* do."

She could feel Holly's nod. "Absolutely never again. It's what *we* do." And Holly held her even harder.

Miranda stayed there a moment and decided that she liked this.

It was firm.

And solid.

And good.

"Hey, I just returned from the edge too. Can I get a hug?" Jon was smiling at her. He looked just as weary, if not as battered, and just as pleased.

Miranda released Holly and considered.

"Hmm. If you have to think about it, then I suppose the answer is no."

But Miranda decided that she *was* pleased to see Jon back safe.

Very pleased.

So she hugged him as well.

He didn't sound surprised like Holly, he simply pulled her in and held her tightly.

That too was very nice.

She rested her forehead against his chest and just let herself be held. Miranda had never been comfortable being held but she could learn to like it.

He kissed her on top of the head. She could feel the scratchiness of his two-day beard along the part in her hair.

"Are we going to have sex now?"

"What?" Jon put his hands on her shoulders and stepped her back a pace. "Miranda!" He said it like she'd been a bad girl.

"I asked if we're going to have sex now."

"Like right now?" He looked around.

Holly, Mike, and Jeremy were still gathered around and looking at her very strangely.

"Maybe we should talk about this later? After we've had our first kiss? In *private?*" He emphasized the last word strongly.

"Oh. Is sex supposed to *always* be a pinkie-swear secret?" She turned to Holly. "Like when you're going to have sex with Mike?"

"Miranda!" Holly practically shrieked.

"Excuse me?" But Mike's grin was so big that it was hard to imagine he was asking a question.

"Oh, that was supposed to be a pinkie-swear secret. Without naming the secret. I see that. Perhaps if we were to name our pinkie-swear secrets we could talk about them without having others know. I could come up with a simple codeword generator that would search for relevant but unrevealing codewords for sworn secret topics. Would that be better?"

Mike squeezed her shoulder. "You just keep thinking, Miranda. That's what you're good at." Mike gave it a Western drawl like he was a character in *Butch Cassidy and the Sundance Kid.* She'd liked that movie.

"We all are. The only times people cease thinking is when they're sleeping, though dream state might argue otherwise, and after we die. Perhaps in certain drug or alcohol-induced states. And—"

Then Jon kissed her. Hard. With his arms wrapped once more firmly around her.

She didn't like having the incomplete sentence dangling from an initial conjunction.

But she kissed Jon back.

Maybe she'd think about the interrupted conjunction later.

86

Mike nudged Holly's shoulder.

"*What?* If you think what Miranda said—"

Mike nodded toward the Antonov AN-124 Condor looming large in the shadowed hangar.

As a group they'd all drifted away from the plane.

Now, Miranda and Jeremy were asking Jon about the flight characteristic variations of the C-5 Galaxy versus the Condor. She noted that Jon and Miranda were still holding hands before she turned to look at the plane.

Apparently it no longer mattered what she thought about that, which was something of a relief.

Two guards appeared on the stairs.

Elayne Kasprak walked between them. They had locked her in a set of chains that cuffed her hands to a thick leather waistband and her ankles close enough that she could just manage to hobble down the steep stairs.

Her hair was matted.

Her clothes were wonked every which way by the

removal of the layers of duct tape they'd used to pin her down. She was just as bloody as Tim and Holly herself had been.

Elayne looked right at them without saying a word.

Not a blink or a nod.

Nothing as she passed by.

Clarissa followed from well behind, with a gun drawn.

Together, Elayne, the two guards, and Clarissa climbed aboard the Gulfstream Clarissa had arrived in.

Holly watched until the jet had been rolled out of the hangar and the doors were closed once more.

"Rough one?" Mike asked softly.

"Yeah. Real close. Too close. I don't know what I was thinking."

"I do."

Holly looked at Mike. He stood at ease; his thumbs hooked in his pockets.

Seeing him and the others alive and safe was almost worth the last forty-eight hours.

"Thinking about sharing it with me?" Holly wasn't sure she wanted to know.

His smile was as easy as the rest of him. "If you'd like."

"I'm guessing I won't, but lay it down anyway." Holly hadn't slept since Kentucky. She'd been around the world in two days and definitely fought one battle too many.

"You're chasing a demon you'll never catch."

"And why's that? I caught one demon today."

She hadn't been a killer like Elayne...had she?

Holly had killed on assigned missions only. She'd been a weapon, not a...what? Elayne would spend the rest of her life paying for her willingness to sacrifice anyone to protect her homeland. Had Holly really been so driven? So ruthless? She didn't know, but she hoped not.

"You'll never catch this one, Holly. Because it's from your past. You talk like you don't have one, but it drives you even harder than Miranda's drives her."

"I've got a past. I just don't talk about it."

"We've all got pasts, but yours is eating you alive. Until you do talk about it. If you don't somehow purge it, it's going to keep—"

"I killed my brother. You happy?" It just came out. She didn't know how or why, it just did.

Maybe because she was tired.

Maybe because she just needed to tell someone.

She checked, but it was still just her and Mike.

"Didn't mean to, but I did."

Mike kept his silence. Didn't give her anything to react to —good or bad.

"There was this flood. In the Outback they're like the Arizona arroyos, only a hundred times worse when they happen. They come out of nowhere. From rain a hundred klicks down some track. Outta the sky blue, suddenly there's a kilometer-wide river runnin' across the land. Just one or two meters deep, it doesn't even look like its moving but it's faster than any joolaroo can ride her horse."

Though it hurt to walk, she couldn't tolerate standing still. Mike walked with her as she slowly circled the big Antonov where she'd nearly lost her life to a Russian Zaslon agent.

"My brother, he was teaching me to drive his ute, that's a pickup to you, and I insisted we could make it across this one flood. I drove into it even as he was yelling at me to stop. I was always a contrary bitch—at sixteen I was even worse, insisting that I could do whatever I was told was impossible. Halfway across, I was laughing at his fears when the car simply floated sideways."

They circled under the massive tail section, which felt as if it was going to fall from the sky on her.

"I swam free as we neared a bridge along the Stuart Highway. The arroyo there is a half kilometer wide and twenty meters deep. You can drop a six-story-tall city block in there and it will wash away...and then the whole world will be drier than a month-old roo carcass twenty-four hours later. He shoved me out and told me to swim for the bridge deck. Made it by a nick."

She leaned against one of the massive wheels of the Condor and tried to stretch out her leg—the knee was badly swollen where Elayne had kicked it.

"He didn't?" Mike asked softly.

"Almost. We clasped hands for an instant, but he let go when he saw it would drag me in with him. My sorry butt landed on the deck, his got washed off the edge. We found his battered ute five kilometers downstream. Found what the dingoes left of his body a week later. My family disowned me. I was sixteen and I lost my whole family in a single day. After my parents made it clear I wasn't welcome back, I hitched out on the first ride I could catch. Two years odd jobbing out at the Mt. Isa mines in the middle of the Barkly. Talk about back o' Bourke; that's real nowhere."

Holly hated the feeling of a pity party thrown for herself and hurried to finish the story.

"Finished high school. Army to SASR until I killed my team on another nowhere bridge to hell. Not much to tell."

And definitely less to think about. She did her best to pretend that she'd been born the day she joined Miranda's team. And now she'd almost died on it. Would that be such a great loss?

"Any plans to stop blaming yourself for all the things you can't change?"

It was a good question. A fair one.

Yeah, she wouldn't mind moving forward at all.

She looked at Mike, smiled at him with her cracked lips and aching face.

Then she rapped her knuckles on the Antonov's fuselage. The thin sheet metal between two ribs konged back at her.

She'd almost died on this plane trying to prove her past wasn't her past.

"I think Elayne did a pretty good job of finally beating that out of me."

87

It was several days before enough rumors had trickled back to the Progress Space Rocket Centre in Samara to draw any conclusions.

First, that the satellite had been lost.

Then, a day later, that the transport plane had blown up in transit.

Another thirty-six hours before Vesna heard that it had been shot down trying to defect to China.

She had listened as Gregor had discussed whether or not to call his American "friend."

"Just to see what she might know about it."

But he'd dropped the idea when an odd rumor, only mentioned once, had reached him.

"They say there was a Zaslon defector," he had whispered to her when they'd gone to bed earlier.

Vesna lay awake all through the night, long after Gregor had spent himself. Even in his sleep, he held her tightly.

She remembered the scary threats of exposure from Gregor's "American" friend.

And the phone call she herself had placed at the "friend's" instruction—only to have it answered by a Zaslon agent.

Vesna had liked the woman who'd answered; she'd been kind and funny. She had also been livid when Vesna had mentioned Arfist, Harper.

Harper was *not* a Russian name.

Was it an American one? She didn't know.

But whoever the Zaslon agent had been, she hadn't *sounded* like a traitor.

Vesna asked herself, "What if she hadn't been a defector?"

Then had the plane really been shot down from the sky?

She'd tried calling the number only once—careful to use a disposable phone.

The phone call had gone to voicemail. Vesna hadn't left a message.

Should she report this?

It was her duty. It was what she was paid for.

But if she reported it, she'd have to expose how she'd heard everything, and that would expose Gregor and his American connection. And she knew exactly what would happen to Vesna herself after they were done interrogating her.

The Zaslon agent's last instruction had been to take good care of her man. *Very good care.*

Yes, Vesna pressed back against Gregor.

Yes. She would listen to the Zaslon agent, say nothing, and do her duty—to herself.

88

Elayne was surprised at her treatment.

Holly and Mike had watched her like she was nothing. That wasn't a surprise.

At least they also hadn't been dancing happily as she'd walked in chains across the hangar floor. Of the others, only the pilot Jon Swift had glanced her direction, quickly looking away as if to make sure the others didn't turn.

As her plane had left the Nevada hangar, Holly and Mike hadn't moved. They'd watched her through the plane's window as she was tied into a Learjet seat far more comfortable than the one on the damned Antonov.

Maybe they weren't so different. She tried to find her anger, but it had burned out somewhere. She'd pushed ever so slightly too far...and now she would pay the price.

The surprise was that she paid the price in comfort, rather than screaming in some illegal rendition site. Instead, she'd been blindfolded and transported to a luxurious prison—that was the most unbreakable building she'd ever seen.

Comfort.

That's what had spoiled the Americans.

She was simply placed in a cell. A comfortable bed, television, books.

Three meals a day and an exercise gym shared with a few other inmates who had pasts just as shadowy as hers. None of whom would ever see the light of day again except in a small courtyard whose high walls gave no indication of where they were.

She had a phone. She was the only one who did.

It was linked to only one number.

Not even a keypad.

She picked it up and it dialed.

Each time it was answered by the same voice.

After three months, far sooner than she planned, Elayne took a breath and didn't hang up the moment it was answered.

It was always Clarissa Reese, the woman from the flight out of Nevada on the other end of the line.

They started slowly, but over time, their conversations grew.

Sometimes they'd speak of men. Sometimes world events or politics. Eventually, they discussed past missions they'd each been on; ones that revealed nothing they didn't both already know.

They spoke as two women who worked in the lethal world of state secrets and deadly opponents.

But they never spoke of the two Condors.

89

At her signal, Mike tipped up the small game timer.

Miranda grasped her right elbow with her left hand, and kept her arm pointed out straight in front of her.

Then she waved it about making *Whoozzz Whoozz* sounds and feeling utterly ridiculous.

"Light sabre," Jeremy shouted.

Miranda nodded and thumped her chest.

"Rey. Daisy Ridley."

She pointed at herself and shook her head, then at Mike and Jeremy.

"Male," Mike guessed.

"Darth, Luke, Obi-wan."

She pointed at him.

"Obi-wan Kenobi."

"Alec Guinness."

"Sir Alec Guinness."

Miranda was lost again. She didn't know what Sir Alec

Guinness had to do with Obi-wan Kenobi. She knew him only from *Lawrence of Arabia* and *Doctor Zhivago.*

The timer had only seconds left.

Holly was laughing aloud, holding on to her ribs as she did so, but laughing. Her eye was better but still scary, now a sallow green against her pale skin. She planned to let her hair grown out naturally, so the black was still disconcerting.

Finally, Miranda shrugged helplessly.

"Younger Obi-wan," Mike called out. She didn't know if that was accurate, but Ewan McGregor was younger than Sir Alec Guinness, so she nodded.

And just as the last grains dropped through the thin neck of the sand timer, Jeremy shouted out, "Ewan McGregor."

Miranda felt such a surge of relief that she forgot she was allowed to speak now and simply gave Jeremy an okay sign.

For some reason, Holly found that immensely funny as well, and laughed—and groaned—even harder.

Miranda sat back on the couch and whispered, "I'm glad that's finally over."

Major Jon Swift slid a hand around her waist and kissed her on the temple. "Well done, you."

Miranda couldn't wait to take him upstairs and find out just how well done something between them could be.

If you enjoyed this, keep reading for an excerpt from a book you're going to love.

..and a review is always welcome (it really helps)...

MIRANDA CHASE RETURNS

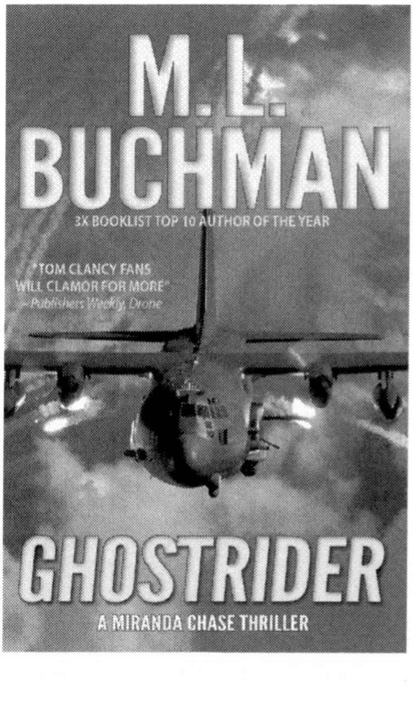

GHOSTRIDER (EXCERPT)

MIRADA CHASE #4

Tacoma Narrows Airport, Tacoma, Washington
(1900 hours Pacific Daylight Time)

Miranda's laptop barely fit on the end of the workbench in her airplane hangar. She was getting squeezed to the side, but she managed to hang on long enough to deliver her latest report.

She selected Upload on the NTSB's secure server. Her report "Airbus A320neo excursion from runway and collision with taxiing 737 at SFO" was complete and ready for final peer review.

It had led to a large number of jokes about Boeing versus Airbus that had seemed irrelevant to the mechanical interactions of the two aircraft or the pilot error.

She had to blink twice at the following screen because it didn't make any sense.

"It's blank."

"What is?" Jeremy didn't look up from where he'd taken

over most of *her* workbench. He'd scavenged a full set of cockpit instruments from a mothballed military C-5A Galaxy jet transport on his last trip to Davis-Monthan Air Force Base's boneyard. He was meticulously dissecting then restoring each one.

She and her team, Team Chase, were sitting in her hangar at Tacoma Narrows Airport. It was a warm summer day and the main doors were slid back to let the sun in. Their "office" in the back corner was comfortable and smelled of a Pacific Northwest summer, all ocean, pine, and fresh mown grass. It was also far quieter than her official office at the National Transportation Safety Board just twenty miles away across the Tacoma Narrows Bridge.

"Our queue."

Mike laughed from where he sat opposite Holly.

The two of them were playing Backgammon across a spare parts crate that had once contained a new cylinder head for an old Douglas DC-3. Mike was playing as if he was reading a good book. Holly clearly felt that Backgammon was a blood sport. She didn't roll her dice out of the cup and onto the board—she slammed it down with a crash that threatened to dislodge the wooden slats from the stout old crate they were using as a table.

"Why is that an issue? I could do with a break." Mike eased back on the old sofa to look at her.

Holly appeared to be fuming at Mike's studied casual style of play. Miranda considered pointing out that the more anxious Holly became, the more casual Mike became. She was still unclear if having an intimate relationship was somehow at the core of their interactions, or perhaps their lack of one. Her attempts at studying human emotions as interacting dynamic systems were still providing erratic results long after any merely mechanical systems would have been clearly delineated.

She returned to the queue, which was far more comprehensible, however unlikely.

"I've been investigating accidents for the NTSB for eighteen years. My queue of open cases has never been empty. There's always been returning metallurgy, additional witness interviews, drafts in need of editing..." And now there was nothing.

Holly seemed to shift modes between one heartbeat and the next; the cheery Australian appeared in a flash. "Well, goodonya, Miranda. It means we're so awesome that we've gone and solved everything. Let's declare a national holiday. Won't last but a minute. Better do it fast. Call your pal Roy and have him declare it right now."

Miranda had actually picked up her phone before she spotted Mike's amused smile. It was interesting that they always seemed to be ready to go three rounds in the boxing ring, yet Mike was Miranda's best gauge of Holly's intentions.

"Ah, a joke." Miranda set her phone back down without calling the President. Besides, it was early evening here in Tacoma, Washington. "I don't want to disturb him as it's almost bedtime in DC. I also note that it's dinnertime and you haven't yet mentioned food, Holly. Are you feeling okay?"

"Would be if Mike played this game faster that a sloth on Xanax. Food, Jeremy."

"Oh, okay. You know, the 1983 version of the artificial horizon instrument was dependent on a gyro mount that should never have lasted as long as they did. The lack of wear is simply amazing considering the number of hours that were logged on that airframe." He moved to a bench microscope.

Mike turned back to the board, rattled his dice briefly and rolled a perfect three-five.

"Yank, bastard," Holly's Australian drawl was thick, which usually indicated she was enjoying herself no matter what her expression and words said to the contrary.

He sealed up the inboard, knocking one of Holly's blots back to the bar. Another three rolls allowed him to get all of his pieces safe before she managed to free her lone piece.

"Hope you roll snake eyes."

He rolled double fives and cleared the point.

Holly managed to avoid being gammoned by getting off a single one of her pieces before Mike finished clearing the board.

Holly glared at the half empty board, his half. "Are you sure there aren't any crashes, Miranda? Maybe if I dropped a plane on Mike's head we could investigate the death of an American weasel."

"Love you too, Harper." Mike began stowing Holly's pieces.

"Not even a little, Munroe." She helped him.

"It wouldn't work anyway." He snapped the case shut and stowed it on top of the rolling tool case.

"Why's that?" She kicked the upside-down wastebasket she'd been using as a seat. She hit it just right so that it flipped with a loud clang of metal, then a ringing wobble before it settled upright.

"Only planes here are both Miranda's, I know you wouldn't risk damaging one of hers."

"Not on your thick head," Holly declared particularly emphatically.

Miranda's Mooney M20V Ultra was the fastest single-propeller piston-engine production airplane there was. And her 1958 F-86F Sabrejet fighter plane was one of the last dozen out of over ten thousand built that was still flying anywhere.

She didn't believe that either would be damaged by an impact with Mike's head, especially since it was unlikely to be significantly thicker than the average human's no matter what Holly said. But dropping one of her planes in such a way that it would impact Mike would imply that it would then hit the ground—and she'd rather not have that happen, notwithstanding the damage to his skull.

During her moment of inattention, Jeremy's reconstruction project had consumed the last of the workbench; a line of engine gauges (N1 and N2 stage RPMs, exhaust gas temperature, fuel flow, and oil pressure) now separated her from her laptop.

She supposed that it was fortunate that there wasn't an accident investigation going on at the moment as she'd have nowhere to work. Over the last eight months, her team had slowly shifted most of their work from the NTSB's Seattle Region office, illogically named as it was placed in Federal Way, into her private hangar at Tacoma Narrows Airport.

Miranda had initially insisted that they use the National Transportation Safety Board's official office as it seemed both proper and convenient. But as her team had become more and more specialized, especially in highly classified military mishaps, the isolation of the hangar at TNA had become a better fit.

"Food it is," Holly stepped up behind Jeremy, and lifted him physically off his stool. He managed to drop his tools with a clatter before she began walking toward the hangar door with him dangling under her arm. Mike stepped up and grabbed his legs as Jeremy broke out laughing.

Lucky for them that Jeremy was little bigger than Miranda herself. She was five-four and Jeremy was an equally slender five-seven. Holly still worked out hard. Perhaps not as hard as when she'd been a Special Operations warrior for the Australian SASR, but she did spend time every day at the weight set beside her and Jeremy's workbench.

Apparently, Jeremy was an easy load.

Miranda picked up her phone and computer, without knocking aside any of Jeremy's instruments, and followed behind them.

Enroute between
Ellsworth Air Force Base, South Dakota
and
Groom Lake, Nevada Test and Training Range
(0300 Mountain Daylight Time)

"Denver Center, this is Shadow Six-four."

"Roger, Six-four. Go ahead."

"Declaring an emergency. Depressurization event. Current altitude three-niner-thousand. Request clearance emergency descent to one-five-thousand."

Missy Collins had only been on the Denver Center Air

Traffic Control desk for six weeks, and she'd never handled an emergency before. She pulled up the checklist on a side screen.

"Confirm. Shadow six-four is declaring an emergency? Please squawk seventy-seven hundred." Seven-seven-zero-zero was the official transponder code for an emergency.

"Confirm emergency."

And right on cue, a plane flashed brightly on her flight-tracking screen. The four-digit transponder squawk code immediately identified the plane's position if not its type or other status.

She checked the status of all other flights in the area.

Nothing intersecting in the next five minutes.

"Shadow Six-four. You are cleared to initiate immediate descent at your discretion. Number aboard?" Next question on the checklist.

"Full crew. Thirteen."

Even as she watched, the altitude readout dropped to thirty-eight, then thirty-seven. Their rate of descent was dangerously fast, even in an emergency situation. In fact...

Kenneth, the head of her section, had been both kind and relentless in training their team. ATC wasn't a job that allowed breaks, yet he insisted on additional training at every opportunity. He'd also showed special interest in her, but she wasn't sure how she felt about that.

Now the training paid off. She slapped the supervisor-call switch, even as she pulled up the plane's filed flight plan, and began studying the sector chart.

Kenneth patched in his headset beside hers, "What are we looking at, Missy?" As always at work, his tone was completely professional. They'd had dinner together after last night's shift. He'd been charmingly roundabout with how he'd propositioned her.

She'd turned him down; he was her boss after all. She also had a boyfriend, technically. Vic was very unhappy that she'd left LA and they weren't on speaking terms at the moment. It was becoming clear that he was more upset about having to pay all of the apartment's rent than about her departure.

"We have a depressurization emergency on military flight Shadow Six-four. Which is listed as..." she inspected the record, "...and AC-130J. Is that a variation of the C-130 Hercules?"

Kenneth whistled softly. "A for attack, C-130 for Hercules airframe, and the J means that it's the newest the Air Force has. The AC-130J gunship." He couldn't help himself but to include a moment of training. She'd heard him do that with everyone.

"Do you know it's V-max airspeed? They're descending at three-seven...three-eight...four-zero-zero knots."

"Max speed on the standard C-130J is three hundred and sixty."

"They're in major trouble." She mumbled out as she searched for any problems along their flight path. There was... "Holy shit!"

Crap! Now that would be on the tape forever if there was a problem.

"Shadow Six-four, Denver ATC. Be aware your max airspeed is very high. Also your direct line of descent includes seven of the fourteeners." They stood in a tight cluster barely southwest of Aspen, Colorado.

"Fourteeners?" Was the plane's radio operator's voice

more strained? She couldn't tell. The military pilots were even more resolute than the airline pilots. It was the general aviation folks who panicked all the time. She hadn't known the word either until Kenneth had told her about them over dinner. Out-of-state pilots weren't used to mountains reaching so high, or the weather systems the mountain peaks generated for thousands of feet higher.

"Mountains over fourteen thousand feet tall. What's your status? Can you divert to Carbondale or Glendale Airport?"

Kenneth wasn't giving her any corrections. She appreciated his oversight though. This was escalating too fast in many ways.

"Total LOC. Negative divert."

Total Loss of Control.

They were falling through twenty-thousand feet at over four hundred and thirty knots, five hundred miles an hour.

"Roger, Six-four." She looked away from the radar to Kenneth. What could she say from the ground to help the pilots. They'd know they were doomed.

Kenneth cricked his neck to the side for a moment then shrugged a little helplessly.

"Denver ATC. Status, Six-four?"

"Negative recovery. Negative control." His voice was dead calm. "Aw, fuck." He said the last softly.

She hailed him again, but there was no response.

Nine seconds later, two new radar images appeared alongside the plane.

"That's the wings," Kenneth whispered softly.

Twelve seconds later it impacted the top of Snowmass Mountain.

Missy looked down at the checklist. She managed to get

her finger on the phone number for mountain rescue, but she couldn't make out the numbers.

"I can't see to call them. I can't, Kenneth. I—"

He rested a hand on her shoulder, and picked up the phone himself. Brushing aside where her tears had blurred the number on the call sheet, he dialed and called out the search teams.

They pulled her off the console and sat her in a small conference room. One of the assistant supervisors conducted the interview, recording and noting down everything she could recall. Kenneth checked in on her several times during breaks in his own round of interviews.

Eighty-three seconds. First-call to crash was just eighty-three seconds. That fast—thirteen people lost there lives. She couldn't get around that fact. How could life suddenly be so short?

When they were done, when *all* of this was done and the investigation was over, Missy knew one thing. She was done with Vic. She was going to take Kenneth up on his offer and hold him as close as she could.

She knew the pilot's final comment, that one final moment when his humanity had slipped past all of his military training, would haunt her for the rest of her life.

Aboard Shadow Six-Four
27,000 feet above Aspen, Colorado
(23 seconds before impact)

As soon as Captain Luis Martinez broadcast the final

report from aboard the diving plane, “Negative recovery. Negative control.” he released his seat harness.

The plane wasn’t quite in freefall, so he fell into the yoke and flight console. “Aw fuck.” Like it was going to hurt anything now other than his ego. No one aboard to see anyway.

He pulled off his headset, and began climbing uphill through the Hercules’ cockpit. Two of the thirteen bodies scattered strategically through the plane had ended up in the aisle and he was forced to crawl over them. The ladder down to the main cargo deck was easier to navigate; he could just pull himself along it.

Danny Gonzalez had left the forward passenger door open.

Luis shrugged into the parachute rig.

He took a moment to ensure that he was oriented properly and then grabbed the bottom edge of the door. It wouldn’t do to fling himself out of the plane and straight into the massive six-blade propeller spinning at a thousand rpm.

The fuselage twisted sharply and he almost lost his grip.

Looking out into the darkness once more he saw that the propeller was no longer an issue—the entire wing had ripped off.

The temperature was a bitch.

Even on a warm June evening, ten thousand feet above Aspen was damn cold. Be lucky if he didn’t have frostbite by the time he got down. But no time to pull on a balaclava—the ground was coming up fast.

He still made a point of flinging himself downward, just in case the tail was still attached.

As soon as he’d ejected, he opened his black tactical

ram-air chute. It was for night insertions deep behind enemy lines, and, like his clothing, had the radar signature of a bird —a small one.

He watched the plane continue down. Less than five seconds after he had his chute deployed, the Hercules impacted at twelve thousand feet atop a high peak. It was supposed to plunge into the back-country wilderness beyond, but it didn't really matter. At over four hundred knots, the destruction was more than sufficient.

The wings landed farther down the slope, bursting into flame as the wing tanks breached. The conflagration spread rapidly upslope. In minutes, the plane would be engulfed as well. Perfect.

Luis turned away and flipped down his night vision goggles. He steered his chute for the extraction point. No one should be at the Aspen racing car track at three in the morning.

Five miles away and two miles down; he had plenty of altitude. The ram-air tactical chute let him tune his glide ratio.

Yes, having the very best gear was only one of the bonuses of this operation.

ABOUT THE AUTHOR

M.L. Buchman started the first of over 60 novels, 100 short stories, and a fast-growing pile of audiobooks while flying from South Korea to ride his bicycle across the Australian Outback. Part of a solo around the world trip that ultimately launched his writing career in: thrillers, military romantic suspense, contemporary romance, and SF/F.

PW says his thrillers will make "Tom Clancy fans open to a strong female lead clamor for more." His titles have been named Barnes & Noble and NPR "Top 5 of the year" and 3-time Booklist "Top 10 of the Year" as well as being a "Top 20 Modern Masterpiece" in romantic suspense.

As a 30-year project manager with a geophysics degree who has: designed and built houses, flown and jumped out of planes, and solo-sailed a 50' ketch—he is awed by what's possible. More at: www.mlbuchman.com.

Other works by M. L. Buchman: *(* - also in audio)*

Thrillers

Dead Chef
Swap Out!
One Chef!
Two Chef!

Miranda Chase
*Drone**
*Thunderbolt**
*Condor**

Romantic Suspense

Delta Force
*Target Engaged**
*Heart Strike**
*Wild Justice**
*Midnight Trust**

Firehawks
MAIN FLIGHT
Pure Heat
Full Blaze
*Hot Point**
*Flash of Fire**
Wild Fire
SMOKEJUMPERS
*Wildfire at Dawn**
*Wildfire at Larch Creek**
*Wildfire on the Skagit**

The Night Stalkers
MAIN FLIGHT
The Night Is Mine
I Own the Dawn
Wait Until Dark
Take Over at Midnight
Light Up the Night
Bring On the Dusk
By Break of Day
AND THE NAVY
Christmas at Steel Beach
Christmas at Peleliu Cove
WHITE HOUSE HOLIDAY
*Daniel's Christmas**
*Frank's Independence Day**
*Peter's Christmas**
*Zachary's Christmas**
*Roy's Independence Day**
*Damien's Christmas**
5E
Target of the Heart
Target Lock on Love
Target of Mine
Target of One's Own

Shadow Force: Psi
*At the Slightest Sound**
*At the Quietest Word**

White House Protection Force
*Off the Leash**
*On Your Mark**
*In the Weeds**

Contemporary Romance

Eagle Cove
Return to Eagle Cove
Recipe for Eagle Cove
Longing for Eagle Cove
Keepsake for Eagle Cove

Henderson's Ranch
*Nathan's Big Sky**
*Big Sky, Loyal Heart**
*Big Sky Dog Whisperer**

Love Abroad
Heart of the Cotswolds: England
Path of Love: Cinque Terre, Italy

Other works by M. L. Buchman:

Contemporary Romance (cont)

Where Dreams

Where Dreams are Born
Where Dreams Reside
Where Dreams Are of Christmas
Where Dreams Unfold
Where Dreams Are Written

Science Fiction / Fantasy

Deities Anonymous

Cookbook from Hell: Reheated
Saviors 101

Single Titles

The Nara Reaction
Monk's Maze
the Me and Elsie Chronicles

Non-Fiction

Strategies for Success

Managing Your Inner Artist/Writer
*Estate Planning for Authors**
Character Voice
*Narrate and Record Your Own Audiobook**

Short Story Series by M. L. Buchman:

Romantic Suspense

Delta Force

Delta Force

Firehawks

The Firehawks Lookouts
The Firehawks Hotshots
The Firebirds

The Night Stalkers

The Night Stalkers
The Night Stalkers 5E
The Night Stalkers CSAR
The Night Stalkers Wedding Stories

US Coast Guard

US Coast Guard

White House Protection Force

White House Protection Force

Contemporary Romance

Eagle Cove

Eagle Cove

Henderson's Ranch

*Henderson's Ranch**

Where Dreams

Where Dreams

Thrillers

Dead Chef

Dead Chef

Science Fiction / Fantasy

Deities Anonymous

Deities Anonymous

Other

The Future Night Stalkers
Single Titles

SIGN UP FOR M. L. BUCHMAN'S NEWSLETTER TODAY

and receive:

Release News

Free Short Stories

a Free Book

Get your free book today. Do it now.

free-book.mlbuchman.com